PRAIS

WHERE SECRETS LIE

"Clever and full of twists—Colleen Coble and Rick Acker have crafted a page-turner that blends the intellectual intrigue of academia with the high-stakes world of artifact smuggling. With an unpredictable plot, complex characters, and a college campus that holds dark secrets, this mystery will keep you guessing."

—ROBERT DUGONI, *NEW YORK TIMES* BESTSELLING AUTHOR OF THE TRACY CROSSWHITE SERIES

I THINK I WAS MURDERED

"It's a high-octane thriller with the grounding touches of Katrina's Norwegian heritage, the hygge of North Haven, and a very sweet romance between two likable, vulnerable people. Romantic suspense comfort food—just like waffles with cloudberry cream."

—*KIRKUS REVIEWS*

"This fast-paced thriller incorporating today's headline news along with compelling family drama proves that the Coble-Acker partnership (*What We Hide*) will continue to produce hits. Recommend to fans of psychological thrillers such as *Lies We Believe* by Lisa Harris and *Criss Cross* by C. C. Warrens."

—*LIBRARY JOURNAL*

"This is a book that grabs you straight out of the gate. Centered around a bang-up concept with a great techno twist, a rich cast of

PRAISE FOR COLLEEN COBLE

characters drives you through a twisty plot that is a white-knuckled ride straight to the end. The suspense was killing me as I read! Make sure you're well-rested before you start *I Think I Was Murdered* because it will keep you up at night."

—P. J. TRACY, *NEW YORK TIMES* BESTSELLING AUTHOR

"A timely and intriguing premise played out in a way that keeps readers guessing."

—STEVEN JAMES, NATIONAL
BESTSELLING AUTHOR OF *SYNAPSE*

"What a roller-coaster ride! *I Think I Was Murdered* gripped me on page one and didn't let go until the epilogue—after a twist that caught this seasoned reader by complete surprise. If you like thrilling suspense, you won't want to miss this novel by Colleen Coble and Rick Acker."

—ANGELA HUNT, AUTHOR OF
WHAT A WAVE MUST BE

"Colleen Coble fans will devour her latest offering, which—with the help of thriller writer Rick Acker—cleverly uses AI, family secrets, and a lost treasure to keep readers guessing until the final satisfying page."

—CRESTON MAPES, BESTSELLING AUTHOR

WHAT WE HIDE

"Bestsellers Coble (*Break of Day*) and Acker (*Guilty Blood*) team up for a heart-pounding tale of stolen artifacts and murder . . . The second-chance romance adds dimension to the well-plotted who-dunit, which leaves more than a few secrets to be uncovered in the next installment. Readers will be on tenterhooks."

—*PUBLISHERS WEEKLY*

"This is an explosive beginning to a new series and a dynamic author partnership between Coble (Pelican Harbor series) and practicing lawyer Acker. Will appeal to fans of the legal thrillers of Randy Singer and Robert Whitlow."

—LIBRARY JOURNAL

"Coble and Acker have forged a seamless partnership with a singular voice. I honestly can't tell where one writer starts and the other ends. *What We Hide* is a crisp and hard-charging start to a legal suspense series that tests the boundaries of yesterday's secrets against today's lies, all while trying to escape tomorrow's verdict. From the courtroom to the shadow of a decaying Gothic university, it's a high-stakes ride through love, second chances, and an ending you won't soon forget."

—CHARLES MARTIN, *NEW YORK TIMES* BESTSELLING AUTHOR

"Get ready to be hooked! Brace yourself for a thrill ride as Coble and Acker masterfully weave a web of suspense in *What We Hide*, where secrets simmer and unexpected twists leave you guessing until the shocking finale."

—KATE ANGELO, *PUBLISHERS WEEKLY* BESTSELLING AUTHOR

"This book has it all. Intrigue, suspense, and the mysteries of the heart, woven together masterfully by the great new pairing of Coble and Acker. Fans of their individual books will not be disappointed. New readers will be delighted."

—JAMES SCOTT BELL, INTERNATIONAL
THRILLER WRITERS AWARD WINNER

"Much is hidden in Tupelo Grove and Pelican Harbor. In *What We Hide*, expert storytellers Colleen Coble and Rick Acker will take you on a riveting ride through a picturesque Southern town inhabited by characters who will pull you in and make you care. Hidden truths find their way into the light—sometimes quickly, often slowly in the face of great obstacles and danger. Once you start reading, you won't put this book down."

—ROBERT WHITLOW, BESTSELLING AUTHOR

"When you combine two brilliant storytellers such as Coble and Acker, the result is a beautiful, well-crafted legal thriller that keeps the reader utterly riveted. If you're looking for a novel that's edge-of-the-seat compelling, emotionally engaging, and nail-bitingly (I know that's not a word, but it fits) suspenseful, look no further than *What We Hide*. With its compelling narrative, well-rounded characters, and intricate plot, this is a must-read, goes-on-the-keeper-shelf book that will stay with you long after the final page is turned."

—LYNETTE EASON, BESTSELLING, AWARD-WINNING
AUTHOR OF THE EXTREME MEASURES SERIES

"*What We Hide* grabbed me with the first chapter and had me reading until two in the morning with its twisty plot and engaging characters."

—PATRICIA BRADLEY, AUTHOR OF THE PEARL RIVER SERIES

WHERE SECRETS LIE

WHERE SECRETS LIE

A TUPELO GROVE NOVEL

COLLEEN COBLE
RICK ACKER

THOMAS NELSON
Since 1798

Published in Nashville, Tennessee, by Thomas Nelson. Thomas Nelson is a registered trademark of HarperCollins Christian Publishing, Inc.

Thomas Nelson titles may be purchased in bulk for educational, business, fundraising, or sales promotional use. For information, please e-mail SpecialMarkets@ThomasNelson.com.

Scripture quotations are taken from the Holy Bible, New International Version®, NIV®. Copyright © 1973, 1978, 1984, 2011 by Biblica, Inc.® Used by permission of Zondervan. All rights reserved worldwide. www.zondervan.com. The "NIV" and "New International Version" are trademarks registered in the United States Patent and Trademark Office by Biblica, Inc.®

Publisher's Note: This novel is a work of fiction. Names, characters, places, and incidents are either products of the authors' imagination or used fictitiously. All characters are fictional, and any similarity to people living or dead is purely coincidental.

Any internet addresses (websites, blogs, etc.) in this book are offered as a resource. They are not intended in any way to be or imply an endorsement by Thomas Nelson, nor does Thomas Nelson vouch for the content of these sites for the life of this book.

Library of Congress Cataloging-in-Publication Data

Names: Coble, Colleen, author. | Acker, Rick, 1966- author.
Title: Where secrets lie / Colleen Coble and Rick Acker.
Description: Nashville, Tennessee: Thomas Nelson, 2025. | Series: Tupelo Grove novel ; 2 | Summary: "USA TODAY bestselling romantic suspense author Colleen Coble and Rick Acker deliver the second book in their compelling Tupelo Grove series (following What We Hide), where a crumbling university, stolen artifacts, deep family secrets, and deadly ambitions all stand in the way of a second chance at happiness"—Provided by publisher.
Identifiers: LCCN 2024057329 (print) | LCCN 2024057330 (ebook) | ISBN 9781400345694 (trade paperback) | ISBN 9781400345700 (hardcover) | ISBN 9781400345717 (ebook) | ISBN 9781400345724
Subjects: LCGFT: Christian fiction. | Thrillers (Fiction) | Romance fiction. | Novels.
Classification: LCC PS3553.O2285 W48 2025 (print) | LCC PS3553.O2285 (ebook) | DDC 813/.54—dc23/eng/20241216
LC record available at https://lccn.loc.gov/2024057329
LC ebook record available at https://lccn.loc.gov/2024057330

Printed in the United States of America

25 26 27 28 29 LBC 5 4 3 2 1

For our amazingly supportive spouses,
Anette Acker and Dave Coble.
This book wouldn't have made
it to print without you!

CHAPTER 1

JESSICA LEGARE KEPT AN ESCAPE BAG IN THE LOWER-LEFT drawer of the desk in her home office. It held a burner phone, fake passports for herself and her son, two credit cards in the same name as her passport, hair dye, a loaded SIG P365, and a heart-shaped silver locket.

The bag was Dior, of course. Jess always carried a Dior purse, so to a careful observer, anything else might be a tip-off that she was up to something. If she ever had to run, she wanted to be halfway around the world before anyone noticed she was gone. She'd been caught flat-footed once—and she got arrested and very nearly spent the rest of her life in prison as a result.

She would not let that happen again.

The man who got Jess arrested, Beckett Harrison, was now in jail himself, facing a long list of felony charges, including murder. Still, Jess didn't assume she was safe. In fact, she knew she wasn't. Even if everything went completely according to plan, there was a good chance she'd need that escape bag.

Should she use it now? She opened the drawer and peered into the shadowy interior, lit only by the glow from the monitors on her desk. She could use one of the cards in the bag to buy tickets to Paris for her and her son, Simon. An Uber to the airport could go on the other card. She could wake Simon and bundle him into the car when it arrived. Twenty-four hours from now they could be safely nestled into one of the little villages dotting the French Alps. They had distant relatives there. Maybe they could build new lives for themselves.

She sighed and shut the drawer. It was a nice fantasy, but nothing more. She and Simon wouldn't be safe in France. They'd just face different dangers. Her best bet was to stick to the plan. Besides, she needed to finish what she'd started. She owed it to her family and herself.

Her computer chimed, notifying her that it was 6:25 a.m. and her video call was scheduled to start in five minutes. She turned on her voice-altering program and opened the call. She kept her camera off. The calling program had end-to-end encryption, but she was taking no chances.

At six thirty sharp, two men joined the call. Both also had their cameras off and used voice-altering software. One had a picture of a gorgeous English cream golden retriever for an avatar, a subtle reference to the fact that his family raised championship dogs a century ago. The other man's avatar was the Punisher's death's-head logo, a not-at-all-subtle reference to how he viewed himself. Though she knew the real identities of both men, thinking of them as their avatars helped her distance herself and remember not to call them by name.

English Cream spoke first. "Greetings, all. Our buyers are getting impatient and starting to ask questions, especially with these new, very valuable pieces of art coming from the digs. We have to get them sold before anyone discovers the new areas being looted. How soon can deliveries resume?"

"Soon," Punisher replied. "Beach is crawling with Coasties

and cops all the way from Biloxi to Pensacola. We're working on an alternate route. Should be good to go in a week or so."

"And I can handle the paperwork, at least for now." Jess hadn't cared about the art they'd smuggled earlier—but this new vein of artifacts was culturally important, and she was eager to get them into the hands of collectors who could pay well. A brand-new Mayan ruin had been located in the jungle, and the treasures it offered were worth a fortune. They included a complete chocolate set and extremely rare codex pages found in a sealed jar. Her conscience twinged at the knowledge that the artifacts they'd found in Central and South America belonged in a museum, but her partners would insist that they be sold for full value.

She pushed away her qualms and focused on how these sales furthered her desire for revenge.

"Good, and what of the other initiatives?" English Cream asked. "Are those proceeding despite the, ah, excitement of the last month?"

Jess nodded, even though no one could see her. "We're very short-staffed, of course." Which was a major understatement—every member of the Tupelo Grove branch of the organization was now dead or behind bars, except Jess. "Nonetheless, everything is on schedule."

"Excellent!" The satisfaction in English Cream's voice came through despite the robotic distortion. "You've done fine work."

The job ahead of her would be hard, but it would be worth it. If only she didn't have to cause her sister so much pain in the process.

Whoever thought young love was the best hadn't walked through the fire to arrive at Savannah Webster's unexpected destination. She smiled at her ex-husband on the other side of the flickering candlelight. Even at thirty-seven Hez retained his lean, muscular build and strong jawline. He commanded a room when he entered, and he still had her heart.

She swept her hand at the familiar dining room. "It feels right to be back here."

Billy's Seafood Restaurant in Pelican Harbor had been the site of landmark moments in their past. He'd asked her to marry him the first time at this very table, and they'd celebrated all their anniversaries here. This spot held tender memories and others with a sharper edge to them. The food and ambience had been a constant throughout their marriage.

He reached across the table and laced his fingers with hers. "Our first real date in ages. This is where I wanted to bring you last summer when I showed up at your office."

If she hadn't been so hardheaded that day, she wouldn't be single right now. "Better late than never. I've been thinking about where and when to have our wedding. What do you think about the gorgeous old chapel on campus? Plans are under way to restore it, and it should be finished by June when the term ends."

"June? Why so long?" He flashed an amorous smile. "Run away with me. I'll pull some strings and we can get married after dessert."

It was a tempting offer, especially with the candlelight dancing in his blue eyes and gleaming off his dark hair. But she shook her head. "I want to do this right, Hez. A clean break and a fresh start. Just getting remarried right away in front of a justice of the peace would feel . . . I don't know, like nothing has changed and we're going to slip back into the old habits that wrecked our marriage the first time."

His eyes grew tender. He gave her hand a gentle squeeze. "I understand. And I agree—as much as I'd love to have you back tonight."

Her heart stuttered and she squeezed his hand back. "Almost as much as I'd love to have you." She took a deep breath to steady herself. He hadn't formally asked her yet, but they both knew they belonged together. "There are practical things we need to think about too. We need to find a house to buy. With Jess's hours, I expect Simon will be with us a lot. My rental on campus isn't big enough for you to have a home office and Simon to have his own room. I'd like a place off campus where Simon can play ball with his friends."

"You're right, and I want to get the Justice Chamber planned too. There's a lot for both of us to do, but I'm ready to restart our life together. That old chapel is beautiful. Do you want to do the whole thing again—white dress and tux?"

"I don't need a big, fancy wedding. Just a sweet ceremony with close friends and family. I don't need a fancy dress with a sweeping train for you to stumble over."

His smile extended to his eyes. "I remember that. In my defense, it was dark outside and I was ducking the birdseed."

"You had a cut on your head where it hit the bench on your way down."

He rubbed his head. "I was afraid I was bleeding all over your dress. I'm glad we aren't replaying that fiasco."

She took a sip of her sweet tea and waited while the server delivered their oysters. "A simple sheath will suit me fine.

Maybe a pale blue one. You can wear a suit instead of a tux. Jess will be my maid of honor, of course. Who do you want for your best man? Maybe Blake?"

"I was thinking about asking Simon. He might actually say yes if he doesn't have to wear a tux."

"Oh, Hez, he would love that! I'd assumed you'd ask Blake or Jimmy. Jimmy's done a lot for you."

"It would be hard to choose between them, but they'd both understand if I ask Simon." He took an oyster shell and slid the meat into his mouth. "Wow, these are good. Have one."

She picked up one and ate it. The salty taste tantalized her taste buds, and she swallowed it down with a cracker. "So good." She gave him a mischievous smile. "We could ask Jimmy to be the ring bearer."

Hez chuckled. "That's quite a mental picture. He'd make four of Simon."

"We could tell the guests he's your bouncer and is there to keep you from backing out."

"Or maybe to keep you from running away."

She shook her head. "I'm not going anywhere. I have a chain in the car ready to use on you, though."

His smile vanished. "I will never leave, Savannah. I learned from my mistakes."

"We both did." She withdrew her hand to take a look at the menu. "The specials sound great, but I must have my favorite shrimp étouffée."

A server carried a bottle of wine and two stemmed glasses past their table. Hez's gaze followed the trajectory as the man delivered the wine with a flourish to the couple next to them. The familiar bottle with its black-and-copper label reminded her of the last time Hez had ordered his favorite Nth Degree chardonnay. After too many refills, she'd had to steady him for the walk back to the Bayfront Inn.

Hez cleared his throat. "I love it too, but I'm not sure it will taste the same with water instead of a good chardonnay." He inclined his head toward the other table. "Looks like a few more people have discovered our favorite label."

His favorite label. She struggled to keep her smile in place. She'd be happy if she never saw another bottle of wine in her life. She'd read that 85 percent of alcoholics relapsed in the first year and 90 percent in the first four years. Knowing Hez, she was sure he was aware of those statistics and was determined to be in the small percentage of people who stayed the course. She didn't understand the struggle he faced, but she wanted to. And she wanted to help in any way she could.

She studied his wistful expression. Was he missing the taste of the wine, or was he thinking of happier times and the things they'd celebrated? Or were good wine and good times inextricably intertwined in his memories? It began to dawn on her that this might be a lifelong battle for him.

CHAPTER 2

HEZ SAT IN THE FRONT ROW OF THE OLD COURTROOM GALLERY, stomach full of razor-winged butterflies. He was a veteran of dozens of felony trials—many in this very courtroom—but he'd always been one of the attorneys dueling in the front or a spectator watching from the gallery. This would be the first time he experienced one as a crime victim—and a witness.

Hez's old friend Hope Norcross stood from the prosecution table at the front of the courtroom. "The People call Hezekiah Webster."

Hez walked down the aisle and across the open space known as the "well of the court" to the witness stand. He could feel every eye on him, and for once he didn't like the sensation.

The bored-looking bailiff pushed himself to his feet as Hez approached. "Raise your right hand. Do you swear to tell the truth, the whole truth, and nothing but the truth, so help you God?"

"I do." Hez took his seat on the witness stand. The courtroom seemed bigger and more intimidating from this perspective. Rows of reporters filled the gallery benches, watching expectantly. A man and a woman in expensive suits sat at the defense table. The defendant was Beckett Harrison, the slimy former provost of Tupelo Grove University who had first tried to steal Savannah's heart and then attempted to murder them both, along with their nephew, Simon. Beckett's dark hair was perfectly coiffed, and he looked relaxed and comfortable, like he was waiting for a board meeting to start. But his brown eyes followed Hez with cold hatred.

The woman beside Beckett watched Hez with an unsettling smile tugging at the corners of her perfect lips. Beckett's attorney, Martine Dubois, wore a charcoal-gray suit and a white blouse that set off her tan. A silver clip gathered her blonde hair at the nape of her neck, accentuating her strong cheekbones and almond-shaped brown eyes, the only features hinting that her mother was half Vietnamese. Hez had known her since law school, and he did not look forward to being cross-examined by her.

Hope arranged her notes on the lectern. She was five years younger than Hez and barely reached five and a half feet, even with the three-inch heels she wore to court. Still, she managed to project strength and confidence—a confidence Hez knew she didn't feel today.

Hope couldn't tell Hez what she thought about the Beckett Harrison case, but she didn't have to. She and Hez had been friends since she first walked into the DA's office as an intern a decade ago and he became her mentor. Ordinarily, she'd be bubbling with excitement over a high-profile trial like this. She couldn't say anything specific because Hez was a witness and not her co-counsel, but her enthusiasm and energy should have been palpable over the past few weeks. They weren't. In fact, she had been tense and unhappy whenever they got together for coffee or a run.

It wasn't hard to guess Hope's problem. There was a right way and a wrong way to try the Harrison case—and she was doing it the wrong way.

The right way to prosecute Beckett Harrison would have been to do it in at least two trials, maybe more. Beckett had committed a series of crimes, including two murders. The case against him for some of the crimes was a slam dunk. But the evidence for others—including both murders—was much thinner, at least for now. Hope could have tried Beckett on the slam-dunk charges now to put him in prison for a few years. Then she could have built her case on the murders and other crimes while he was safely behind bars and charged him whenever she was ready. Instead, she had charged everything at once. That decision would have come from the DA himself: Elliot Drake.

Drake was up for reelection, and he considered himself an excellent candidate for governor someday. Future governors didn't bring piecemeal cases that would barely merit a mention in the local newspaper—they brought big, splashy cases that would capture the media's attention statewide. So Hope was stuck trying a big, splashy case that she could well lose.

Compounding Hope's problem, Beckett had hired a smart lawyer. Defense attorneys usually wanted months or even years to prepare for trial because the prosecution had a huge head start since they'd finished investigating the case before bringing charges. But Martine correctly read the situation and pressed for the earliest trial date she could get, gambling that her odds of an acquittal would only go down if both sides had time to do a full investigation.

Hope cleared her throat. "Please state your name for the record."

Hez turned to the jury box and spoke directly to the jurors, just like he'd always coached witnesses to do. "Hezekiah Webster."

"When did you first meet the defendant?"

"The day I started investigating the murder of Ellison Abernathy."

"Why were you investigating that?"

"My wife, Savannah—or, well, she was my wife at the time—she found the body and the police initially showed interest in her. I'm a former prosecutor, so I was representing her."

"Did you suspect that Mr. Harrison might be the killer?"

"Not at first, but I should have."

"Why?"

"Because he immediately insinuated himself into the investigation for no obvious reason. He had no law enforcement background or investigative expertise. Also, he had a very busy job and he wasn't particularly close to Abernathy, and yet he somehow always had time to work on this case." Hez shook his head, annoyed at the memory of his stupidity—which had nearly gotten Savannah, Simon, and him killed. "I should have suspected that he was trying to figure out whether he was a suspect and divert suspicion away from himself."

"When did you first begin to think that he might be the killer?"

"It wasn't until I saw his number on the phone of his co-conspirator, Erik Andersen, that I—"

COLLEEN COBLE AND RICK ACKER

Martine rose in a fluid motion. "Objection. Assumes facts not in evidence. Specifically, assumes that the defendant and Mr. Andersen conspired together."

"Sustained." Judge Achilles Hopkins leaned over the bench and arched a bushy eyebrow at Hez. "You know the rules of evidence as well as I do, Mr. Webster."

Hope smiled. "Let's take it step-by-step, Mr. Webster."

Hez's face grew hot. It had been a stupid mistake brought on by nerves. He started over, with Hope helping him to "lay a foundation," as all rookie litigators were taught to do, before launching into the story of how he and Savannah caught Beckett's crony, former TGU European history professor Erik Andersen, red-handed with a smuggled artifact. Andersen tried to call Beckett, but Hez had grabbed the phone before Andersen could press Call.

Hope walked Hez through the rest of his investigation of the murder and smuggling case that dominated his life during the past few months. The jurors listened raptly, and one elderly woman was literally on the edge of her seat. But Hez couldn't help seeing the holes in the case Hope was building. Someone knocked out Hez while he was outside Beckett's home, but it probably wasn't Beckett. He had been inside talking with Savannah—and denying that he had anything to do with the artifact smuggling or anything else. Hez found a bug in his office light fixture, but there was no proof that Beckett planted it. Only the evidence from Erik Andersen's phone and home— all of which later vanished—connected Beckett to the artifact smuggling. And nothing at all tied him to the scenes of the two murders or the knife used in both.

The only direct evidence tying Beckett to either murder was

a security-camera video that appeared to show him stealing a fleece from Hez's former client Jessica Legare. That fleece was later found soaked with Abernathy's blood, wrapped around the murder weapon, and buried on Jess's property. But the video only caught the thief's leg, which had a scar that resembled one on Beckett's left leg.

The best evidence in Hope's entire case was what Beckett did after Hez and Savannah found the video. Beckett kidnapped them and Simon, knocked them unconscious, and took them out on Bon Secour Bay, where he planned to kill them all. Fortunately, Hez had been wearing a wire, so the police had heard everything Beckett said. Even so, law enforcement barely arrived in time.

Hope milked this part of Hez's testimony, drawing out every detail. He understood why she was doing it, but reliving that day was brutal.

"What did you see when you woke up on the boat?"

"The first thing I saw was Savannah's face, right over mine. She looked terrified."

"Then what happened?"

"She kissed me and told me she loved me." Hez took a deep breath and fought to keep his voice steady. "I think she wanted me to know before we both died."

"Did you think you were going to die?"

"Yes."

"Why?"

"We were lying in the bottom of a boat with our hands and feet bound. Beckett had already threatened us, and that was before we had hard evidence that he was a murderer. His intentions were clear, and he removed all doubt a few seconds later."

"What did he do?"

Hez forced himself to look at Beckett, who returned his gaze with a stony stare. "He came over holding a pistol and said he really enjoyed seeing us helpless. Then he kicked me in the stomach."

"Then what happened?"

"I thought he might start shooting any second, so I tried to get him talking. If I was going to die, I wanted you to have as much evidence as possible to prosecute him for murdering us." He pushed his mouth into a half smile. "Fortunately, he's more of a talker than a thinker. You know the old law enforcement saying: 'We never catch the smart ones.'" Hez savored the spasm of impotent rage that flashed across Beckett's face. He hoped the jury saw it too.

"What exactly did he say?"

The jury would doubtless hear the tape several times over the course of the trial, but Hez knew the impact live testimony could have, and he was sure Hope did too. He turned to the jurors, making eye contact with each one as he spoke. "He said he'd rented the boat and bought the gun using my credit card. He told me that he planned to make it look like a murder-suicide—that I was unstable and killed my wife and nephew before turning the gun on myself. He said it would be how the world remembered me, my epitaph."

He paused as the memory rushed back over him. "I'll never forget the look on his face. He was smug, proud of himself. He was about to kill three people, including a child, and he was patting himself on the back."

"What happened next?"

"I heard another boat approaching and then a Coast Guard air horn." He smiled and shook his head. "I'll never again complain about how loud those things are." Several jurors smiled and one suppressed a chuckle.

Hope turned to the judge. "No further questions at this time. Pass the witness."

CHAPTER 3

EVEN THE OLD GATOR BOO RADLEY WASN'T AS TERRIFYING as what waited on the other side of the door. Savannah smoothed her damp palms on her navy skirt and took a deep breath before trying on a smile. It felt more like a grimace to her. The undercurrents of uncertainty had been hard to miss in these final days of tenure approval. She should have been a shoo-in, but Tony Guzman's résumé was formidable. While her PhD came from the University of Alabama with honors, Tony's had come from Yale. Alabama was a good school, but it couldn't compete with an Ivy League one.

With her smile in place, she twisted the doorknob and stepped into the conference room in the administration building with her head high and confident. "Good morning."

Professor Charlie Hinkle's warm brown eyes smiled back at her from under his white brows. He was serving as acting head of the history department, and his white hair stood on end, as if he'd run a distracted hand through it. She didn't know the acting provost, Gerald Saunders, well, and she almost wished Ellison Abernathy back from the grave. At least he was a known personality, even if they'd often clashed.

Gerald, with his thick black hair, put her in mind of an aging

Elvis, and she resisted the urge to break into a rendition of "Don't Be Cruel." She bit the inside of her lip to choke back the nervous laughter struggling to erupt.

"Have a seat." Gerald steepled his hands in front of him on the table. He waited until she slid into a chair at the other end of the conference table. "You have an impressive résumé, Savannah. Your family's long history with TGU is much appreciated too."

She absently fondled her bracelet before forcing herself to stop. They'd given her five years' experience full credit when she was hired two and a half years ago, and she'd come with full expectations of being granted tenure. She was a Legare and that meant something here. "Thank you. I love TGU and my students. I have many fond memories of running through the swamps and open fields in my youth. It's wonderful to be back." She wanted to add "permanently," but it felt presumptuous. She had to be granted tenure. The future she planned with Hez centered around TGU and the surrounding community.

"We have two very talented individuals competing for the same position. I wish we could offer tenure to both you and Professor Guzman."

The *but* hovered in the room like an early morning fog off the swamp. Her stomach tightened at the sympathy on Professor Hinkle's gnomelike face. "I wish that were possible too. Tony is an excellent professor."

She'd sat in on Tony's lecture on the Neo-Babylonian Empire and had noticed how enthralled the committee had been when he'd mentioned protecting ancient sites in Iraq. He'd worked to recover priceless artifacts looted from Iraqi museums as well. It wasn't even his specialty, but he'd been passionate and knowledgeable about all of it. But her expertise in pre-Columbian artifacts had made a huge contribution to the university already. No one else had her wide breadth of experience and knowledge about the Willard Treasure—not only the artifacts themselves but the history behind them as well. That had to count for something. The university press was going to publish her book on the Willard Treasure too. That was big news.

Gerald exhaled. "I'm sorry to tell you we have decided to offer Professor Guzman the tenure position. We'll have to eliminate a professorial position and switch the course load to adjuncts, so there's just not room in the budget for both of you. I know you were hoping for a different outcome."

The news stole her breath, and nausea roiled in her stomach. "I—I understand. Tony is an excellent choice, and I wish him well."

"I've already written you a glowing letter of recommendation," Hinkle put in. "Several other members of the committee are doing the same. I hate to see you go, Savannah. I'm sure you'll land a wonderful position soon. I hate losing you."

She couldn't wrap her head around the realization she had to leave this haven she'd found. Her legs wobbled when she stood. "Thank you for the recommendations. I appreciate them so much."

She fled the room before she disgraced herself by crying or throwing up. Finding another job wasn't as much of a problem as having their lives upended when they'd already been through so much. Jess had guaranteed Hez his legal clinic here. How could she tell him he had to relocate now? He needed the stability of his beloved law while he continued the road to recovery. They both did.

Ella was buried in the family cemetery, and Savannah wanted to be able to visit with her baby girl at any time. She couldn't move clear across the country where it would require a flight to sit by her daughter's grave and watch the mourning doves pecking seeds in the grass.

Savannah shut the door behind her and, breathing heavily, leaned her back against it. Hez was testifying right now, and she couldn't talk to him. Did Jess already know? Savannah escaped the building and rushed to her sister's office across the green space. Tears burned in her eyes, and she wished she could blame it on the stiff January wind that made the fifty-five-degree weather feel like the forties. She entered Jess's building and spotted her open door.

The clatter of Savannah's heels on the marble tile alerted Jess as Savannah rushed toward the room. Eyes wide, Jess stood and came around the side of her desk. "Savannah, what's wrong?" She tucked a strand of chin-length blonde hair behind her left ear.

Savannah stopped and pressed a hand to her midsection. "I didn't get tenure, Jess. They offered it to Tony. I have to find another job."

Jess's mouth opened and closed before she clenched her jaw. "The rats. I'm sorry, Savannah."

"I shouldn't be surprised. Tony is a terrific professor. If I were on the committee, I would have picked him too." She stepped past her sister and yanked a tissue from the box on Jess's desk. "I don't want to leave here. I want to be with you and Simon." She blew her nose. "Where is he anyway?"

"He's at the gym playing basketball with some of the guys. I told him to be back here in an hour." Jess gripped Savannah's upper arm. "There's just enough time for some coffee and a cinnamon roll at University Grounds. Some carbs will settle your nerves. Try not to worry. I'll help you find something."

Savannah let her sister tug her toward the door. By the time Jess had to be back for Simon, Hez would be out of court, and they'd have to decide together what came next.

Martine took Hope's place at the lectern. "Good morning, Mr. Webster." Her voice held a hint of a French accent from her Paris childhood. "Let's start with a standard preliminary question that Ms. Norcross forgot to ask. Are you under the influence of alcohol or any other substance that might impair your ability to testify accurately and completely?" The gleam in her dark eyes said that she knew all about Hez's past.

Hez smiled. He'd expected her to try to rattle him. "Nothing except caffeine."

"I'm glad to hear it. Mr. Harrison was friends with Savannah, wasn't he?"

"Yes, though that was before he tried to kill her."

Martine's full lips twitched. "We'll get to that. As her friend, it would make sense for him to be concerned for her welfare, correct?"

"I suppose."

"And that would explain why he was so interested in seeing her cleared of an unjust murder charge, right?"

"I don't know. You'd have to ask him that." Which almost certainly wouldn't happen. No competent defense lawyer would put the defendant on the stand in a case like this. A prosecutor like Hope couldn't comment on Beckett's decision to take the Fifth, but Hez was a mere witness today, so the same rules didn't apply to him.

Martine's eyes narrowed. She adjusted her notes on the lectern, knocking a pen off in the process. She bent over to pick it up, flashing her ample cleavage at Hez. He suppressed a chuckle and kept his gaze fixed on the back of the courtroom. She had told him about this trick over drinks when they dated briefly before he met Savannah. She called the tactic "blinding 'em with boobs" and used it to knock difficult male witnesses off-balance.

Martine straightened. "The video allegedly showing Mr. Harrison with Ms. Legare's fleece does not show his face, correct?"

"Yes."

"In fact, the only reason you think it shows Mr. Harrison is the scar on his leg, correct?"

"That, plus the fact that his build and gait are the same as the man in the video. Plus, he had been in Ms. Legare's office on multiple occasions and likely knew she kept a fleece there."

"Are you aware that Mr. Harrison is an avid cyclist?"

"I've seen him dressed in bike shorts on occasion."

"Are you aware that many cyclists have scars on their legs?"

Hez shrugged. "I know a lot of bikers, and I've never seen a scar exactly like that."

"But some of them do have scars?"

"Yes."

"Did you ever see the murder weapon in Mr. Harrison's possession?"

"No."

"Did you ever hear him threaten to kill either Ellison Abernathy or Peter Cardin?"

"No."

"Did you ever see him act aggressively or violently toward either of them?"

"No."

"Did you ever see a trafficked artifact in Mr. Harrison's possession?"

"No."

"How about fraudulent documents designed to allow the sale of such artifacts? Did you ever see him with any of those?"

"No."

"Would it be fair to say that you never liked Mr. Harrison?"

"We weren't friends, if that's what you mean—but I didn't really have anything against him until I realized he was a murderer and was trying to pin his crimes on my client, Ms. Legare."

"But he was friends with your ex-wife, correct?"

Hez felt his blood pressure rising at the memory of seeing Savannah and Beckett together. "Yes."

"Close friends?"

Close enough that Hez once walked in on Beckett giving her a shoulder massage. Hez did his best to purge the image from his mind. How had Savannah let such a sociopath into her life? "You'd have to ask them," he forced out.

"Did their friendship bother you?"

Hope stood. "We're getting pretty far afield. Counsel is simply harassing the witness now."

Martine wrinkled her forehead. "Harassing? No, Your Honor. I'm merely demonstrating that the witness is biased against Mr. Harrison."

Hope leaned forward. "The defendant kidnapped and tried to kill the witness, his wife, and his nephew. I think we can stipulate that the witness probably doesn't have warm feelings for the defendant."

The judge nodded. "You've made your point, Ms. Dubois. Move on."

"Thank you, Your Honor." Martine turned back to Hez. "In each of the attacks you claim occurred, you admit that Mr. Harrison did not act alone, correct?"

"Yes."

"In fact, aside from him allegedly striking you on the boat, he never touched you in anger, correct?"

"Yes."

"In every other case, someone else struck you, clamped a drugged cloth over your mouth, and so on, right?"

"Yes."

"And one of these violent individuals was on the boat with Mr. Harrison at the time of the alleged attempted murder, correct?"

"There was another man on the boat, but I don't know whether he was the same one who had attacked me before. I never saw their faces."

"Are you aware that the other man on the boat with you, Deke Willard, has a long criminal history, including convictions for assault with a deadly weapon and attempted murder?"

"I didn't know anything about Mr. Willard at the time, but I subsequently learned about his past."

"Mr. Harrison had previously stated that he was attempting to protect you, Savannah, and Simon from dangerous individuals, correct?"

Hez blinked. Was Martine really trying to portray Beckett Harrison as a frightened pawn trying to protect them from Deke Willard? "Yes—but it's pretty clear from the surrounding circumstances that he was lying."

"Is it possible that your bias against Mr. Harrison has colored your memory?"

"No."

Martine picked up her notes. "Pass the witness."

The judge looked at Hope. "Any redirect?"

She stood. "No, Your Honor."

The judge leaned over the bench and peered down at Hez. "Thank you, Mr. Webster. You're excused."

Hez got up and walked out of the courtroom on stiff legs. The adrenaline crash hit as he stepped out into the cold January sunshine. All he wanted to do was get to the old couch in his condo and take a nap. He'd never realized just how exhausting it was to testify.

The lawyer part of his brain refused to shut down, though. His testimony had gone about as well as it could, and Hope had made the right decision in forgoing redirect. She'd gotten everything she could on direct, and Martine hadn't done any damage that could be fixed on redirect. Still, she had done damage.

Was it enough to establish reasonable doubt in the minds of the jurors?

CHAPTER 4

THE BLACK IRON STAIRS TO HEZ'S CONDO CLANGED UNDER Savannah's feet as she climbed to the second floor. A fishing boat motored toward the Pelican Harbor dock, and another boat blasted its horn out on Bon Secour Bay. The scent of crab cakes should have made her hungry since she hadn't eaten since last night. She hadn't touched the cinnamon roll Jess had insisted on buying her. Her stomach was still in knots from the news.

The door was locked, and she pressed the doorbell. It seemed forever until Hez opened it. His hair askew and sans tie and suit jacket, he blinked blearily down at her. The welcoming smile that appeared fell away when he finally focused on her face.

She threw herself into his arms, and the familiar scent of his cologne soothed her agitation. "Were you sleeping? Just hold me a minute."

His arms came around her. "I didn't get much sleep last night, so I took a nap on the sofa after I got back." He hugged her tightly to his chest, and his heartbeat sped up under her ear. "What happened?"

She lifted her head to stare up at him through her tears. He wouldn't expect her to be strong the way Jess had. Hez always understood. "They gave tenure to Tony. I'm out." Her voice wobbled at the end, and fresh tears blurred her vision. "I—I can't stay here, Hez. I have to find a new job somewhere else."

"Oh, babe." He folded her close again and rested his chin on her head for a moment before he stepped back and guided her into the living room. He dropped into the armchair and pulled her onto his lap. "Cry it out, and we'll talk."

The sound of his deep, confident voice coupled with the security of his arms was enough to stop her tears. She gulped and wiped her face with her palms. "I'm okay. I should have expected it. I mean, Tony Guzman is a first-class professor. It was wrong of me to expect my family connections to sway anything. It should be based on merit alone—and it was."

His fingers rippled through her hair in a soothing gesture. "He's good, but he's not better than you. Your book about the history of the university should have been something the committee took into account too. They've lost a star."

His voice still sounded groggy, but she'd never known him to nap in the middle of the afternoon. He really must have been tired. "Your new clinic is here, Hez. I'll try to find something close enough for us to at least see each other on the weekends."

His fingers in her hair stilled. "Not going to happen, Savannah. Now that we've found our way back to each other, I won't let anything come between us. We can check out Birmingham universities. There are several, and I could go back to work for Jimmy or set up shop just about anywhere."

"But what about your clinic?"

His palms cupped her face, and he stared into her eyes.

"You're more important to me than anything else. A clinic like mine is a draw to law students. Someone will want it eventually. Maybe the timing isn't right yet."

She slid her arms around his neck and pulled his face down for a kiss. His arms tightened around her, and his kiss drove out the pain and humiliation of the morning. Her smile and optimism returned when he lifted his head. "I don't know how you do it, but I knew you'd make everything right again. We've weathered far worse than this setback."

Her pulse resumed its normal rhythm, and she laid her head back on his chest. "It's only about four hours to Birmingham. We could visit Ella's grave any weekend we wanted."

His fingers resumed their path through her hair. "I could check out Mobile for a job too. It wouldn't have to be Birmingham. Being close to Ella's grave is important to both of us. We have options, babe. The only thing that isn't an option is splitting up." His final words ended in a yawn. "I should make coffee and try to wake up. I've never been on the witness stand, and I didn't realize how grueling it was."

She patted his arm. "Did Beckett's lawyer give you a hard time?"

He nodded. "It was Martine Dubois. Do you remember her?"

Savannah remembered her very well. She first met Martine on one of her and Hez's early dates. Martine spotted them at an outdoor table at Maria's and walked up. She commented that Hez had been working out and squeezed his upper arm. She then left her hand on his shoulder as Hez introduced Savannah, and they chatted for a couple of minutes. Then Martine trailed her hand across the back of Hez's neck as she walked away. Savannah was sure Martine was making a power move, but Hez insisted she was just a friend and touched people a lot. "She didn't go easy on you even though you're friends?"

He chuckled. "That's not her style. She wouldn't go easy on her own grandma if she thought it might hurt her chances of winning."

"How did it go?"

"I think my testimony helped the case, but Hope has an uphill battle for conviction on the two murders. Beckett will probably get convicted on the kidnapping and attempted murder charges but acquitted on everything else."

She winced before kissing him again and sliding off his lap. "I'll make coffee. You need it good and strong. You have anything to eat in the fridge? I'm starving."

"Leftover shrimp bisque. There's enough for both of us. I'll go get a breath of fresh air. That should wake me up. We can take a walk along the water and make plans."

She kicked off her pumps and padded on bare feet to the kitchen. She dumped an extra scoop of coffee in the grinder and washed out the carafe, then grabbed the old filter and grounds. When she opened the trash, she froze.

An empty bottle of Mondavi cabernet sauvignon lay atop the rest of the garbage.

Her lungs squeezed, and she couldn't draw in a breath. Hez had been so groggy when she arrived. Was this the reason? The fingers of her right hand crept to the comfort of fondling the bracelet on her left.

Maybe someone had given it to him and he'd dumped it down the sink. She hadn't smelled alcohol on his breath, but she'd been so upset, she might not have noticed. Tears burned her eyes again, and she swallowed hard. Was their newfound happiness a sham?

———

Hez pushed himself out of the armchair as Savannah went into the kitchen to make coffee. He opened the door leading to the condo's little balcony and walked out, letting the chilly breeze blow the last wisps of grogginess out of his head. He surveyed Pelican Harbor's quaint little French Quarter. The cries of seagulls mingled with the pleasant hum of voices on the street below and jazz from a couple of better-than-average street musicians. A pair of mourning doves cooed from the power lines across the street. The familiar smells of fresh coffee and hot beignets drifted up from Petit Charms. Most days, he would have been tempted to go down for a sweet snack and jolt of caffeine, but he had no appetite after Savannah's tenure news.

This place had just started to feel like home, but it wasn't. They would have to pick up and start over somewhere else. He could set up shop basically anyplace that had a courthouse and affordable office space, but what about Savannah? What if another school denied her tenure in a couple of years? How many chances would she get? Had TGU been her best shot?

She seemed to be holding up well, but this must have been a real gut punch—and one that she wouldn't recover from quickly. She'd feel it every time she set foot on her beloved TGU campus.

He shook his head. She said he'd made everything right

again, and he wished that were true. She deserved to be happy. He shoved his hands in his pockets and fidgeted with the contents. The longing to be husband and wife again only intensified with each day. One day soon she'd be his again. He'd be able to roll over in the morning and find her warm and still groggy in the same bed. That time couldn't come soon enough for him.

"Hez?" The brittleness in Savannah's voice told him something was wrong even before he turned around.

Her auburn hair stood out from her head as if she'd raked her hands through it. Her green eyes were wide and disbelieving in her white face. She held out a bottle like an accusation. A wine bottle.

A chill went through him. "Where did you get that?"

Her voice was barely above a whisper. "Your trash."

His heart stopped. "I—I have no idea how it got there."

"Hez, this is Mondavi cab. You always used to have a couple of bottles in the kitchen before—" She stared down and blinked.

"Before Ella died and I became an alcoholic." He rubbed his forehead. "I know. Look, Savannah, I never saw that bottle before. Someone must have planted it in my trash." He winced inwardly as soon as the words were out of his mouth. He sounded so desperate and paranoid.

"Why . . . why would someone do that, Hez? And who would know about your go-to wine from three years ago?"

He shook his head as the implications of the bottle in her hand sank in. Someone had broken into his apartment. Someone who knew a lot about his personal history. "I don't know, but I'll figure it out."

She drew a shaky breath. "I know recovering from alcoholism is really hard. I'll be there for you, no matter how long it takes."

Her words cut through him like a cold knife. "I haven't had a drink in over a year. I swear it. I swear it before God. Someone is trying to frame me." His brain whirred, spitting out half-formed theories. "Augusta hasn't caught the smugglers yet—maybe it's one of them. But how would they know I drank Mondavi cab? The mole in the police department! That's it! There must be something in the file on Ella's death that—"

Her shoulders started to shake and a ragged sob broke from her throat. "I—I can't do this. Not now."

"Savannah, you have to believe me. I—" He reached out to touch her arm, but she flinched away.

"I'm sorry, Hez. I have to go." She turned and fled.

"Savannah, wait!" He started to follow her, but she was gone. He heard the front door open, followed a moment later by the clatter of steps on the outside stairs.

He stood alone in the middle of the empty apartment and sighed. He reached into his pocket and pulled out a small box. He opened it. A diamond sparkled in the rays of late-afternoon sun slanting in through the living room window. It was the same diamond he gave her the first time but reset in a new band with five small rubies, one for each year of their first marriage. He'd been waiting for the right moment to give it to her.

Would that moment ever come?

CHAPTER 5

SAVANNAH PARKED IN THE LOT ACROSS FROM UNIVERSITY
Grounds and dodged a rusty blue pickup on her way across
the street. After she'd shot a panicked text to her best friend,
Nora Craft had promised to meet her here. Once upon a time
the building that housed the coffee shop had been Hotel Tupelo. An investor had bought the grand old place with its high
ceilings and had turned it into retail and office space, but it
maintained its stately exterior.

She slowed to calm her racing heart and glanced around
the quaint town of Nova Cambridge. It had always reminded
her of a smaller, shabbier version of Oxford, Mississippi.
The weedy cobbled streets held cozy 1920s bungalows inter-
spersed with grander, newer homes. The little university town
was strategically located near all the things she loved while
maintaining its individuality. Just offshore, Mobile Bay and
Bon Secour Bay kissed and merged, and close by was the road
leading to the Sanctuary Animal Refuge over a little bridge
with Mobile Bay on one side and Weeks Bay on the other. It
was fifteen minutes from Pelican Harbor and about the same
to Foley if she wanted bigger stores and more people.

A familiar voice called out her name, and Savannah turned

to see her sister hurrying toward her on the sidewalk. The Dior bag on her arm was a pop of bright green against her tan slacks and sweater. Savannah tried to force a smile, but her eyes filled with tears.

Jess touched her forearm. "Savannah, I'm so sorry I didn't have more time to talk when the tenure news came down. You want to discuss your options a little more? I'll help you find another job. Simon is at a tutoring session with Will Dixon, and I'm free for however long you need me."

Savannah knew Jess valued her time above all else, and her willingness to offer comfort spoke volumes. "I think Nora is already inside, and I'd love to have you join us."

They went up the steps to the wraparound porch. The outdoor tables and chairs were taken by college students in TGU sweatshirts. She opened the door for her sister, and they stepped into the warm space scented with espresso, cinnamon, and cider. Nora waved to them from a table by the window. She was a forensic tech with the Pelican Harbor PD, and the two of them had bonded in a grief group. Nora was in her thirties with thick brown hair cut in a bob. She had been Savannah's spiritual mentor as well as a sounding board for the trials of the past two years.

Savannah managed to hold her composure on the way to join her. She spotted several other professors inside who avoided eye contact. News like hers traveled at warp speed through a university, and no one ever knew what to say when someone was on their way out. She'd been in their shoes before, but she'd never expected to face this fate.

She settled next to Nora and slipped out of her jacket. They ordered coffee and sandwiches before Nora poked her glasses back into place over her brown eyes and leaned over to squeeze her hand. "What's the SOS about?"

"I didn't get tenure. They gave the job to Tony Guzman." When her friend's eyes widened, Savannah tried to smile and failed. "I would have given it to him too. He's a terrific teacher and scholar."

Jess tapped her red nails against the tabletop. "He's not even in your league. You've always told me God doesn't make mistakes, but I think he blew it on this one. TGU doesn't deserve you."

"When do you need to leave?" Nora's voice shook. "What about applying at one of the other nearby universities? That way you could still stay in the area."

"I'll need to be out in the summer so they can move in someone else." The thought of her sweet cottage belonging to another professor tightened Savannah's throat. "I need to consider what's best for Hez too."

"I assume you told him?" Nora asked. "You guys will get through this. Maybe a fresh start will be good for both of you."

Savannah tore her napkin into strips as she nodded. "He's willing to start over wherever I can find work."

"I agree with Nora," Jess said. "Get out of here and make a fresh start. Hez has contacts in Birmingham. Or maybe you want to start over in Florida or somewhere else near the water."

Savannah pushed the paper strips aside. If Jess wasn't here, she would have already told Nora about the bottle she found in Hez's trash. It was something she needed to air, but her sister was bound to jump to the wrong conclusion. Even Hez's help through the jail ordeal hadn't endeared him to Jess. But Savannah couldn't hold it back any longer.

Her fingers stilled, and she stared at Jess. "That's what he said too. Right before I found an empty bottle of Mondavi cabernet sauvignon in his trash."

Shock settled over their faces before they looked away. It was one thing to be upset with Hez herself and another thing to hear anyone else condemn him.

The server brought their coffees and sandwiches. When he left, Nora eyed Savannah over the top of her coffee mug. "I'm sure you didn't let that slide. What did he say when you confronted him?"

"He denied it was his and said someone must have planted it there."

Jess put her hand to her mouth. "You can't go back into a toxic relationship like that, Savannah. How can you even work through things if he denies the truth? I know how you value honesty."

"He's never lied to me before."

"You sound like you believe him," Jess said.

"Maybe I do."

Jess hesitated for a heartbeat. "Is it possible he's deluding himself? Or could he have forgotten it? He took a hard hit to the head a few months ago. Did he complain of a headache or anything like that?"

Savannah took a sip of her coffee. "He seemed fine. When his drinking was at its worst, he had some memory issues. It's possible that's what happened. I could have him ask the doctor about the effects of the concussion."

Nora took a toothpick out of her BLT club. "Memory loss from one bottle of wine? That seems doubtful to me considering his history."

Jess shook her head. "Not from one bottle of wine—from a serious blow to the head. I've heard of people having memory problems and even personality changes years after a head injury. What if he has memory issues and maybe other problems, which alcohol makes worse? He might not even realize it."

Had Hez seemed off recently? Savannah searched her memory. Nothing came to mind, but they'd both been so busy she couldn't be sure. "I suppose it wouldn't hurt for him to check with his neurologist."

"Have you considered premarital counseling?" Nora asked. "It would be a way to get into the deeper issues. You have a lot to work out—both of you. The kind of trauma you've been through isn't something you ever get over, but you can learn to handle it better."

"I haven't said anything to him about it, but I will." It had been the right decision to tell them what had happened. She felt stronger and more ready to deal with it than an hour ago. In the past, she'd run away from their problems, but she couldn't make that mistake again. Hez was in a better place too, and she had to believe they could make their way through this new challenge.

"So who do you think put the bottle in your trash?" Hez's cousin, Blake Lawson, asked Hez as the two of them jogged along the asphalt trail bordering Bon Secour Bay.

"Good question." Light rain dampened the shoulders of Hez's red-and-white TGU sweatshirt. The rain was the tail end of a blustery overnight storm that had scattered driftwood, seaweed, and dead fish over the beach. The rank stench was nauseating. Hez's snaggletoothed rescue mutt, Cody, loped along beside him, occasionally pulling at his leash to get closer to a particularly smelly piece of debris left behind by the waves. "My best guess is someone from the Pelican Harbor Police Department. My landlord is the police chief, and she's the only other one with a key to the condo."

Blake turned his head, surprise in his blue eyes. "You think Jane Dixon planted the bottle?"

"Not Jane . . . but someone in her department." Hez had trouble talking while keeping up the eight-minute-mile pace set by his cousin, but he wasn't going to ask to slow down. "Someone who could walk into her office when she's out and no one would get suspicious. We already know there's a mole in the department."

"Have you told anyone around here that you used to drink?"

Hez shrugged. "It's not exactly a secret. And I've started going to an AA group, so anyone who shows up there would know. But I don't think I've ever mentioned that the Mondavi cab used to be my favorite wine."

"So how did someone discover that? Or was it a coincidence?"

"Probably not a coincidence. I'm guessing there's a mention of Mondavi cab somewhere in the police file on Ella's death. We always used to have a bottle or two in the kitchen." A new connection clicked in Hez's head. "That also explains the candy. We found Justin's peanut butter cups with Simon after he was kidnapped last year. That was the candy Ella was trying to get to when she drowned. That would have been in the police file too."

"Have you talked to Jane?"

"I called her yesterday, but I'll stop by today to mention the candy connection."

Wispy cowlicks waving in the breeze, Cody lunged toward a group of seagulls gathered around a trash can blown over by the storm. The birds squawked and flapped away—and Cody instantly grabbed whatever they'd been eating.

"Leave it!" Hez yanked at the leash as Cody frantically gobbled garbage. "Leaveitleaveitleaveitleaveit!"

Cody ate even faster, deftly managing to avoid dropping any morsels as Hez dragged him away from his feast. Cody managed to swallow past the constriction of his collar, then looked up at Hez with a triumphant grin.

Hez sighed. "Know a good vet?"

Blake chuckled. "You know I do." He and his mother ran an animal sanctuary near Gulf Shores, and they had one of the best veterinarians living at the park. She also happened to be the love of Blake's life who'd recently returned to town.

Hez shook his head. "You'd better not throw up on the police chief's handmade rugs." Cody gave him another grin and went back to scanning the beach for targets of opportunity.

They ran in silence for a few minutes. Gray waves crashed on the shore, and gulls cried overhead as they rode the gusty sea breeze. Hez kept Cody on a very short leash. Hez felt bad for dumping his worries on his cousin when Blake was dealing with his own problems at the animal park.

"I'm not sure I get it," Blake said. "Why would someone do this? I mean, if Beckett's cronies are still after you and they got into your kitchen, wouldn't they poison your food or something? Or at least leave a threatening note? What's the point of breaking into your apartment just to leave an empty wine bottle in your trash?"

Those same questions had nagged at Hez ever since Savannah walked out with the bottle. "I don't know—but I'm going to find out."

CHAPTER 6

HEZ APPEARED CLEAR-EYED AND SOBER, AND HE PATTED the bench beside him overlooking the sparkling Bon Secour Bay. Maybe his drinking had been a fluke. Savannah sat beside him, feeling the warmth of his body on the chill winter day. She threw the last crumbs of her beignet to the gulls and ordered Marley, her black Aussie, and Cody to leave them be.

The two dogs were becoming best friends, and they made a strange sight together. Marley with his trim athletic build that was all Australian shepherd and Cody, who looked like no other dog she'd ever seen. He seemed to be made out of leftover parts from random breeds: Chihuahua legs, Great Dane ears, greyhound body, and an elegant—but crooked—Chesapeake Bay tail.

The gulls stopped their squawking long enough to gobble up her offering before demanding more. She opened her hands to show them. "All gone. You'll have to find someone else." The nearest gull pinned her with a black-eyed stare before fluttering off to a group of teenagers fishing out on the pier. "There's Jane."

"I asked her to meet us here. I want to talk to her about the mole in her office. Someone planted that bottle in my trash."

That unbelievable story again. Savannah's mood deflated, and she laced her fingers together. She couldn't help him if he wouldn't admit to the truth. She pinned a smile back in place as the police chief, Jane Dixon, reached them. Even when she was in uniform, it was hard to miss her resemblance to a younger version of Reese Witherspoon but with chin-length light brown hair. Even at barely five-two, Jane was a force to be reckoned with.

Jane carried a cooler and set it on the grass beside the bench. The dogs sniffed the container before dashing off after a butterfly. "I brought fish to feed Pete."

As if he'd heard his name, a brown pelican flew down to join her. She crooned to him as she tossed him fish. "People are used to me doing this every day and won't think anything about it. You want to talk about a mole in my office?"

Hez leaned back and extended his arm across the park bench behind Savannah. "The file on Ella's death probably mentions her love of Justin's peanut butter cups. It's not something Savannah and I talk about. That detail had to come from the file. And someone put an empty Mondavi cab bottle in my trash. I think there has to be a mention of that in the file too."

With the last of the fish gone, Jane shut the cooler lid and wiped her hands on the grass. "I reviewed the file after your text. I found a mention of the peanut butter cups, but there was nothing about that brand of wine."

"You're certain? I don't know how else anyone would know I used to drink that brand. I haven't had any type of alcohol in over a year. I want to find out who planted it. And why."

Jane's hazel eyes were blank and professional. "I'm taking the idea of a mole very seriously, and I'll continue to dig to find him or her." She gave a polite nod. "I'd better get back to work. Thanks for the information."

Savannah tried to analyze Jane's just-the-facts demeanor. She hadn't dismissed Hez's assertion that a mole had planted the bottle, but she hadn't tried to encourage it either. Maybe she thought it was as crazy as Savannah did. Her breaths grew shallow and her palms were slick at the thought of pushing him about this, but she had to. She couldn't tuck her head under her wing like the gull at her feet. She loved Hez too much to ignore the danger.

Hez shifted on the bench and withdrew his arm. "Well, that was disappointing."

Savannah curled her fingers into her palm. "She'll keep digging." She put her hand on his knee. "I love you, Hez, and I'm committed to you. You know that, right?"

His gaze searched hers. "I love you too. I never stopped. It feels like there's a 'but' in there somewhere."

She shook her head. "No 'but.' I want us to be as solid as possible for our new beginning. What would you think about getting premarital counseling? I made plenty of mistakes the first time, and I don't want to fail you again."

"Babe, I failed you. We both know it was my fault."

"The fault of a marriage's failure is always on both sides. I want us to start again the right way with our marriage centering on the right things—love and faith. I never doubted you loved me and Ella, but life took us into uncharted waters. I should have told you the minute I saw you drifting deeper into your work and away from me and Ella. And after she died, I should have intervened when I saw the wine bottles piling up. And you should have talked to me about how you were feeling. If we make sure we know what to do next time, our marriage will start out stronger."

He slipped his arm around her and leaned in close enough for her to catch the tantalizing scent of his skin mixed with soap. His lips brushed her ear. "Have I told you how beautiful you look this morning? I'd do anything for you. You know that."

His reply bolstered her courage for the next step, and she leaned into his embrace. "How have you been feeling?"

He nuzzled her neck. "Fine."

"I think you should have a checkup, just to make sure. Maybe a CT scan to make sure everything is okay." He pulled away, and she felt him stiffen. "A concussion can cause memory issues."

"This is about the wine bottle, isn't it? You don't think I picked up a stray empty bottle along the road and plunked it in my trash, then forgot. You think I bought it and drank until I passed out. I wouldn't forget something like that, Savannah. I'd have a hangover, and I'd know." His voice was tight, and he didn't look at her.

She touched his arm and felt the tense muscles under his shirt. "I just want us to be honest and open with each other. I'm not going anywhere, Hez."

He finally turned a furious gaze on her. "Do you think I'm drinking again, Savannah? Do you not believe me when I tell you someone put the bottle in my trash?"

She tried to cup his face with her hands, but he shook off her touch. "I don't want to fight."

"Neither do I, so I'd better leave." He called a reluctant Cody to him and clipped on his leash.

She rose and took a step toward him. "Hez, don't be mad."

He didn't answer, and she sensed his despair and hurt from the stiff way he walked toward his car. She'd handled this all wrong.

"Bye, Mom!" Simon called as he climbed into the cab of Will Dixon's spotless silver pickup, decorated with TGU Gators stickers.

"Bye, Simon!" Jess called back. She watched from the pillared entrance of her house as they drove down the long curve of her driveway and disappeared around the corner. That was the first time he had called her "Mom" instead of "Mum." His English accent was melting away faster than ice cream on the Fourth of July. Six months from now, he'd probably have an impeccable southern drawl. She chuckled at the thought.

Simon had made the change from an upper-crust Essex boarding school to an Alabama public school with surprising ease. Of course she'd planned on putting him in an Ivy League prep school, but he had been adamant about attending public school. She couldn't argue with that really—the local schools had fine faculties thanks to TGU's influence on the area.

Having Will as a tutor certainly helped. Simon's only academic deficit was American history, a subject he easily could have learned on his own. Will was a good teacher, but he was an even better surrogate big brother. Simon idolized him, and the fact that Will was the starting quarterback for the Gators had given Simon instant social standing at school. It was a pity they'd be separated soon, when TGU imploded and Will was forced to transfer to another school.

Her watch buzzed against her wrist. Almost time for her call with Punisher and English Cream. She sighed and went back inside.

She did a quick sweep of her home office for bugs. She had no reason to suspect anyone was spying on her, but if she waited until she suspected something, it would probably be too late. Satisfied that the room was clean, she flicked on her computer. The gorgeous dog and grim death's head appeared on her monitor.

English Cream started the conversation. "Greetings, all. I see deliveries have resumed and we're even making a dent in our backlog. Nicely done."

"Thanks." Jess had put in a lot of late nights to make that happen. It was nice to have her work noticed. "I'm still short-staffed, but I can hold up my end."

"And I'm holding up mine," Punisher added. "The new over-land route adds a day and some costs, but it works. What about the money angle?"

"The vehicle is almost finished," English Cream said. "The funds are available for transfer. When will the debt con-solidation be complete?"

Jess tapped her newly manicured nails on the desktop. She hadn't expected English Cream to be ready this quickly. She had been so busy getting the deliveries back on schedule that she hadn't made much progress on the university's finances. "Not yet. I'm working on it."

"Better work fast. Someone will be watching soon. You need to do better." Punisher seized on her shortcomings, as always. Their relationship in real life at least was better, but it was his way of making sure she performed to his expectations.

COLLEEN COBLE AND RICK ACKER

He was right. Jess needed to get as much done as possible while TGU had no president or permanent provost. Once those positions were filled, her actions might be scrutinized. "Well, at least we don't need to worry about the lawyer watching."

Punisher gave a harsh laugh. "Heard about that. Guy can't think about anything except that bottle."

The bottle ploy had worked even better than Jess had hoped. She had surreptitiously copied Hez's key while she and Simon were at his condo for a dinner with him and Savannah. Then it had been a simple matter to slip in while he was testifying in Beckett's trial and drop the bottle in his trash. She'd expected him to find it that evening. That would have rattled him plenty and kept his focus off TGU's finances—but having Savannah find it must have been devastating. No wonder he was obsessed with that bottle.

She tried not to think about the pain in her sister's face when they met at University Grounds. The double whammy of the tenure committee's decision and the wine bottle must have hit her like a sledgehammer. But Jess didn't have a choice, did she?

"What about our police source?" English Cream asked. "Has the lawyer tied the bottle to them?"

Jess's ergonomic chair squeaked as she leaned back. "Yes, but the lawyer is wrong, of course, so that's just taking him down a dead end. If anything, it's leading him away from the source."

"I see." English Cream paused for a moment. "What about you? What will you do if he accuses you?"

Jess had thought of that too. "I'll deny it, of course. It doesn't matter whether he believes me. Even if he blames me, he'll chalk it up to our, ah, personal history." This wasn't the first time she'd done something that undermined Hez's relationship with Savannah. He'd never connect the university's finances to Jess putting a wine bottle in his trash.

"Good. Very good." Jess could almost see English Cream's little nod of approval. "Perhaps we should accelerate our plans—strike while the lawyer is distracted and key supervisory positions are vacant."

"Right," Punisher said. "Best time to rob a store is when no one's watching the register."

Jess's fingers dug into the armrests of her chair. She couldn't let TGU implode while Savannah was still there. Jess had a golden parachute carefully packed for herself, but her sister didn't. Savannah would be in free fall—jobless and with a black mark on her résumé. And she might try to interfere with the university's collapse. She could get hurt. "We should stick to the original timetable. Acting sooner creates too many risks."

"I think not," English Cream replied. "We move when the money is ready to be transferred."

"Right," Punisher put in. "No time like the present."

Jess's gut clenched. She had to save her oblivious sister from the Mack truck barreling toward her, but how?

CHAPTER 7

THE PAST TWO DAYS HAD MOVED AS SLOWLY AS TURGID swamp water. Savannah had tried to keep busy by working on her résumé and not worry when Hez answered texts with one-word responses. On paper she looked like a wonderful candidate, but she feared finding another job wasn't going to be easy.

Before she stepped into Petit Charms, she shot a glance up at Hez's balcony, but there was no sign he was home. Just as well. If he had time to think it through, surely he'd see her suggestion made sense. Wouldn't he? She shook off her worry and stepped into the sweet aroma of powdered sugar and sweet dough.

Her order of six beignets was ready, and she paid for them and a coffee. As she turned to leave, she spotted Helen Willard and two men at a round iron table. Helen always looked like an approachable grandmother with white hair curling around her face. She was barely five feet tall and turned a smile on everyone—except a Legare. Savannah recognized Helen's sons, David and Michael.

Though her last conversation with Helen had turned sour, she approached the three of them with a smile. "Good morning. I wanted to let you know my book was accepted for publication, and I'd love to give you a copy. I think you'll like it. I made sure to recognize the huge contributions to TGU made by Willards over the years."

Helen squared her narrow shoulders. "Why would I be interested in the words of a con artist? You tricked me to get access to the Willard letters for your own purposes. The least you could have done was to be honest with me. Legares have cheated us through generations. I have nothing to say to you."

David lumbered to his feet. His gut strained at the constraints of a too-tight belt as he leaned over to help his mother up. "She's not herself today. I'm sorry for her harsh words. I know you were trying to be kind." He offered his mother a beefy arm.

Michael rose as well and took his mother's other hand. He was about the same height as his brother, though his fine-boned but muscular build contrasted with the burly David. His blond hair was going gray at the temples, but Savannah had seen plenty of women give him an appreciative glance or two.

Savannah sent an apologetic smile at the group and exited first, practically running for her car. She should have known better than to approach the elderly woman. Her hatred of the Legare family wasn't misplaced. Political winds of change at TGU had blown the old lady right out of her home, and she now lived in a run-down bungalow.

Anticipating a sweet treat to soothe the morning's confrontation, she sped along the short drive to her office. Her phone rang as she shut her door behind her and set her coffee and beignets on the desk. Her gut clenched when she glanced at the screen.

He rarely called, but maybe he'd heard the news. "Hey, Dad."

"Savannah, the presidential search committee wants to talk to you. Are you free right now?"

"Sure. I don't have class for another hour."

"We'll be right there." He hung up without saying goodbye.

She didn't have the bandwidth to wonder what the committee wanted. Maybe they were considering Jess as a possible candidate. Jess would be an excellent president.

Savannah scarfed down a beignet, then slipped down the hall to the bathroom, where she washed the powdered sugar from her hands and made sure her face didn't have a dusting of white. After she got back to her office and took a sip of coffee, her father bustled into the room with two other committee members in tow.

Her head was a blur as her father introduced the trustees, Harry Winslow and Ira Duncan. She'd never had a need to meet the trustees, though she was sure Jess would know them. They refused her offer of beignets, and Savannah pulled chairs into a circle and gestured for them to be seated. Her dad wasn't one to sit. Standing was his way of maintaining control.

He crossed his arms over his chest. "I'm not going to beat around the bush. The university has always done best with a Legare at the helm. We didn't want to contact you while you were up for tenure, but now that you've been turned loose, you're free to consider what's best for TGU. We want you to take the vacant president's seat."

"Me? I've never had a management position like that."

"You and Hez cracked that ring robbing us blind. If not for the two of you, we could be bankrupt soon. You showed wisdom and strength in your dogged search."

"And you solved two murders." Ira Duncan appeared as ancient as one of the artifacts, and his voice was faint and shaky. "You dug hard. You and Jess would make an outstanding team. Two Legares at the top. It couldn't be a better situation to transform TGU. Would you consider taking the job?"

"I—I don't know. I'll have to think about it."

"I'm sure if you think about it, you'll see it makes perfect sense," her dad said.

"What about my classes?"

Her father waved his hand as if to shoo away gnats. "We can spread out the load with the other faculty."

The trustees rose and moved toward the door with her father. "We have an excellent package for you, but your dad assured us money isn't a major motivator for you." Ira paused and looked her in the eye. "We know you care about TGU. It's in your blood, and that deep love can turn things around for us. We'll await your decision."

Savannah saw them out with her head stuffed full of conflicting thoughts. They weren't wrong. She did love the university, and she'd hate to see it fail. Besides, Hez's plans for the legal clinic could move forward. She envisioned buying a house near Jess's where she could watch Simon grow up. Saying yes felt like a no-brainer, but she'd talk to Hez and seek his opinion. Maybe her life wasn't about to be upended.

Half a year had passed since Hez last set foot in Jimmy Little's office, but it felt like much longer. A lot had changed—at least for Hez. Jimmy looked exactly the same—he even wore the same ratty Crimson Tide sweatshirt he had on the last time Hez visited the office on a Saturday.

Jimmy was an enormous man who had struck terror into SEC quarterbacks on the gridiron until a knee injury ended his football career twenty-five years ago. Now he dominated courtrooms the way he used to dominate the line of scrimmage. He had a successful firm, Little & Associates, where Hez had worked before going down to TGU. Jimmy still kept an office with Hez's name on the door in case he decided to come back. Jimmy was also Hez's Alcoholics Anonymous sponsor, which was the main reason Hez had made the four-hour drive from Pelican Harbor to Birmingham. Jimmy would understand what it meant to have the love of your life find an empty wine bottle in your trash.

"I'm sorry to hear about Savannah's tenure situation." Jimmy shook his massive head. "There are lots of good schools in Birmingham. I'm sure one of them would snap her up."

"Fingers crossed. She's working on her résumé now, and I wouldn't mind coming back up here."

A hopeful gleam came into Jimmy's brown eyes. "I could let you have some office space for the Justice Chamber. I'd even make it rent free if you'd take a few cases for me."

That got Hez's attention. Little & Associates occupied the ideal spot for a law office—right between Birmingham's two main courthouses. It even had a nice view. "Wow, that's very generous, Jimmy. I'll let you know what we decide to do."

"Let me help you decide. I know lots of people at all the top schools in town. I'd be happy to make some calls for Savannah." Jimmy's leather chair groaned as he leaned forward.

"Hey, let me take you guys to dinner tonight! I've known you for two years, but I've never met Savannah."

Hez squirmed at the reminder of their long separation and the divorce that followed. Had they finally overcome the dark chasm between them—or had the last few months been an illusion? "Actually, she's not here. I came up by myself."

Jimmy's bushy salt-and-pepper brows shot up. "Oh? Why's that?"

"Partially because I wanted to eyeball possible office space for the Justice Chamber and she's not ready to visit schools yet. But also . . . well, it's kind of a weird story." Hez told Jimmy about the mystery bottle, ending with Savannah's suggestion that he see a neurologist.

Jimmy let out a long whistle and leaned back behind his hand-carved walnut desk. "That's crazy, man."

"I know, right? It doesn't make any sense. I don't know what to do next."

"I do."

Hez sat up straight. "You do? What?"

"See your neurologist."

The bottom fell out of Hez's stomach. Even Jimmy doubted him. "I thought you'd understand."

"I do understand—and I believe you."

Hez's temper flared. "So why are you literally telling me to get my head examined?"

"Because she asked you to, and it's not a crazy request. You just said this doesn't make any sense to you. Why should it make any sense to her?"

"She should trust me."

"It sounds like she's trying hard to do exactly that. Look at it from her perspective: she can either assume you're lying or assume you're being as honest as you can, but you took a hard shot to the head a couple of months ago."

"Or she could believe me when I say someone must have planted the bottle."

"Which you just said doesn't make any sense," Jimmy shot back. "So you're saying she should believe something that doesn't make any sense. Listen to yourself!"

Hez was cornered, but he didn't want to admit it. He sat in silence and looked at the national championship ring in a case on Jimmy's desk. The thing looked as heavy as a paperweight and as wide as a napkin ring.

Jimmy sighed and continued more gently. "Look, this thing may make sense after you've done some more digging. It probably will—no one hunts down evidence better than you. But for now, you've got to ask yourself: Would you rather be right or be with her?"

CHAPTER 8

SAVANNAH KEPT SNEAKING GLANCES AT THE CLOCK. WOULD this class ever end? Hez would be as blown away by the job offer as she was, and she couldn't wait to get his take on it, but it would have to wait until he got back from Birmingham. *University president.* She wasn't under any illusions that it was anything more than her father using his influence, but that didn't matter. She could do good work here.

The students gathered their books and backpacks and filtered out the door. Savannah grabbed her purse and slung it over her shoulder, but before she stepped away from her desk, she heard the staccato of heels on the hallway floor. It had to be Jess. No one else walked with that purposeful stride in pumps.

Her sister hurried into the classroom and shut the door behind her. Her navy suit deepened the color of her hazel eyes, which were fixed on Savannah. "I saw Pierre and the rest of the committee come into the building. Were they here to see you?"

"They were." Savannah exhaled and sat back down in her chair. "They offered me Abernathy's job. They want me to take over as president of TGU. I still can't believe it."

Jess took a couple of steps closer. "You're not going to take it, are you? I haven't said much because of my confidentiality clause, but, Savannah, you'd be foolish to try to save the university. It's going down. The fallout from the murders and the smuggling of artifacts affected our enrollment, and that's only going to get worse. Get out of the blast radius while you can. The way I see it, it was a good thing not to get tenure. It left your options open."

"We've always worked well together. The two of us could turn things around. I know we could. We'd have Hez's legal support too. A trifecta of sharp minds."

Jess's eyes narrowed. "You're parroting your dad. That's more of Pierre's scheme to harvest as much money from TGU as possible. All he cares about is his fat university-funded trust fund. If he was concerned about the university, he wouldn't have put Abernathy in charge. He knew he was a corrupt incompetent, but Pierre got a promise from him to turn a blind eye to the embezzlement. Think it through, Savannah. Why would he suggest a history professor with zero executive or fundraising experience to take over as president? I'm sure he thinks you'll do the same."

Savannah stiffened. "I didn't realize you thought so little of my skills."

"You know I love you, but sitting at the helm of a failing university is a big job. It will be a lot of hours and high stress. Do you want that when you're trying to start over with Hez? Especially now that he's started drinking again."

"He says he didn't drink that wine." Savannah winced inwardly at that feeble statement.

"And someone just magically put it there. Listen to yourself.

Surely you aren't swallowing that line. Don't be gullible about him or this job offer. Did you stop to think about why they didn't offer *me* the job? Wouldn't that be the logical thing to do with my experience? He knew I'd take all that stolen money out of his trust. He's afraid of me." Jess's lips curved in satisfaction. "And that's exactly how I want him to feel."

Her sister wasn't wrong. The ill will between Pierre and Jess worsened every year. "But we have to at least *try* to save the school. The three of us make a formidable team."

Jess folded her arms over her chest. "Why should we save something that's rotten at the core? We didn't create this mess, and we risk our reputations to save it. If it goes down, it will take us with it."

"Are you going to quit?"

Jess lifted her chin. "I don't know yet. Maybe it would be worth my reputation to stick around and watch the place fall to ruin."

"I know Hez thinks it can be saved."

Jess rolled her eyes. "Oh please. How reliable is Hez? I know he's a brilliant attorney and means well, but his behavior lately calls everything into question. If he truly believes he didn't put that wine bottle in the trash, he's having blackouts. Otherwise, he's lying. Neither option bodes well for helping us. Or for your marriage for that matter."

Savannah didn't want to examine her sister's logic. Hez's face when he thought she didn't believe him still pierced her heart. He was depending on her to help him get through this. "I don't believe it's as bad as all that."

Jess leaned forward. "I handle the financials, Savannah, and I am telling you it is. I don't want you left holding the bag. You realize you'd be blamed if you're at the helm when it all falls apart, right? I'm already planning my landing spot, and you should do the same."

"Where's your landing spot?"

A mysterious smile lifted Jess's lips. "You'll know when it's time. I haven't decided what to do just yet, but no matter what happens here, I want you safe and protected from the fallout. You have to believe me—get away from here before the nuclear blast levels everything."

No matter what, Jess had always tried to give Savannah good advice. The ring of truth and genuine concern in her voice proved Jess believed what she was saying. Savannah's inclination to take the job wavered. Maybe she and Hez would be better off in a low-pressure environment. What if staying here increased the stress Hez felt and the drinking got worse? She didn't want her desire to save the university to doom their fresh start.

But could she really walk away from the place that generations of her family had devoted their lives to? "I'll talk to Hez."

Irritation flashed across Jess's face. "You do that. Maybe he can talk some sense into you." She turned and strode away.

Savannah gathered her purse and followed. This decision wasn't going to be easy.

Hez stepped out of the neurologist's office and took a deep breath. The wild, fresh scent of the sea was especially crisp after the big tropical storm that came through a few days ago. Hammers rang on the roof of the nearby courthouse as workers replaced lost shingles. Some parts of the county had been hit hard—Blake, Jenna, and their crew had stayed with Savannah while they waited for the floodwaters at the Sanctuary Animal Rescue to recede.

A knot of tension relaxed between his shoulders. He hadn't realized how stressed he'd been over this. He'd had to swallow a big lump of pride, but he didn't regret it. The doctor had listened carefully and hadn't seemed to doubt Hez's story, but she did a thorough exam and ordered a CT scan without hesitation.

Hez felt fine and he hadn't noticed any memory lapses—but would he notice? No one seemed really convinced by his theory that someone planted the bottle in his trash, and even he didn't find it to be a compelling story. He only believed it so firmly because it really happened to him. Or had it?

It would be good to get the test results.

Hez did his best to push the whole thing out of his mind as he walked across the courthouse square.

A familiar voice called to him. "How are you doing?"

Hez turned to see Martine Dubois walking toward him. "I'm fully recovered from your cross-examination, thanks."

Martine laughed, forming little crinkles at the corners of her brown eyes. She patted his cheek. "Sorry about that. You were a tough witness—too tough for my client and me. I assume you heard the verdict?"

Hez nodded. As he'd predicted, Beckett had been convicted of kidnapping and attempted murder, but he was acquitted on all the other charges. "I did. Beckett got off very easy, though I admit I'm biased. Nice work."

"Not as nice as I'd hoped, of course, but it could have been worse. We'll see how things play out post-trial."

"Oh?" Hez arched an eyebrow. "What kind of post-trial motions are you bringing?"

"The usual stuff—mostly some evidentiary rulings that should have gone the other way."

Hez shrugged. "I took a look at the court file and the rough transcript. The prosecution's case seemed pretty solid. Hope did a good job."

A secretive smile tugged at the corners of Martine's mouth. "She did, but maybe I'll be able to pull a rabbit out of my hat anyway. See you around."

Martine walked off before Hez could respond. Tension started to creep back into his shoulders as he watched her retreating back. She was gloating about something, but the question was, what? Hez had a bad feeling about the answer.

He pulled out his phone and called Hope. She answered on the second ring. "Hi, Hez." Did her voice sound tense, or was he just projecting?

"Hey, Hope. I just ran into Martine Dubois. We chatted about the Beckett Harrison trial, and she acted all mysterious about post-verdict proceedings—like she had a secret ace up her sleeve or something. Any idea what's going on?"

Hope let out a long sigh. "Let me know if you ever need an assistant for that legal clinic you're starting. I may be looking for a new job soon."

"Why? What happened?"

"I'm under orders to keep it confidential until tomorrow's hearing, but I'm done following Elliot Drake's orders. Besides, you have a right to know. Drake made a deal with Harrison."

Hez groaned. This was exactly what he'd feared Martine was hinting at. Drake viewed the DA's office as little more than a platform for his personal ambitions, and he would make whatever deal he thought would benefit him. Martine would have figured him out in thirty seconds, maybe less. "What kind of deal?"

"I'm not entirely sure. I wasn't part of the negotiations." Her voice dripped acid. "I do know that Harrison hired an old friend of Drake's who just happened to have made a big contribution to his last campaign. Martine and this guy showed up at Drake's office to meet with him. I wasn't invited, but afterward I was told to draw up a stipulation and take Harrison's proffer. The good news, I guess, is that Harrison is going to testify that Deke Willard murdered both Ellison Abernathy and Peter Cardin. So Drake will probably get the murder conviction he wanted."

Hez grimaced. He doubted Willard committed either murder, at least not alone. Beckett had been the mastermind, and probably the killer. "And what's the bad news?"

"After Harrison testifies, we'll stipulate to Martine's post-trial motions. The verdict will be overturned and Harrison will be a free man."

Free to come after Savannah again.

CHAPTER 9

SAVANNAH SPOTTED HEZ'S SILHOUETTE OUT ON THE PIER, and her pulse kicked as she parked her car. They'd parted on a strained note two days ago, and she didn't want the unease between them to continue any longer. She thought he would be intrigued by her news, and talking it over might heal the breach between them.

She tucked her jacket a little closer around her and got out into the wind at the Pelican Harbor waterfront. Gulls squawked above a shrimp boat chugging across the bay. The salty breeze lifted her hair in a tangle across her face as she hurried to join Hez.

He turned at the sound of her shoes on the wooden pier, and his smile emerged. Her chest eased until she got closer and saw the shadow in his blue eyes. Was he still mad at her? She checked her initial response to kiss him until he opened his arms.

She stepped into his embrace. "I missed you, Hez." There was no reservation in his tight hug or his tender kiss. Whatever had caused that expression must not be about their relationship.

He released her and led her to the wooden bench built into the side of the pier. "I can see in your eyes that you're about to burst with something to tell me."

She pushed her hair out of her face, but the wind snatched it again. "I can tell you're worried about something. You go first."

He settled his arm around her shoulders. "I saw a neurologist today."

Her chest tightened. "There's something wrong?" Her mind ran through the possibilities—a brain bleed, a tumor. Something had caused that shadow in his eyes.

"I don't have the results of the CT scan yet. The doctor should get them later today. She said she'd call when she had them. My pupils aren't dilated though, and she didn't see anything problematic in the initial consult. She checked my gait and balance. The test will tell her more, though."

She leaned into his side, and her relieved breath fogged the cool air. "I know you did it for me, so thank you. I'll feel better if we know for sure you're all right." Though she didn't mention the wine bottle, she knew it had to be uppermost in his mind. "If the initial exam went well, why do you still look so upset?"

He pulled her closer and rested his chin on top of her head. "There's more. I ran into Martine." He told her about the conversation and how unsettled it had left him. "I called Hope, and she told me Beckett has struck a deal. His conviction is being overturned, and Deke Willard is taking the fall. We both know Beckett was the mastermind and probably the killer. Whatever Deke did, he didn't do it alone."

Savannah shuddered. "How can Drake just let him go like that? Doesn't he care about justice at all?"

Hez shrugged and lifted his chin off her hair. "Drake's political ambitions outweigh his sense of right and wrong. It happens more than I'd like to admit. And with Beckett walking free around Nova Cambridge, maybe it's for the best you didn't get tenure. Who knows how he might try to harm us to get revenge? You'll be safer out of his line of sight."

He wasn't going to like her news, and she didn't know how to feel about it herself—especially now that Beckett would be on the loose. She turned in his embrace so she could see his expression. "My father is part of the selection committee for a new president. He and the other members came to see me today. They offered me the job."

His eyes went wide. "The president's job? How do you feel about it?"

"Jess doesn't want me to do it." She told him about Jess's desire to get her away from the fallout.

"She's not wrong. I'd hate to see your father's bad decisions take you down. Jimmy offered me a spot for the Justice Chamber in Birmingham and even offered to help you get a position with one of the universities there. He's got the clout to do it too. Beckett would be hundreds of miles away, and you'd be safe."

"Jess said I needed a good landing spot. Birmingham would be perfect for that."

"It really would. We'd be close enough to Nova Cambridge and Pelican Harbor to visit whenever we wanted, but far enough away that we wouldn't be affected by the problems down here." He gave her shoulder a squeeze. "We could buy a nice place in the suburbs—maybe Mountain Brook. It's a beautiful town with great public schools. I'm not trying to persuade you one way or the other, but we have choices."

She could see every detail of the idyllic scene. They would live on a quiet, leafy street with great schools and parks. Every morning, they would have breakfast in a sun-filled kitchen. Then they would get in the car and drive to the neighborhood school, where she and Hez would drop off their new child—or children?—for a top-notch education. The two of them would drive into the city, where she would be a tenured professor and Hez would lead the crusade at the Justice Chamber. It would be perfect, except . . .

What about TGU? Two years ago, she would have told herself there was nothing she could do, that it wasn't her fault, that she and Hez deserved some happiness after all they'd been through, that she didn't need to think about what happened at TGU. She would have turned her back on the whole mess and embraced the bright dream in front of her. Now it wasn't so easy.

"It's hard to let Beckett waltz back in and figure out a way to continue his illicit business. My dad will install another corrupt president and continue to milk TGU for every penny. I'm not sure I can walk away and let that happen. Doesn't the injustice get to you sometimes, Hez? It seems the bad guys often win."

He grimaced. "Oh, it gets to me. Sometimes I want to walk away and never see the shenanigans pulled behind closed doors again. But I can't do it. If those of us who value justice turn our backs, the little guy will have no chance in the system. So I stay and fight, along with thousands of others who care."

She cupped his face in her palms. "And your integrity is one of the reasons I love you. How can I walk away now? If good people do nothing, evil wins. My father wins. Beckett wins.

TGU will fall, and I would have to live with the fact that I stood back and let it happen."

He remained silent for a long moment. The furrows on his brow deepened. "It's not going to be easy, babe. Beckett will be out as soon as Deke Willard's trial is over, maybe even sooner. We have to assume he'll come after us. I don't want you to have a target on your back."

She let her hands fall back to her lap. "I don't know if I can save it, but my family's legacy will be no more if TGU closes. Thousands of students and university employees will suffer if I fail. Beckett doesn't scare me. I dealt with him once, and I can do it again." TGU anchored most of the good memories of her childhood, and she couldn't bear to let her father strip away her family's legacy. It was her legacy too—hers and Hez's. Their daughter's grave, nestled with those of her mother and her grandparents, looked down on the beautiful buildings and tree-lined streets. "I have to try to save TGU."

"If anyone can do it, you can." He swept his hand toward the water. "Your heart is as big as the ocean."

She smiled and leaned in for a lingering kiss before pulling back and searching his gaze with her own. "You'll help me, won't you, Hez? A university president needs a good special counsel."

"You know I will. Together we're a force of nature. And Jess will help. Besides, I wouldn't mind another shot at Beckett. We never got to the bottom of the smuggling, and I'll bet he was involved."

"You'll start the Justice Chamber here? The publicity might help TGU."

"I'll get right on it. When you take over, you can assign me some space to begin."

Her heart was lighter with the decision made and Hez fully on board. But neither of them had mentioned the wine bottle. Maybe it was best to leave it that way until they heard about the scan.

Jess took a deep breath and wiped her palms on her gray wool slacks. These calls were never fun, and this one would be worse than most—possibly the worst yet. She might as well get it over with. She opened her videoconferencing app. English Cream and Punisher were already on.

Punisher spoke first. "You messed up. Badly. You disappoint me."

Jess winced but kept her voice cold and professional, with just a hint of sarcasm. "Nice to talk to you too. How's the weather?"

Punisher cursed. "You're lucky we're not in the same room."

Jess wouldn't let him intimidate her. "That makes two of us."

English Cream's polished veneer cracked for an instant. "Enough!" He paused and went on with his normal smoothness. "You should have foreseen and accounted for this possibility and you didn't. Do not let that happen again. Now, how do you propose to fix the problem?"

Jess chose her words carefully. "By keeping a very close eye on it, which will be much easier now. You remember the old adage 'Keep your friends close and your enemies closer'? Better still to keep your enemy close and make him think you're his friend."

Punisher scoffed. "The lawyer thinks you're his friend?"

"For this purpose, yes. He thinks we're on the same side, that our interests are aligned when it comes to business matters."

"That's a fair point," English Cream acknowledged. "How close of an eye can you keep on him and the, ah, other individual?"

Jess leaned forward. If she could persuade English Cream, Punisher might fall in line. "Very close. Our offices will all be on the same floor. I'll make a point of dropping in on both of them unexpectedly. We'll meet regularly, maybe even daily. Any financial questions they have will come to me first. I'll know the instant they suspect anything."

Punisher grumbled something unintelligible. "Unless they suspect you."

English Cream spoke before Jess could respond. "Do you have a better solution?"

"Yeah, I do," Punisher shot back. "We were gonna act while those positions were empty, right? Make them empty again."

An icy dagger stabbed Jess's heart. "No! We can't just kill them!"

English Cream backed her up. "Agreed. More suspicious deaths at this point will simply draw more law enforcement scrutiny and make our lives harder."

Punisher was silent for a moment. "Well, if either of them looks in the wrong place, they're dead. Remember that."

CHAPTER 10

THE PRESIDENT'S OFFICE HAD BEEN CLEARED OF EVERY stick of Abernathy's furniture and personal belongings when Savannah stepped through the door. Her great-grandfather Luc had been a master woodworker, and he'd built the quarter-sawn oak bookcases attached to the walls on either side of her. The faint scent of carnauba wax mingled with the stronger overtones of the new creamy-white paint on the walls. Light streamed through the wall of mullioned windows and heightened the patina on the gorgeous old marble floor.

Devoid of its furniture, the office felt massive the way it did when she was small. It still held the whisper of her grandfather Andre's presence. He hadn't been flashy like her father but steady with a kind voice and gray eyes that saw the fear she always carried with her as a little girl. If only he were here now to answer her misgivings and calm her feelings of inadequacy. She was about to be the first female president to occupy this space. Proving her worth to take the helm of this place she loved was a huge undertaking.

She bit her lip. "You can do this, Savannah," she whispered.

"Where do you want the rug and the library table?" a gruff voice said from behind her.

She turned to see two deliverymen carrying the piece of furniture. "Right there." She gestured to the spot where her grandfather used to sit with one bank of bookshelves behind him. The table matched the bookshelves and wasn't nearly as grand as the desk Abernathy had used, but she'd been thrilled to find it in storage. Her grandfather had told her the simplicity of the table had been chosen to highlight the beauty of the wood itself. He'd always positioned it so he could see out the window into the small garden spot, and she wanted to do the same.

A third man came in behind them with the new rug, and it only took a few minutes for the room to take shape. She balanced the wide room with her library table and comfortable chairs on one side and a seating area with a leather sofa and coffee table on the other. Both had a beautiful view of the garden.

Savannah placed her briefcase on the table and turned at the familiar staccato of Jess's heels on the marble. She braced herself for the confrontation with her sister.

Jess's eyes widened as she took in the new decor. "I-is that Grandpa's library table?"

Savannah caressed the smooth wood. "It's still gorgeous, isn't it?"

"But why? How can you maintain discipline and authority in a space that looks like a parlor instead of an office?"

Savannah's smile withered. How did Jess always manage to puncture any joy she felt? She pulled herself to her full height and gestured to the chairs on the other side of the table. "Have a seat. Hez should be here any minute."

"I'm here." Ignoring Jess, Hez entered the room and whistled at the transformation. "I could work here." He crossed the Persian rug and kissed Savannah before he dropped into the chair beside Jess.

His presence repaired the damage Jess had caused to Savannah's confidence. "You two are vital to the plans I have for TGU. The three of us—the Council of Three—have a lot of work to do to turn this rudderless ship around." She reached into her briefcase and withdrew a notepad. "Jess, you go first. How will you clean up the mess the financials are in?"

Jess looked a little bewildered, but she reached into her bag and pulled out a laptop. "As you know, there were a lot of off-the-books income streams and debts. A lot of shady corners have to be brought into the light of day, and I'm working as fast as I can to accomplish that. I hope to have us in order within the next quarter." A smile played around the corners of her lips, and her voice held a quiver of glee.

It didn't take any real insight for Savannah to guess the source of that joy in her sister's face. Jess would take delight in hacking off a large chunk of Dad's trust fund. The very thing he was most eager to protect was about to hit the chopping block, and Jess would be only too happy to take the blame.

"That's great news. I want a weekly report on your progress." Savannah noted the shock on Jess's face at the order. She'd get over it. "Hez, how about the Justice Chamber?"

Hez smiled and leaned back in his chair. "The Justice Chamber has its first client."

"Already?" Savannah eyed the spark of mischief in his eyes.

"TGU will be our first client." When Jess started to object,

COLLEEN COBLE AND RICK ACKER

he held up his hand and continued in his commanding courtroom voice. "I know it's a bit unorthodox, but justice starts at home. My students will jump at the chance to clean up their school. It will set them up for fighting corruption and injustice wherever they find it, no matter the cost. My first target will be the smuggling I believe is still going on. We're going to track down who's behind it and put a stop to it."

Jess shut her laptop with a snap. "That's a ridiculous plan, Hez. We have enough work to do to recover our reputation without you focusing more attention on Beckett's actions. Find an innocent person to help. The media attention on that would soon have the public forgetting all about what Beckett did."

"Hez is right," Savannah said. "The evidence he's found is compelling, and besides, nothing new can be built on a rotten foundation. We have to root out all of the corruption." She nodded at Hez. "You had another point?"

He nodded. "I've also uncovered a sleazy online diploma mill Abernathy used to generate quick cash. That's going to stop right now."

Jess gaped at him before giving a grudging nod of approval. "I heard about that. You're right—it's very sleazy and gives us a poor reputation. I tried to get Abernathy to stop it, but he was always about the bottom line."

Wait, were they actually on the same page? Savannah hid a smile and consulted her notes again. "The final item is security. Jess, Hez has reason to believe Beckett will be out looking for revenge when the Deke Willard trial is over. We need to beef up security. Oscar Pickwick isn't going to stop anyone from barging in here with a gun." The old guard was more interested in his *Pokémon Go* game than in evaluating risks to the university. "I want you to find money in the budget to hire some real guards."

Jess went pale and gave a slow nod. "We'll have no choice if Beckett is out." She glanced at her watch. "I have a Zoom meeting in fifteen minutes. That report will be on your desk every Monday morning."

Hez said nothing until Jess pulled the door shut behind her. "You handled that like a boss, my love."

Savannah couldn't hide her smile. "I think Jess was too stunned to object." It had been one battle, and the war was far from over.

Hez didn't like the look on his neurologist's face. She wasn't smiling as she pulled up his CT results, and small lines of concern creased the corners of her mouth and the space between her brows. She turned her monitor sideways so they could both see it. It showed a CT scan of Hez's head. She pointed to a spot just inside the left wall of his skull. "See that?"

Hez looked closely and saw a small, pale crescent. "Yes, what is it?"

"It's a subdural hematoma, bleeding on the brain. It's typically caused by a head injury like the one you suffered."

Hez stared at the image. "Could that be affecting my memory?"

The doctor shrugged one shoulder. "Probably not. Most researchers think memory is controlled by the temporal lobes, and that's on your left parietal lobe. But no one knows for sure. Brains are weird."

That wasn't the most reassuring thing he'd heard a doctor say. "So, uh, can it be treated?"

"Sure. The most common treatment for a small hematoma like that is to drill a hole in your head and drain the blood."

He forced a smile. "I always said I didn't need another hole in the head, but maybe I do."

She gave a polite chuckle. He guessed she'd heard that joke before. "Maybe, maybe not. When I got this image, the first thing I did was check the scan you got right after your injury two months ago." She pulled up a slightly different image and pointed at the same spot. "This shows a hematoma in the same spot that's pretty close to the same size. The angle is slightly different, which makes it less visible." She cleared her throat. "We, um, missed it at the time."

Hez squinted at the screen. The crescent was there, but it was very, very faint. "Yeah, I can see why."

The doctor relaxed, and her lips curved into the first genuine smile of the meeting. "To be honest, I was a little nervous saying that to a lawyer. Thanks for being understanding."

"Of course. Mistakes happen, even to lawyers."

Her smile broadened. "The delayed diagnosis may actually turn out to be a good thing. If I'd noticed the hematoma two months ago, surgery would have been the clear choice. But that's not true today. I've consulted with a radiologist, and we're fairly certain the hematoma hasn't grown. Since you also don't have any classic symptoms of intracranial pressure, I'm inclined to take a 'watchful waiting' approach for now. I want you to come in next week for a follow-up scan. After that, you should have scans every few weeks until we're sure the hematoma is stable and the underlying injury is fully healed. In the meantime, avoid strenuous physical activity and anything that might result in a blow to the head."

Hez breathed a sigh of relief. "That's great news! I—" His phone rang and Hope's number appeared on the screen. "I'm sorry. I should take this. Can I step outside for five minutes?"

The doctor waved her hand at the door. "We're done. Just make a follow-up appointment at the desk before you leave."

Hez took the call as he walked out of the office. "Hey, Hope. What's up?"

Her voice was grim. "Beckett Harrison was just found dead in his cell."

CHAPTER 11

SAVANNAH CRUMPLED THE PEAT MOSS INTO THE RAISED flower bed the gardeners had constructed for her in the garden outside her new office window and worked it into the soil. The aroma took her back to gardening in this very spot with her great-grandpa when she was a child. Sunshine peeked through the overstory of tupelo and oak trees around the perimeter of the garden space and warmed her arms from the cool breeze. The azaleas waiting to be planted should thrive in the shady garden.

She stood and studied the old school whose future was now in her hands. Tupelo Grove University's fading grandeur with its weedy lawns and old buildings was still beautiful. The towering oaks festooned with moss and the tupelo trees on the quad were her favorite sight. From here she could see the brick paths she'd walked as a student herself. Old Boo Radley would be sleeping on the grass by the pond this time of day. It was up to her to save it all.

She spotted Hez coming her way, and her automatic smile faltered at his somber expression. "What's wrong?"

He thrust his hands into the pockets of his khaki pants. "I thought I'd find you in your office."

"It seemed fitting to revive my great-grandpa's azalea garden." She yanked off her gardening gloves and gestured to the stone bench flanked by boxwoods. "There's no one else out here. What's happened?"

He perched on the edge of the bench and pulled her down beside him, then took her hand. "I got a call from Hope. Beckett was found dead in his cell."

She caught her breath. "Murdered?"

"Hope doesn't have the autopsy back yet, but it looks suspicious. He was found hanging in his cell, but he didn't seem suicidal and bruises marked his hands and arms consistent with a struggle."

She clung to his hand and tried not to imagine the grisly details. "Any suspects?"

"I asked Hope the same thing, but she said not yet. Deke Willard was in his cell and nowhere close to Beckett, but Deke could have arranged for someone else to do it. And a couple of other Willards were in jail in Bay Minette. They stick together, so any one of them could have done it."

Conflicting emotions struggled for dominance as Savannah tried to make sense of it all. She'd once thought she and Beckett might have a future together, and some of the better memories of their long friendship still lingered. He'd tried to kill them, but thinking about his last moments in that cold cell made her shudder.

The breeze blew auburn strands of hair across her eyes, and she brushed them away. "Do you think his murder was more than just making sure he didn't testify against Deke?"

"It could have been more. Like I told you and Jess, I'm not convinced the smuggling has stopped. And there's still the mole in the Pelican Harbor PD. I'll talk to Jane and Augusta about it tomorrow. I've got a lot to catch up on with work."

The mention of the mole turned Savannah's concern to that wine bottle in Hez's garbage. "You saw the neurologist this morning, didn't you? What did the CT scan show?" She'd wanted to go with him for the report, but he hated it when she hovered.

His blue eyes flickered, and he glanced away. "Um, there was a spot on my brain. The doctor called it a hematoma. It was there on the earlier scan as well, but they missed it."

She listened to his explanation of the doctor's watch-and-wait approach. "No bike riding, Hez." His rueful smile came, and she grabbed his arm. "I'm serious. No biking, no running. If your blood pressure goes up, it could make that thing bleed more."

"I'd better go then, because your stress is raising my blood pressure right now." He squeezed her hand, and his eyes crinkled in a wider smile. "You're even more beautiful when you're agitated." A finger brushed her cheek. "Your eyes are spitting fire, and your cheeks are flushed."

She inhaled and tamped down her emotion. "So that's the cause of some memory loss?"

"The doctor didn't think so. It wasn't in the right place to cause that."

What did that mean about the bottle in the trash then? Had Hez lied to her about drinking it and throwing away the bottle, or could he be dealing with memory loss from some other cause?

She squelched the impulse to question him about the wine again. Hez was a grown man, not a child. She didn't need to harp on the matter or tell him what to do. Now wasn't the time to ask about counseling either. He had enough on his plate. "I suppose you'd better get to work."

He slipped both arms around her and pulled her against his chest. "I've got a few minutes. How's it feel to be TGU's president?"

"A little terrifying. I'm gulping water from a fire hose trying to learn everything at once. I don't know what my dad and the trustees were thinking to have a complete newb take over."

He twirled a lock of her hair around his finger. "You'll pick up what you need to know. You have the most important skills for this job—love for TGU and the students, great attention to detail, and an aptitude for learning and networking with who can help. You're bringing a fresh perspective to the job too."

She relaxed into his embrace and inhaled the familiar scent of his spicy cologne. "You always say the right things. I picked up the phone once this morning to call and resign."

He pressed a kiss against her ear. "You're no quitter, Savannah Webster. I'm sure your great-grandfather would be busting his buttons to know you're at the helm here."

"I wish he were here to advise me now. I found some of his old journals in storage. I'm going to go through the volumes and see if there's any wisdom in them I can glean. He was a professor first before he took over too. I brought his journal and the journals of two other presidents to my office. My great-grandfather might have been just as intimidated as I am now." She laughed and shook her head. "Or maybe not. He was never a man to show hesitation or weakness."

"I wish I'd met him."

"I've been thinking about him and my great-grandmother

a lot lately. They lost a son to pneumonia in the thirties, and I went with my great-grandma to take flowers to his grave a few times. He's buried not far from Ella. We'd sit there and she would talk about how grief is part of life and how her son's death made her more sensitive to the sorrows she saw on other people's faces. I didn't understand it then, but I do now. Maybe that's why God allows us to grieve—so we understand."

He shifted beside her, and she knew the mention of God had unsettled him. He still struggled with accepting the truth that God had forgiven him for Ella's death, and he struggled even more with forgiving himself. Had that guilt driven him back into the numbness wine offered? She didn't want to believe it, but she had to find the truth.

The brief February daylight was nearly gone though it was only six when Savannah parked in the lot at Mac's Irish Pub in Pelican Harbor. All afternoon she'd thought about the situation with Hez and her worry had grown.

She found Nora inside the front door waiting to be seated, and the hostess led them to a booth in the packed restaurant. They placed their orders for shepherd's pie, and while they waited for their sweet tea, Savannah studied the signed dollar bills stapled to the wall and gathered her thoughts to unload on her best friend.

The server brought their tea and an appetizer of Reuben egg rolls. Nora selected an egg roll. "How's your first week as president going?"

"It feels like a disaster. There are a million things to handle, some of them going all the way back to before Abernathy's murder. We didn't have an interim president, and it shows. The more I dig, the more leaks I'm finding that have been sinking the university for decades."

"At least you have Hez and Jess to lean on. Did Hez tell you about Beckett?"

"He came by late morning to tell me. It was shocking."

"Hez has been in touch with Jane about working together to catch the smugglers too." Her eyes behind her glasses were shrewd. "How are things going with you? Did Hez get the test results back?"

Savannah nodded and reached for an egg roll. "He has a hematoma, but the doctor doesn't think it would cause memory loss."

"But what about the drinking?"

"Exactly my worry. He didn't bring it up, and like a coward, I didn't either. I didn't want any stress to raise his blood pressure and make that hematoma worse." She took a bite, and the strong Reuben flavor exploded on her taste buds. "Mmm, good," she mumbled. She swallowed and shook her head. "I didn't even bring up premarital counseling because of it too. Maybe taking this job was a really bad idea. Saving the university isn't worth losing my marriage, even though I'd hate to see TGU fail. But trying to work on both could leave me with neither."

"Don't try to borrow trouble, girlfriend. All you can do is one thing at a time. I know you believed God put you in this position to save the university. Do you still believe that?"

Did she? Savannah's certainty had waned in the stress of the first few days on the job. She gave an uncertain nod. "I think so. The students need it."

"Then focus on that and let God worry about tomorrow. And try not to worry. It solves nothing, and it disrupts our trust and faith. I know it's easier said than done, and I'm far from perfect at it myself." Nora laughed. "I'm pointing one finger at you and four back at myself."

There was a sparkle in Nora's brown eyes that hadn't been there before. Savannah took a sip of her drink. "How are you doing? You're always listening to me and so rarely complain yourself."

"I'm in a better place finally. And I—I met someone." A smile curved the corners of her lips, and she glanced up shyly as if she wasn't sure Savannah would approve.

Savannah straightened. "What? Who? I want all the deets."

"His name is Graham Warner. He's been to the grief group the last two weeks." She gave Savannah a pointed look. "If you'd shown up, you would have met him."

"I know, I know. It's been crazy. I'll be there on Thursday, even if it's only to meet Graham. What do you know about him?"

"He's the bookstore manager at TGU actually, and he lost his wife two years ago. He just started in January." Nora sipped her sweet tea. "He was impressed I was your bestie. Not because you're the president but because your book was accepted for publication. And isn't that just like God to give you a fresh joy to go with the struggles? I can't wait to read it, and I'll bet you can't wait to hold it in your hands."

"I'll probably cry," Savannah admitted. "It's a dream come true, but I never thought it would happen."

"I'm thrilled you wrote the Willard history. I'm a Willard myself, and that past helped shape me. It's part of the culture in our area too. I've always hoped the university press would find someone to write about it."

Savannah set her glass on the table. Nora had always downplayed her connection to the Willards and claimed not to see them much. "How exactly are you related?"

"My mother is Helen's niece, so it's not all that close."

The server brought their food, but Nora's revelation troubled Savannah at some deeper level. Could Nora know anything about the Willard connection to Beckett's death?

CHAPTER 12

HEZ TOOK A DEEP BREATH AND PREPARED TO WALK INTO the Justice Chamber for the first time. The nameplate holder beside the door was still empty, but a sheet of paper with JUSTICE CHAMBER in forty-point font had been taped to the scarred oak door. He didn't care that the sign was crooked.

He opened the door and flipped the light switch. A fluorescent light buzzed to life, illuminating a small office containing a much-used table, a tiny desk bearing an old computer, and four unmatched office chairs. Gray light dribbled in through a drafty trefoil window, a flourish added by a long-dead architect who loved Gothic cathedrals. The office's prior occupant had warned Hez about the window and left an ancient space heater in a corner by the desk.

Hez plopped a box on the desk and pulled out a coffee maker, which he immediately set up on the corner of the desk. He loaded it with a rich dark roast and started it. First things first.

As the aroma of brewing coffee filled the office, he unloaded the rest of the box—notepads, highlighters, sticky notes, pens, accordion folders, coffee mugs, and other necessities. Finally, he took out a plaque that read *"But let justice roll on like a river, righteousness like a never-failing stream!" (Amos 5:24).* He looked at it for a long moment, then hung it over the desk.

The plaque was an office-warming gift from Savannah—and really the whole office was her gift. The law school couldn't find room for Hez's clinic, so Savannah had flexed some presidential muscle and found them space in Connor Hall. The history department had two vacant offices, thanks to her departure for the administration building and Erik Andersen's disappearance the prior semester. After a week of quick office moves, the Justice Chamber now occupied the second least desirable office in the building. The least desirable office remained empty next door, so the legal clinic had room to grow.

"Aah, that smells awesome," a male voice said.

Hez turned to see Eduardo Hernandez filling the doorway with his broad shoulders. Ed was a scholarship swimmer and first-year law student. He'd apparently come straight from practice, and his collar was damp where it touched his black hair. "Grab a mug and a seat. We'll begin as soon as the other two arrive."

Ed filled the largest mug. His brown eyes were downcast, and Hez frowned. "Anything wrong, Ed?"

The young man hunched his shoulders. "I think I'm going to have to leave school." His voice was bleak, and there was a shine to his eyes. "I wanted to be the first lawyer in my family."

"What's happened?"

"My scholarship just got eliminated." His gaze darted to Hez. "My family doesn't have the money for tuition, so this will be my last semester."

Hez put his hand on Ed's shoulder. "I'll see what I can find out. Maybe the new president will have an idea."

Ed's head came up. "You'd do that for me?"

"You bet. Don't give up hope." Was there any way he could pay these students for their help at the Justice Chamber?

As Ed replaced the carafe, two women walked in together. One was Toni Casey, a thirtyish blonde with a professional air who looked like exactly what she was: an accountant who had spent a few years in the business world and then decided to go to law school. The other was tall and had long black hair—she must be Dominga Steerforth, a favorite student of Savannah's. Dominga had expressed interest in law school, so Savannah suggested she volunteer for Hez's clinic.

Once everyone was caffeinated and seated, Hez got started. "Thanks for coming to the inaugural meeting of the Justice Chamber. Our mission statement is up there on the wall." He pointed to the plaque. "I thought we'd need to go to the public defender's office or legal clinics to find clients in need of justice, but our first client found us. In fact, you could say it *is* us." He spread his arms. "This university—our university—needs our help in at least two areas. First, you might have heard about a smuggling ring using TGU as a front to traffic pre-Columbian artifacts looted from Central and South America. The DA and the U.S. Attorney's Office claim they have it all wrapped up, but I'm not so sure. Ed, you worked on a smuggling case last semester. Do you want to take a look at this?"

Ed savored a sip of coffee and smiled. "It would be my pleasure. If we can shut this down, maybe there will be more money for scholarships."

Dominga, who had been eyeing Ed since she walked in, leaned forward. "I can help. I took Professor Webster's course on pre-Columbian history. It's a really interesting area and I learned a lot."

Hez suppressed a smile. "Okay, great. I'll give you my file and the investigative leads I've gathered so far." He turned to Toni. "The second problem may be more up your alley. Are you familiar with the TGU Extension School?"

She frowned. "I've heard the name. It's basically an online program, right?"

Hez nodded. "Right. TGU's last president, Ellison Abernathy, set it up. He told the board it would be a great way for people who are working full-time or aren't around here to benefit from TGU's excellent programs. It wouldn't cost the university anything because an outside company could administer it for a percentage of the revenue. All the profits would go into TGU's scholarship fund for low-income students."

Toni's eyebrows went up. "I'm not sure why that's a problem. It sounds like a good business model. Part-time and off-campus students get a good education on flexible terms, and the university gets free money for a good cause. That should be a win-win."

Hez grimaced at the memory of what his preliminary investigation had uncovered. "It should be, but it's not. The Extension School admits unqualified students and charges them the maximum they can borrow from government loan programs. The courses are low-quality recorded lectures from Abernathy's friends, who often aren't even TGU professors. And the scholarship fund hasn't gotten a penny. The whole thing has actually been a lose-lose."

Ed sat back and folded his arms. "I'll bet someone's winning."

Toni nodded. "Yeah, all that student loan money has to be going somewhere. Do we have any financial data for the Extension School?"

"We do." Hez lifted his mug and inhaled the rich scent before taking a sip. "They have to submit quarterly data to the president's office, but no one looked at it until last week. It's also not very clear, and . . . well, let's just say Excel and I are not friends."

Toni smiled. "I'm besties with Excel. Send me the spreadsheets and I'll take a look. I can also do some poking around and see what I find."

Hez grinned. "I was really hoping you'd say that." He drained his mug and pushed back from the table. "Okay, let's go do some justice."

Savannah's eyes burned from so much computer work. The sun touched the glossy leaves on the roses outside the arched window of her home office, and if she didn't have so much work to do, she'd get some sweet tea, then wander outside to wait for Simon to get off the bus from school. He was staying with her for a few days while Jess was in New York City to meet with TGU's lenders. If Jess could whip up a little magic there and consolidate the university's debt at a decent rate, it might be a glimpse of sunny skies for TGU.

The yellow bus came around the corner of the street and put out its stop sign. Her nephew bounded down the steps. Moments later the front door slammed. "I had a po'boy delivered for you from Little New Orleans," she called. Since arriving in Nova Cambridge, Simon had become obsessed with the area's po'boys—due to Will Dixon's influence—and she'd had a Cajun shrimp one delivered. "It should still be warm."

He appeared in her office a minute later with his sandwich on a plate and a sweating glass of sweet tea. "You're the best, Aunt Savannah." He plopped onto the love seat along the wall.

He was ten going on thirty, thanks to his self-sufficient nature. He had his mother's blond hair and his father's blue eyes, though Savannah didn't like to think about his lecherous dad. Simon had already taken possession of her heart as she'd watched him navigate the change from English boarding school to all-American kid.

The enticing aroma of Cajun spices and shrimp made her mouth water, and she realized she'd skipped lunch. She peered through bleary eyes at the numbers on the screen. "How'd school go?"

Talking with him was always the highlight of her day whenever he slept over. Ella would have been in grade school by now, and they would have talked over her day like this too. Would she have been as open as Simon was? Savannah liked to imagine lazy afternoons with her Ella. She glanced at Simon's happy expression as he ate his po'boy. If she wasn't working on an important report, she would have shut off her computer and joined him for sweet tea.

"I was gobsmacked. I aced my history test thanks to Will."

She looked up from the screen. "Well done! I'm proud of you."

"Thanks." He chomped on his sandwich, and his cheek bulged before he chewed it into submission and swallowed.

She spotted movement through the window. "Hez is here." A wash of pleasure at the sight of his dark hair and trim build lifted her out of her mild discontent at the computer work she'd been immersed in all day. She rose and stretched, then finger combed her hair before she went to open the door. His focused gaze went soft at the sight of her, and the warmth in her chest spread to the rest of her.

She kissed him, then stepped aside for him to enter. "How'd it go?"

"Great!" He smiled over his shoulder at Simon, who had followed her. "I think you've grown two inches, kiddo."

Savannah followed him and Simon into the living room. "Want some sweet tea or coffee?"

"I've been downing gallons of coffee all day so I'm all caffeinated. Dominga, Ed, and Toni came in, and the Justice Chamber is official." His smile beamed out. "It feels great, and I wanted to come by and show you where I put the plaque you gave me." He swiped on his phone and turned the photo around to show her its prominent position above his battered desk. "I can see it when I start work every morning."

"An attorney of your caliber deserves a better desk. If you save TGU, I'll find it in the budget."

His grin vanished, then came back full wattage. "Um, about that budget. Can we pay the students anything?"

"I thought experience would be their only required compensation."

"Ed Hernandez is losing his scholarship."

She listened to the rest of the story with a rock in her throat. "I don't see where I can come up with funds for that, Hez. We're already in the red now. Tell you what. If the Justice Chamber plugs some of the scammy leaks in our budget, I'll see what I can do."

"What's the Justice Chamber?" Simon asked. "Is it an office or something?"

"It helps people who need justice," Hez said. "Right now it's helping us save TGU."

"You're an awesome lawyer, Uncle Hez. You can do anything."

Hez bent down to rub Marley's ears. "Good dog," he crooned. "The problems are huge, and the Justice Chamber only has four people including me. It's going to take a while to unravel it all."

Savannah watched him with a bemused smile. They'd changed their romantic dinner plans for tonight when Jess jetted out of town, and though Savannah was thrilled to have Simon, she wished she and Hez had more alone time. They'd both been so consumed with saving TGU that they hadn't had a chance to talk about wedding plans, and she'd hoped to bring up the topic tonight.

"Do you need more help?" Simon asked.

Hez's message alert went off on his phone and he pulled it out. "I need all the help I can get. Three student volunteers is all I've got, though. But we'll get it done." He frowned at the phone. "I'll have to run back to the office. Ed locked himself out. Want me to stop and pick up dinner somewhere? Maybe pizza?"

"Sure. There's a movie I thought the three of us might watch. It's an action movie, so you and Simon will like it."

"I want to help save TGU," her nephew said.

She yanked her attention away from Hez. "It could be dangerous, Simon. You were nearly killed a few months ago. None of us want you that close to danger again. Your job is to get good grades in school and make new friends."

His blue eyes widened, and he turned an accusing glare Hez's way. "Mom is in danger and you let her go off to New York without help?" He dragged his phone out of his pocket and tapped on it. "I'm making sure she's okay."

Savannah patted his shoulder. "She's fine, Simon. It's just a business meeting. Hez didn't mean she was in danger now."

"No one is going to stop me from protecting my mom. It took all these years before I got to live with her again, and I can't lose her." His voice cracked.

How had they managed to mess up this conversation so badly? They should have been paying more attention to his questions. She'd better end the discussion before she messed it up even more. "We'll talk to your mom about it. No promises, though."

His defiant expression didn't change. "I'm going to look out for my mom."

She cut her glance to Hez. They'd have to figure out something Simon could do or he'd be going rogue again, and that had disastrous consequences last time.

CHAPTER 13

JESS'S HEART SKIPPED A BEAT WHEN SHE SAW THE TEXT
from Savannah: *We need to talk about Simon. Call when
you can.*

She pushed back from the mahogany conference room
table, drawing startled looks from the two men with her. She
turned to the older of the two. "Sorry, James. I need to take a
short break. Do you have an empty office I could use to make
a call?"

James Hornbrook looked at her, his icy-blue eyes missing
nothing. He nodded once. "Of course. The southeast conference room is empty. You can use that."

She thanked him and walked down the hall to the room
he'd indicated. Its floor-to-ceiling windows offered spectacu-
lar views of Manhattan. The familiar spire of the old Chrysler
Building dominated the view to the east. The Empire State
Building stood to the south, and One World Trade Center
reached up above Lower Manhattan like a crystal needle. Her
old Upper West Side condo and the Central Park paths where
she used to push Simon in a stroller were to the north. She
couldn't see them, but she could feel them behind her. This
used to be home.

She glanced over her shoulder toward the north wall of the conference room. One of James's beloved cream-colored golden retrievers grinned at her from a large picture hung on the wall. She shut the door, but she didn't assume her call would be private. Hornbrook Finance, LLC, was rumored to have hidden microphones and cameras in all of its conference rooms and offices, and she didn't doubt it.

She dialed Savannah's number and paced along one of the windows as the phone rang. Jess forced herself not to think about what might have prompted her sister's text. If anything had happened to Simon . . .

Savannah finally answered. "Hi, Jess. Thanks for calling me so quickly. Hez is here too. I'll put you on speaker."

Jess's blood pressure went up at the mention of Hez's name. "What's going on? Why do we need to talk about Simon?"

Savannah cleared her throat. "He heard Hez and me talking about the Justice Chamber, and he wants to join."

"What? That's out of the question, of course."

"That's exactly what we told him." Savannah sounded exasperated. "But he immediately got defiant and said no one was going to stop him from protecting you."

Hez chimed in. "And we all remember what happened the last time he tried to do that on his own."

Jess closed her eyes and rubbed her forehead. "I'd hoped he'd learned his lesson."

Savannah's voice softened. "Did you ever learn not to try to protect Mom?"

The memories cut like broken glass. Pierre flaunting a new affair in front of Mom, who knew she was trapped and could never leave him. Mom escaping into booze and pills. Jess urging her to fight back, then lashing out at Pierre when her mother couldn't or wouldn't. Pierre casually telling Mom to "control your bastard girl." Savannah trying to separate them before the confrontation turned physical.

Sometimes she succeeded, sometimes she didn't. It happened over and over. And all the while, Mom spiraled further down. Jess had been helpless to stop it—but she wasn't helpless now. She couldn't save her mother, but she could make Pierre pay for his crimes. All of them.

Jess stared out over the cityscape without seeing it. "What do you suggest?"

"Let Simon help. Keep your friends close, your enemies closer, and your headstrong ten-year-old closest of all."

Hez laughed, but Jess winced. Savannah's line was too close to the one she'd used about Hez. "That won't work. He can't help me analyze confidential financial data, and it wouldn't be responsible to give him access to it anyway. Plus, I can't take him out of school every time I need to make a trip to New York." And there was no way she would let James or his minions get anywhere near her son.

Hez's deep voice came through the line. "I can find some jobs for him to do for the Justice Chamber. He can scan documents, organize files, pick up office supplies from the storeroom, and stuff like that. He'll be involved, but he'll also be safe—certainly safer than if we tell him no and he decides to freelance."

He had a point, and Jess couldn't think of a better alternative. She sighed. "Okay, fine."

She ended the call and turned to go back into the meeting. She had done everything she could to keep Simon outside the blast radius of the bomb she was building, but he kept worming his way closer to ground zero. First, he managed to get himself expelled from his British boarding school and wound up in Nova Cambridge. Now he would be working with Hez at the Justice Chamber, which was the second most dangerous place he could be, regardless of what job Hez gave him.

The most dangerous place for Simon was with her, of course. She wanted that with all her heart—and had to fight against it with all her strength. They would be together when all of this was over. Until then, she had to keep him safe.

It felt like a family of bees had taken up residence in Savannah's chest as she waited in her office for Jess, Hez, and her father to show up. Confrontation wasn't her strong suit—not with anyone and certainly not with her arrogant and strong-willed father. She'd spent a lifetime kowtowing to his wishes and demands, and old habits were hard to break.

After a longing glance at the flowers blooming in the garden outside her window, she settled in her chair before lighting a pine-and-vanilla candle. The scent filled her lungs, and the tension knotting her shoulders eased. She might as well spend the next hour doing something useful. After logging in to her computer, she called up the proof she intended to show her father. How did she segue into the topic? The cowardly part of her wanted to let Hez start the conversation, but this was her job, not his. She needed to gather her courage and do what needed to be done.

A sharp rap sounded on her closed door, and it opened before she could call out. Her father strode through and shut the door behind him with a decisive click.

She straightened and gulped back the initial bolt of panic. "Dad, you're early. Our meeting isn't until ten." The library table that served as her desk didn't feel substantial enough to protect her from the rage vibrating from her father's fiery gaze.

He advanced toward her workspace. "I wanted to speak to you before anyone else shows up. One of Hez's law students has been poking around the Extension School, and you need to put a stop to it. I hope you aren't letting your sister manipulate you. Her vendetta against me is obvious—if she can't find anything concrete to accuse me of, she'll make up something."

Savannah could have pointed out dozens of instances where he was at fault in the complicated family relationship, but she bit her tongue. Dad never admitted to wrongdoing, and in all her thirty-five years, she'd never once heard him apologize to anyone. "Jess isn't involved in the investigation, Dad. Hez has been in charge of it, and he's a man of the law. He's not going to fabricate anything, and I see no reason to distrust the results of his investigation."

"Well, you should have serious doubts. The rumor mill is in full swing, and I heard the leadership is considering some very counterproductive proposals. Is this true?"

"I'm not going to get into our decisions until our meeting."

He placed both hands on the library table and glared down at her. "I did a huge favor for you, Savannah Elaine Legare."

"It's Webster." Wrong move. His glare intensified, and she had to force herself not to cower.

"It's thanks to me you're sitting in this office. If I hadn't intervened after you were denied tenure, you'd be begging for another job far away from Ella. Are you going to stand back and let your own father be railroaded with false accusations? I thought better of you, Savannah. I've dedicated my entire life to education. Surely you remember all I've done for TGU."

How dare he use Ella in this battle. She struggled to tamp down the rage bubbling in her chest. "I'm grateful to you and the TGU board for entrusting me with the future of our family's heritage. But, Dad, it's very vulnerable. Once I started looking at our situation, it was clear something is very wrong. We have to fix things before TGU ends up in bankruptcy. I know how much you love TGU." *For what it can do for you.* "I know you want me to do the right thing even if it's personally painful to some of us."

He rubbed the space between his eyebrows. "I trust you not to do anything we'll both regret." His voice vibrated with unspoken emotion. He turned and stalked over to jerk open the door. The slam that followed knocked a book over on one of the bookcases.

Savannah rose to put *Fahrenheit 451* back in place. She'd stood up to her dad for the first time in her life. It was something her mother had never done, and Savannah had followed that example for as long as she could remember. She let that fact sink in. It felt good—really good. Until the tone of his final words sank in. It felt like a threat. What exactly did he mean?

CHAPTER 14

HEZ TAPPED HIS PEN ON THE GLASS-TOPPED CONFERENCE room table. Jess sat across from him, brown leather padfolio open on the table in front of her. Savannah occupied the seat at the head of the table. The empty chair opposite her was for Pierre, who hadn't arrived even though the meeting had been scheduled to start five minutes ago. It was a power move, which Hez would have countered by starting the meeting four minutes and thirty seconds ago. But this wasn't his meeting—or his father.

The hand-carved oak door swung open, and Pierre walked in. He wore a blue oxford shirt and khaki slacks, in contrast to the suits worn by everyone else. Another power move. A smile creased his tan, handsome face, showing too-perfect teeth. "Ah, there you are. I thought we were having a little chat where I could answer a few questions. I didn't realize this was a formal meeting." He gave a smooth chuckle as he sat. "Y'all look so serious, like a bunch of undergrads interviewing for your first jobs."

Savannah's smile was so tight it was almost a grimace. "Thanks for coming." She pressed a button on a little control panel in front of her. "We'll be recording today's meeting, like all official executive proceedings from now on. This meeting of the Ad Hoc Committee on University Affairs will now come to order."

Pierre grinned and leaned back in his chair. "All right, Madam President. What's on the agenda?"

Jess frowned, but Savannah's expression stayed neutral and professional. "The TGU Extension School. We're shutting down the current operation and bringing it in-house. We'll restart it next year under all new management."

Pierre's grin vanished. "Only the board can do that!"

Savannah cut her gaze toward Hez. "My lawyer says otherwise."

Hez nodded. "The university bylaws give the president broad powers to deal with 'fraud and perfidy' at the university."

Pierre eyed him warily. "That's for cases of cheating on exams and that sort of thing. Why do you think it applies to the Extension School?"

Hez leaned forward. "Because the entire thing is a fraud, Pierre. It charges exorbitant tuition for low-quality taped lectures. The profits are supposed to go into a scholarship fund, but there never are any profits. All the money is sucked up by administrative fees charged by something called Education Management, LLC. Education Management does hardly any actual work. It just takes money that should be going to the scholarship fund." Hez fought to keep the anger out of his voice. "Most Extension School students need to take out loans to afford the classes, so they're getting saddled with enormous debts in return for garbage degrees stamped with the TGU seal."

Pierre shook his head. "That's certainly not how Ellison described the Extension School when he founded it. I don't see what any of this has to do with me, though."

Hez folded his arms. "We know who owns Education Management, Pierre."

Pierre looked at him stone-faced. "Do you now?"

"It took a lot of digging, but yes. You did your best to hide it, but we can prove that you, Ellison Abernathy, and Beckett Harrison founded Education Management—and that most of the profits are being funneled into your trust. The final piece of evidence came out of the probate case for Abernathy's will." Hez opened his padfolio and took out a letter on TGU letterhead, which he slid across the table to Pierre. "This is a formal request for the return of all unearned fees. If Education Management doesn't comply, the university will sue."

Pierre flicked a glance at the letter, but he didn't pick it up. He turned to Savannah. "This is completely unacceptable."

Jess tapped a perfect nail on the tabletop. "You don't get a vote."

Pierre kept his eyes on Savannah. "I wasn't talking to you."

Savannah cleared her throat and swallowed. "The committee's vote was unanimous."

Pierre's face went white and then red. He half rose, planted his palms on the table, and glared at Jess. "You did this! You set this whole thing up!"

She regarded him with icy calm. "I wanted to sue you personally and have the process server deliver the papers in the middle of the night. You can thank your daughter for preventing that."

Pierre jabbed a finger at Jess. "This is not over!"

Jess's smile was pure venom. "No. No, it's not."

The sound of jazz echoed from down the street, and the scent of beignets floated from Petit Charms below Hez's condo. Savannah glanced around the balcony with awe at the romantic space he'd created for dinner. A white linen cloth covered the iron table and candles flickered in the dim light. There were even cushions on the hard chairs.

She turned to smile at him as he came through the sliding glass door. "I'm so glad it's warm enough to eat outside. What a surprise to see all this."

He set a tureen beside the salad on the table. "I thought you needed a reward for the rough waters you faced this week."

She picked up a blue-and-white plate. "Are these your grandmother's? I wasn't sure what happened to them."

"I found them in the garage at my place in Birmingham. I'd forgotten about them."

Back then he'd forgotten a lot of important things in their lives. She set the plate back in place. "I've always loved them."

He held out the chair for her, and she settled in it. "I remember."

She caught the aroma of shellfish. "Shrimp bisque?"

He nodded and sat in the chair next to her. "I haven't made it in a while, but there are some things you never forget."

She saw other unforgotten things in his eyes: his love for her and their life together, his commitment to make amends, and his regret for all that had led them to this point. Those same things crowded her chest as well. She speared the blackened salmon Caesar salad with its homemade dressing and savored the hit of heat on her tongue. "I haven't had this since . . ."

"Since we separated," he finished for her. "I've lived mostly on takeout, and it felt good to be creative in the kitchen." He aimed a smile her way. "I'm so proud of how you handled your dad over the Extension School exit. It had to have been hard confronting him with how he's fleeced TGU."

"I felt a little like David facing Goliath, but I didn't back down. Whenever I wanted to waver, I took a quick peek at your face and reminded myself how rock solid your evidence was. People like my dad think they'll never get caught, and when I saw your expression, I remembered how much evil you've taken down in your career. You're a good example."

His smile faltered. "Not in everything." He lifted the lid of the matching blue-and-white tureen and grasped the ladle. "I found the North Sea shrimp you love. Save room, though. I made mint chocolate chip ice cream."

She eyed the champagne flutes. Did she dare ask what he planned to put in them? A bottle of something waited on ice in the wine bucket on the other side of the table. She couldn't read the label. If he pulled out a bottle of sparkling wine, how would she handle it? He couldn't drink, of course, but what if he offered her a glass? She moistened her lips. "You're spoiling me."

"I plan to do that for the rest of our lives." He reached for the bottle in the wine bucket. "It's sparkling water with a hint of citrus. I think you'll like it." He filled their flutes.

Relief made her lightheaded, and she took her drink and sipped it. "Delicious." And not alcoholic. Was she always going to be on edge, wondering if he was secretly drinking? The thought of tiptoeing around the topic forever depressed her.

His hand went into his pocket and he fiddled with something, and there was something in his expression she couldn't quite read. Fear? Hope? He removed his hand and picked up his spoon again.

She reached for her spoon and savored the bisque. "Jess's rage with Dad practically suffocated us all in that meeting room. I wish I knew how to bring peace between them."

"Pierre will never apologize. Men like him never take the blame for their actions, so it's unlikely there can be any resolution."

"Jess could forgive him even if he doesn't apologize. Her hatred is destroying her life."

"Forgiveness is hard." He reached across the table and took her hand. His thumb made lazy circles on her palm. "I don't take your forgiveness for granted. I don't deserve it, but I'm thankful for it."

His touch made her forget the delicious food. "And I'm thankful for yours. Not everyone gets a second chance like we have."

His other hand went to his pocket again. That expression, half hope and half fear, returned. What was he thinking? She pulled her hand back. "I'll clean up and make coffee since you made dinner." She cleared the dishes and tableware and carried them into the kitchen. He'd cleaned up as he went, like usual, and all she had to do was load the dishwasher. The trash caught her attention. No. She put coffee beans in the grinder and removed the old filter with its grounds. It had to go into the trash though, so she pressed her toe on the lever to open the lid. No wine bottles were in the nearly empty bag when she dumped the filter into it, and she almost gasped with relief.

Of course he wasn't drinking. The bottle last time had been a fluke. He didn't even remember it. Her gaze cut to the recycling bin. Before she could stop herself, she lifted the lid and peeked inside. No bottles there either. But would he drink if he knew she was coming? No, he'd be careful. She moved to the pantry cabinet and found nothing but pasta and canned goods.

"Looking for something?"

She whirled with her hand to her throat. Heat rushed to her cheeks, and her tongue went dry. "Y-you scared me."

"You still think I'm drinking, don't you? Savannah, I'm not."

His mouth flattened to a hard line, but his blue eyes held a depth of sadness that broke her heart. She couldn't lie to him. "I'm sorry, Hez," she whispered. "I'm worried."

He regarded her with that heartbroken expression for a long moment as his hand went to his pocket again. He gave a slight shake to his head and pulled his hand out. "I think you're right, and we should start counseling. We clearly have trust issues we need to resolve."

When he left the kitchen, she exhaled and went on wobbly legs to sit on a stool at the island. What was she supposed to do—put on rose-colored glasses and ignore the past? She wished she could.

CHAPTER 15

HEZ YAWNED AND A SHIVER RAN THROUGH HIM. A WINTRY gray drizzle fell outside the Justice Chamber's drafty window. The chill clung to him despite the hot mug of coffee he held with both hands. Even the space heater in the corner hadn't warmed him up.

He rose and stared out the window at his view of Legare Hall, the unfinished Gothic-style building that had fallen into decay. It was supposed to be Pierre's greatest monument to himself, but the domed grand foyer had partially collapsed. The college had vague plans to convert it into student housing, but Hez didn't see how they could ever afford it.

He shivered again and turned away. The cold wasn't just external. He had felt it ever since he caught Savannah going through his trash last night. Every last detail had been perfect until that moment—especially the look in her beautiful green eyes when they talked about their future together. Even the weather had been perfect, allowing him to quickly move their dinner out to his balcony five minutes before she arrived. It seemed like the ideal moment to give her the ring he'd had in his pocket all night.

And then he made the mistake of following her into the kitchen.

He hadn't slept much last night. The same unanswerable questions kept cycling through his mind. Would she always be searching the trash and checking his breath? What—if anything—could he do to make her trust him again? How could they get remarried if she didn't trust him? He gulped his coffee and the hot liquid slid down his throat, but it did nothing to warm the icy bleakness in his heart.

An energetic young voice broke into his gloom. "Hi, Uncle Hez!"

He turned to see Simon walking in, an excited smile on his face. He carried a TGU thermal mug and a new binder with a carefully lettered label that said *Justice Chamber*.

Hez couldn't help smiling too. "Hi, Simon. I'll make you something hot to go in that mug of yours."

"Thanks, but Aunt Savannah already got me a hot chocolate at University Grounds. So when do we get started?"

"When the others arrive. Toni and Ed are in the same Civil Procedure class over at the law school, and it just got out a couple of minutes ago. Dominga should be on her way too." As he was speaking, female laughter floated in from the hallway.

A moment later, the three students walked in together. Dominga had her hand on Ed's arm and laughed at something he'd said. Toni trailed behind, wearing a knowing smile. She cast a curious glance at Simon, but she said nothing.

"Great to see everyone." Hez gestured to Simon. "As you can see, our merry band has grown. This is my nephew, Simon

Legare. His name might sound familiar to you in particular, Toni."

Her brows went up. "Are you related to Jessica Legare? She was a big help in my investigation of the TGU Extension School."

Simon beamed with pride. "I'm her son."

Hez raised his mug to the former accountant. "Toni did an outstanding job. She uncovered a major fraud, which TGU's management is working to fix. I have a good feeling about how that's going to turn out."

Toni smiled at the compliment. "Thanks, Professor Webster. Ms. Legare has already given me leads on three other potential scams. She's been very supportive of the Justice Chamber."

It felt strange to have Jess be very supportive of anything Hez did. Even when he defended her in a murder case, she had been so secretive and controlling that he had almost withdrawn. He was surprised at her level of cooperation now, but he shouldn't be. They both had an interest in cleaning up the university's finances, and Jess had the extra motivation of killing some of Pierre's sleazy golden geese in the process. Hez needed to learn to trust her.

"That's terrific. Open new case files if you haven't already and load any documents you receive. Simon can help you with scanning." Simon opened his binder and wrote down his assignment. Hez turned to the other two. "Ed and Dominga, how's your investigation going?"

"Not quite as fast as Toni's." Ed nodded to his fellow law student. "But we're making good progress. Dominga searched gallery listings, and she found five pre-Columbian artifacts with TGU provenance documents—and two of them were previously unknown Huacho wood masks. I suspect they're currently looting a rich mother lode of items. She checked with Professor Guzman, who confirmed that the documents were forged. One of the forgeries is dated less than a month ago."

Hez straightened. "So after Beckett Harrison's arrest and Professor Andersen's disappearance? Are you sure?"

Ed pressed his lips into a grim line and nodded. "Your hunch was correct. The smuggling is still going on, and it's ramping up. Valuable items are being lost to the underbelly of the black market."

Hez bit his lip for a moment. Provenance documents from a respected university dramatically increased an artifact's value, but they took some expertise to fake. "Did you ask Professor Guzman who might be forging the provenance documents now that Andersen and Harrison are gone?"

Dominga leaned forward. "We asked, but he didn't have any ideas off the top of his head. He said whoever is doing it is being more careful now."

"Hmm." Hez drummed his fingers on the arm of his chair. "Maybe we should come at this from another angle. The Coast Guard and police have been keeping a close eye on the beaches. Do you have any idea how the smugglers are doing it?"

A wide grin split Ed's face. "We do indeed. A little birdie told me all about it. We're still nailing down a few things, but another shipment should be coming soon. We might be able to catch them."

Hez pumped his fist. "That's awesome! Who's the birdie? Our friends over at the DA and U.S. Attorney's Office will want to know for their warrant applications."

Ed's grin faded. "Uh, I promised not to tell. The source is

very nervous. Do you think they can get warrants without the identity?"

Hez considered for a moment. "Maybe, but we'll need to give them as much corroborating detail as possible. When and where the shipment will be delivered, means of delivery, contents of the shipment, and so on."

Ed nodded. "We can get most of that from the source. We'll also independently verify whatever we can."

Simon listened to Ed with rapt attention. "That sounds cool! I can help too."

Hez cleared his throat. "That . . . might not be the best idea, Simon." Defiance sparked in Simon's eyes and he opened his mouth to object, but Hez hurried on before his nephew could speak. "We need you to work with Toni. She has three new leads, and she's the only one working on them. Ed and Dominga are both working on a single investigation."

Taking his cue, Toni nodded. "Yes, I could really use your help—and you'd be working with your mom too."

Simon's rebellious look vanished. "I'd like to work with my mom."

Hez breathed a sigh of relief. Poking around in the university's finances would be much less dangerous than trying to catch smugglers. Plus, Jess was one of the most formidable people he'd ever met. Standing next to her was probably the safest place in the world for Simon.

Bookshelves lined the wall behind Pastor Forrest Walsh's office, and Savannah studied the titles of the theology books while their pastor took his seat at the tidy desk. The tension in her shoulders radiated up her neck. Why was she so nervous? This should have been an easy counseling session, but the betrayal in Hez's eyes when he found her going through the trash still stung. Maybe Pastor Forrest could straighten out this fear in her head.

The pastor and his wife had dealt with his own addiction before God had called him into the ministry. If anyone knew how to emerge from this kind of situation, he would. Maybe he could help Hez face his problem.

Pastor Forrest's brown eyes were wise and kind. "So the two of you are about to be remarried. Congratulations. I've often done premarital and postdivorce counseling, but never both at the same time." He chuckled. "When were you divorced?"

"About six weeks ago," Hez said.

The pastor's brows rose. "The ink is barely dry. Why do you think it's a good idea to remarry so quickly?"

Savannah shot Hez a glance. "The divorce was kind of a misunderstanding. We still love each other, and Hez thought he could show me he wanted what was best for me by filing for divorce. I was about to tell him I didn't want it any longer, but it was a little too late."

"I never stopped loving Savannah. We just had a lot of problems to work out."

The pastor shifted in his leather chair. "It's not unusual to hear divorced couples say they still love each other. But since it wasn't enough the first time, what has changed since your marriage fell apart?"

Savannah launched into Ella's death, Hez's drinking, and the destruction that followed. "It was a difficult time, and we both want a second chance." What had changed for her? She wasn't able to answer his question, not really.

His attention turned to Hez. "How do you feel about all of this, Hez? What has changed for you?"

Hez shifted in his chair. "I stopped drinking and started attending AA. I realized I was a workaholic, and I left my high-pressure job and came to TGU to start a legal clinic. I wanted to be closer to Savannah and start over. When I realized she wanted her freedom, I gave it to her even though divorce was the last thing I wanted." He turned toward Savannah and caught her gaze. "If there are any other changes I need to make, I'll make them."

"I can hear the sincerity in your voice, Hez," the pastor said. "You've already made some huge changes. Congratulations on your hard work. How about you, Savannah? What has changed for you?"

That question again. She wet her lips, and her heart rate accelerated. "I've been trying to get better at confronting emotional problems instead of running away." What a lame answer. Hez had worked tirelessly on his issues, and she still found it hard to confront hers. Maybe she was the one who needed to change the most. She'd hurt Hez deeply by looking for wine bottles, but how did she get past this fear?

The pastor's expression went neutral. "Is there anything specific you know you need to work on?"

"The trauma of Ella's death still hurts, but at least we can talk about it now." She darted a glance at Hez. "I-I'm worried he's started drinking again. He says he hasn't, but I found an empty wine bottle in his trash, and it's hard to believe someone else put it there as he claimed."

Hez twisted in his chair to look at her. "I don't blame you, Savannah. But how can we think about marriage again if you're constantly going through the trash and checking my breath? Will you ever trust me again?"

Her eyes blurred at the pain in his voice. "I want to, Hez, but it's so very hard. Mom always said she was quitting booze and pills, and I trusted her. I believed her every time. And a few days later, I'd find her drunk or drugged out of her mind. And that's how I'd find you."

He took her hand. "I know, honey, and I'm sorry. But I've changed."

She was barely aware of her tears spilling over until she felt their heat on her cheeks. "You never knew her, Hez. She was so beautiful and vibrant. She was a gifted poet, and her work was extraordinary. Everyone loved her too, until the booze and pills changed her. She became a pathetic wreck who never got out of bed. That's why I left you the first time. I couldn't stand to watch that happen to you. It changed you. And now you seem to be back, really back. But what if you go down that road again? I couldn't bear it." Despair erupted from some dark place where she'd stuffed it. She clutched herself and rocked back and forth in her chair as she sobbed out her fear.

Hez started to leave his chair and move toward her, but she shook her head. "Th-that's why I was going through the trash. I want to believe you, Hez. Desperately. But my fear is greater right now, and I don't know how to change that." She whispered the last words before shame choked them back. He'd mustered up enough faith to trust her with his heart again, and she'd failed him. How did she get past this terror of seeing him walk her mother's path?

"That's a hard spot, Savannah," Pastor Forrest said. "Childhood trauma can be difficult to navigate, and it sounds like yours was particularly bad."

She raised her head and took the tissue he proffered to mop her face. "I've blocked out some of it. My sister remembers details I can't face. I should probably work harder at remembering those details. If I do, maybe I can let them go."

"I think a qualified Christian counselor might be exactly what you need. This isn't straightforward premarital counseling, and it's likely going to take some deeper work to help you. I have someone in mind, an empathetic woman in Pelican Harbor." He scribbled on a sticky note and handed it to her. "Here's her name and number. I think you'll find her helpful."

She stared at the note through blurry eyes. "B-but what about the premarital counseling?"

"If you don't deal with it, your trauma will rear up in ways you aren't expecting. I'm sorry."

Shock dried the last of her tears. She hadn't expected she would be the one with the most problems.

CHAPTER 16

A PELICAN SWOOPED DOWN TO SCOOP UP A FISH IN THE waves off the pier, and Savannah imagined how that fish must feel. The same hopelessness swirled in her chest as she fingered the paper Pastor Forrest had given her. Hez hadn't said much and, even now, sat beside her on the bench with his gaze far away.

She stared at the name. Melissa Morris.

Hez moved closer and slipped his arm around her. "You okay, babe?"

"It's a lot to take in to realize the divorce was m-my fault."

"That's not what Forrest said."

"It was implied. I'm the one who needs additional counseling for ch-childhood trauma. I never came to terms with what happened to Mom, so I just left when you started down the same path. If I'd handled things right when you started drinking, we wouldn't be here now."

His warm lips pressed against her temple. "I doubt I would have listened. I was desperate to numb the guilt. We can't go back and change things. All we can do is learn from our mistakes and go forward."

COLLEEN COBLE AND RICK ACKER

She knew she needed to press the issue about whether he was still drinking, but he'd been so sincere in his denial with Pastor Forrest. Whatever had happened, he clearly didn't believe he'd emptied that wine bottle, but nothing else made any sense. And her reluctance to bring it up again showed her how much she needed that counseling. "I think I'll make an appointment."

The wind caught her hair and blew it into his face, but he didn't brush it away and only pulled her closer. "It hurts to see you cry like you did in his office. I didn't realize until then how your mother's drinking affected you. And then I started that cycle all over again. No wonder you couldn't deal with it."

"I should have been stronger."

"No, I shouldn't have put you through it in the first place. I'm sorry, babe. More sorry than I can say. You are my whole world, and I let you down. I promise I'll do better. Just trust me."

She couldn't look at him and stared out over the whitecaps. "I do trust you, Hez." It was easier to say than to do. That hard kernel of distrust lodged in her chest, and she didn't know how to dissolve it.

He tipped her chin toward him. "Then why can't you look at me and say that?"

Her eyes blurred, and she blinked away the moisture. His expression was so earnest, so sincere. Yet so hurt. She desperately wanted to believe him. "I trust you with my life. I always have."

He gave a slight nod. "I know you want that to be true, and maybe with counseling it will be. That will take time. I'm glad we didn't get remarried right away. What did you say that night at Billy's? We need a clean break and a fresh start so we make sure we don't fall back into the habits that broke us apart. I'll prove myself to you. I'm not ever giving up on us."

"I'm not either." A hiccupping sob erupted from her throat. "Thank you for sticking with me."

The pain in his eyes softened. "You had me in the palm of your hand from the first moment we met. I don't think it's possible to stop loving you. Even the bottle couldn't eradicate it."

She leaned in to kiss him and vowed to fix the damage inside her that childhood trauma had caused. More than anything in the world, she wanted to build a new life with Hez.

Hez paused to drink in the sight of Savannah as he walked into the president's office. The morning sun streaming through the mullioned windows brought out gold highlights in her auburn hair and warm tones in the old wood of the library table she used as a desk. She wore a cream blouse and a green blazer that matched her eyes. A picture of a tuxedo-clad younger version of himself on their wedding day grinned at him from the middle of a collection of photos on the credenza. Would a new version of that picture ever take its place?

Doubt clouded Hez's heart after the counseling session last night. The old helpless despair in her face as she described her mother's losing battle with addiction made him want to sweep her into his arms and comfort her. But the fear and pain etched deep into her soul were beyond his power to heal.

He would have faced an uphill battle even without the trauma of her childhood. As Jimmy had pointed out, Savannah's lack of trust was entirely logical. Hez was an alcoholic, most alcoholics relapsed, and she found a wine bottle in his trash. Ergo, the only rational conclusion was that he had relapsed. His denials only meant that he was probably a liar in addition to being a drunk. Rehashing things on the pier hadn't gotten him very far. Dredging up her feelings had taken everything she had.

He really had only one hope of proving otherwise: catch whoever planted the bottle. His gut told him the same person was at the heart of the corruption threatening TGU. And with luck, the trap he and the Justice Chamber had laid was about to catch them.

"Excuse me," Jess said from behind him.

"Sorry." He stepped into the office and out of her way. "I was just admiring the view."

Savannah's smile was tired but warm. "Are you buttering me up to ask for something? If so, the answer is yes."

"Nope." Hez sat in one of the chairs opposite Savannah and Jess settled in the other. "In fact, I come bearing a gift: the smuggling operation on a silver platter."

Jess twisted in her seat to look at him. "Smuggling operation? Do we even have proof that's still going on?"

Hez nodded. "The students in the Justice Chamber have done a really terrific job of connecting the dots. They found smuggled artifacts listed for sale by art galleries, including at least one with a fake TGU provenance letter dated after Beckett's arrest."

Jess frowned. "Are you sure? Every time I go down to the beach or out on the bay, I see cops and Coast Guard. How can smugglers possibly get through?"

"They're using a new route. Instead of bringing in shipments by sea, they're smuggling them in semitrailers loaded with legitimate cargoes. Drug-sniffing dogs don't notice anything, of course, and the artifacts are usually small enough that they can be hidden from a visual inspection."

Jess arched a skeptical eyebrow. "Can you prove any of this? What evidence do you have?"

Hez hesitated for a moment. Jess had zeroed in on his weak point. "We have an anonymous source."

That didn't satisfy Jess, of course. "What kind of source? A smuggler? Someone in an art gallery?"

Hez grimaced. Jess would have made a good lawyer. She had a natural gift for cross-examination. "I don't know. The source talked to one of the Justice Chamber volunteers and insisted on confidentiality."

Jess rolled her eyes. "This sounds like a college prank."

Hez smiled. "The DA's office disagrees. So did Judge Hopkins."

Jess's eyes widened. "What did you do?"

"I presented our evidence to the DA. The source had enough corroborating details to persuade them. They went to the judge and got a warrant."

Jess stared at him for a moment, then slowly shook her head. "If you're wrong, this will be a huge embarrassment for the university."

Hez shrugged. "We'll know tomorrow. The source says a shipment is coming through in the middle of the night. There's going to be a surprise party waiting for them."

For the first time in Hez's memory, Jess was speechless. He savored the moment. And really hoped she was wrong.

CHAPTER 17

THE PALE MOONLIGHT OUTLINED THE EDGES OF THE SHRUBS and trees with silver. Savannah crouched with Hez behind a sprawling wax myrtle bush a couple of miles from Elberta, and the bayberry scent from the crushed leaves wafted to her nose. The temperature had plunged into the thirties, and her foggy breaths blended with Hez's. She could make out the outlines of police cars, engines idling and lights off, on either side of the crossroad. Hez's car was parked a quarter mile away to allow the police to make full use of the scant cover.

Hez slipped his arm around her and pulled her closer. "You're cold. You should have stayed in the car where it's warm. We have no idea how long this might take. The semi is supposed to show up around one, but it could take longer."

His whispered breath warmed her ear. She snuggled against his warm bulk and inhaled the faint scent of his soap and cologne. "I wanted to help you listen and watch, and when the police start pulling out statues and other pieces, I'll be able to tell if they're artifacts." So far all she'd heard was the bleat of a goat at a nearby farm and the low growl of the police engines keeping the officers warm.

His fingers squeezed her upper arm, and she relished the

unspoken approval. After their counseling session, she'd been more determined than ever to try to get past this fear lurking inside. She couldn't let this second chance with Hez slip away because of childhood trauma. She had her first counseling session with Melissa Morris tomorrow.

Headlights appeared in the distance, and she held her breath when the vehicle rumbled closer. The sound of the big diesel engine told her it was a semi hauling a trailer even before she could pick out the details of the truck. "Just like you said," she whispered against his ear.

He nodded and they watched it pull to the stop sign. A police car pulled in front of it and another one blocked the back. Officers spilled from the vehicles, and one of them yanked open the driver's door. "Out," he said.

The driver uttered a string of curses as he climbed out of the cab. He stood with his hands on his hips as officers opened the back of his truck and clambered inside. "What's this all about?"

Hez helped Savannah up, and they walked to the back of the trailer to watch the action. Officers ripped open shrink-wrap on the pallets of boxes and began to go through the contents. Savannah stamped her feet to bring a little warm blood to her toes. This wouldn't be a quick task—not with that many pallets of boxes. At the front of the truck, the driver continued to harangue the officers, and his language grew even more colorful as the minutes stretched out.

"Got something here," one of the cops shouted after about an hour. He came toward Savannah with a wrapped statue. "This what we're looking for?"

Her mouth went dry. Finally they had some evidence. She

took the Bubble Wrap off the item. "Could one of you shine a light on it for me?"

A female officer promptly complied, and Savannah's bubble of anticipation deflated. The statue was of two children holding hands. "It's not an artifact, just a piece of decorative art for a living room." She handed it back to the officer, who shrugged and took it back to the truck.

What if this was a bust? Hez's information indicated the truck would have several hidden illegal artifacts, but the smugglers could have gotten wind of the trap. But that didn't make sense either because wouldn't they have avoided the area and gone a different direction?

The minutes ticked by into hour two of the search as she and Hez watched. The officers looked for hidden panels in the sides and under the floor, but nothing was inside but what was on the pallets.

Two hours later, an officer shook his head. "We're done here. It's clean." He shot Hez a disgusted glare as they clambered down out of the trailer and headed to their vehicles.

Hez sighed and took Savannah's hand. "Let's get to the warm car. I don't know what went wrong."

"You can go, sir," one of the officers told the driver. "Sorry for your inconvenience."

"Sorry! Is that all you can say? You delayed me two hours for nothing." He snorted and stomped toward the cab of his truck. He glared at Savannah and Hez as he passed. He reached the cab and pulled open his door.

The interior light shone on his face and Savannah frowned when she got a good look at him. She'd seen him before, but where? She gasped when recognition clicked into place and clutched Hez's hand. "That's Joseph Willard V, known as Little Joe. I met him when I was researching my book."

The man shrugged off his denim jacket before he climbed into the truck, and she spotted a Punisher tattoo on his arm. She struggled to remember what she knew of the various branches of the Willard clan. Little Joe had gotten a business degree, hadn't he? Why was the man driving a semi in the middle of the night?

———

Jess's hand shook as she powered on the computer in her home office. A poisonous cocktail of caffeine, adrenaline, and fatigue coursed through her veins. She took a deep breath and tried to calm her racing heart. Tonight had been a very close thing—and it wasn't over yet.

She'd been going nonstop since she walked out of the meeting with Hez and Savannah fifteen hours ago. A tense series of calls and videoconferences with Punisher and English Cream punctuated her day as they scrambled to find the source of the leak and figure out what to do with the shipment, which was already on a truck in Texas by the time Jess left Savannah's office.

The big problem was that they had no idea where the ambush would take place. Hez hadn't revealed the location during the meeting, and Jess couldn't press for more information without raising his suspicions. Their mole in the Pelican Harbor Police Department was no help because the DA had kept the PHPD in the dark and worked solely with state police, presumably because Hez had told the DA about the mole. So Jess and English

Cream decided—over Punisher's loud objections—to keep the truck on its regularly scheduled route and send it into the ambush. The smuggled artifacts had to be in New York for an auction today, so they were pulled off the truck in a dark wayside outside Chunky-Meehan, Mississippi, before it reached Alabama, and given to a courier. A second courier took the provenance documents from TGU to New York so everything arrived at the auction house on time. It had been expensive and nerve-racking, but they had managed to pull it off.

Now came the finger-pointing. At least none of them should be aimed at her. Still, she braced herself for the fireworks as her monitor came to life. Punisher and English Cream were already online.

"Explain yourself, little Fury," Punisher barked, referring to her avatar: an image from an ancient Greek vase showing one of the Furies, goddesses of vengeance and justice. "How did you let this happen?"

So she was somehow still to blame. Of course. She was in no mood to play nice. "Simple. I made the mistake of going into business with you."

"Watch your mouth!"

Her raw nerves snapped. "Watch your back! Someone in your organization talked. That's the only explanation."

"She's right," English Cream said. "You have a traitor in your midst. I don't know the details of the shipping routes and schedules and neither does she. Only your people do. If it hadn't been for our friendly Fury, we all would be paying a heavy price for your leak."

Punisher cursed. "I'm already paying a heavy price. The load of furniture in that truck was late thanks to the cops, and I had to pay a penalty. If we'd taken care of the lawyer like I suggested, this wouldn't have happened."

English Cream sighed. "No, something different and worse would have happened. We've been over this already. Take care of the leak."

Punisher snorted. "Oh, we will. We're gonna find it and plug it. Permanently."

Savannah entered her office building after ten. Her first appointment with Melissa Morris had gone well, though she felt wrung out from the emotions of recounting everything to her. It had been cathartic, and she felt a tiny sliver of hope. Melissa had given her a Bible passage to memorize from Isaiah 43 about forgetting the past. She especially liked the part about God doing a new thing and making a way in the wilderness. That wilderness was in her past, and with God's help, she could find her way.

She reached her office door and found Hez pacing the marble floor outside. "Hez, what are you doing here?" He wore the same jeans and TGU sweatshirt as the night before. Lines of fatigue fanned from his tired, red eyes, and his scruffy chin told her he hadn't shaved this morning either. "Did you get any sleep?"

He shook his head and continued to pace. "I've been here since three this morning. There has to be a bug here at the university, Savannah. Has to be! Our intel was rock solid, so there's no other explanation for my failure last night. I've searched the Justice Chamber, my office, and the conference room. I came here to wait for you and Jess to arrive so I could search your offices. Jess arrived at seven, but her office was clean. So it has to be here in your office."

She examined his tone for an accusation but didn't find even a hint of blame. So why did she feel so defensive? "I know I'm late. I had my first counseling session this morning." She expected him to grill her about it, but he seemed too intent on his mission to ask any questions.

She unlocked the door to her office and flipped on the light. Hez went straight to the bookcases and pulled out every volume. He ran his fingers along the undersides of the shelves as well. Savannah went to her library table desk and pulled out her chair before squatting under it to examine the underside. Nothing. Her chair was clean too.

After twenty minutes of searching, Hez dropped into the armchair. "I don't understand this. I was sure a bug was in here. Did you tell anyone about the roadblock?"

She stiffened. "Of course not. I wouldn't do that."

"Not even Nora? Or a passing comment to someone?"

Was he accusing her of leaking the information? His mention of Nora stirred her unease at her discovery that Nora was a Willard. Had she told Hez about it? She didn't think so, but maybe she should. "I—I didn't tell Nora. She's a Willard, but the connection is distant and she doesn't see them much."

He leaped to his feet. "What? Why didn't you tell me?"

She didn't like his raised voice and tried to chalk it up to his fatigue. He couldn't be accusing her of anything. "It didn't seem important—like I said, she doesn't see them much."

He ran his hand through his thick dark hair. "Savannah,

that was crucial information. Nora is the mole! It makes perfect sense since she's in the police department. You must have said something to her."

"You're wrong! I haven't even seen her or spoken to her on the phone." *Keep your cool.* She took a couple of deep breaths before answering in a softer tone. "Nora has never been anything but trustworthy. Even if I'd said something to her, she would never betray me. You need to go home and get some sleep. This is your exhaustion talking."

He rubbed his forehead. "I have a class to teach. I barely have time for a quick shower and more coffee."

"Then go home and take a nap after your class. That's an order from your president." She forced a smile so he didn't take offense.

He didn't so much as crack a tiny grin before heading to the door without answering her. He didn't kiss her goodbye either, and he left the door standing open. She exhaled a shaky breath and sank onto her chair. What had just happened? She'd never expected Hez to blame her for last night's failed ambush. Her thoughts spun through everyone she'd talked to in the past twenty-four hours. This couldn't be her fault.

Jess poked her head in the door. "What's up with Hez this morning? He looked like he'd been on an all-night bender. He's never rattled, but he was not himself." She entered the office and shut the door behind her.

A shiver of dread rippled down Savannah's back. She hadn't been close enough to him to smell his breath, but it didn't sound like he'd had time to drink.

That never stopped him before.

She shoved away the unwelcome thought.

"He's trying to figure out how the smugglers knew about the ambush."

Jess adjusted her navy skirt. "I don't think they did. If they knew the cops were waiting, wouldn't they have made sure they didn't come down that deserted road? I think it's clear his intel was off."

Savannah wanted to tell her sister about Hez's accusatory tone, but it would only heighten the tension between the two people she loved most in the world. "I'm sure he'll figure it out." And once he thought about it, he'd be back with an apology.

CHAPTER 18

FOR THE THIRD TIME, HEZ READ THE OPENING PARAGRAPH of the paper he was grading—and he still didn't understand it. Ordinarily, that meant a low grade, but today he wasn't at all sure whether the problem was on the page in front of his eyes or with the brain behind them. He'd been up too long, had too much coffee, and had too many balls in the air. And if he was honest with himself, he was too old for this sort of thing. Thirty-seven felt a lot different than twenty-seven after pulling an all-nighter.

He leaned back and rubbed gritty eyes. His joints creaked, and he could feel a migraine knocking on the back door of his skull. Maybe Savannah was right that he needed to go home and take a nap.

Savannah. His mind went back to his visit to her office this morning. He hadn't exactly been at his best. His old workaholism came back with a vengeance after his humiliation at last night's roadblock. He hadn't been able to think about anything except what had gone wrong. He'd needed to figure it out immediately. Sleep was out of the question, of course, so he had headed to TGU, started the coffee maker in the Justice

Chamber, and begun hunting for the bug he was certain the smugglers had planted.

Seven hours and a pot and a half of coffee later, he was pacing in front of Savannah's office. What did she see when she walked in? A man who had really changed? Or the guy whose obsessive streak helped ruin their marriage the first time? Why should she trust her heart to someone who turned into a brittle monomaniac the instant something went wrong?

He sighed and pushed himself out of his chair. Time to go home, take Cody for an easy jog along the beach, and get to bed early. Tomorrow he'd prioritize her, no matter how much he wanted to hunt clever smugglers. Maybe he could take Savannah out for a relaxed dinner, or maybe they could spend a day hiking this weekend. Maybe both.

His phone buzzed as he walked out of the building. He didn't recognize the number, but it was local. He hesitated for a couple of rings. He wasn't expecting a call, but maybe it was related to last night, and he could always hang up if it was a spammer. "Hello?"

"Professor Webster, it's Toni." Her voice shook. "Someone broke into my car and stole my phone. Another law student had your number and let me call you on his phone."

A jolt of adrenaline pierced his fog of fatigue. "You think this might be related to the Justice Chamber?"

"Maybe. I was at the gym. When I came out, my window was smashed. They didn't take my wallet or laptop—just the phone."

Hez's tired brain whirred. "The smugglers knew about the roadblock. They might also know that our tip came through the Justice Chamber."

"I tried calling Ed and Dominga. They didn't answer, but there's no reception at that old track where they run this time of day."

"On my way there now."

Hez ended the call and ran past Connor Hall, an old brick-and-limestone edifice that moldered among banks of azaleas and rhododendrons about two hundred yards from the law school.

He rounded the corner of the last building and took in the scene at the old track in an instant. Ed lay prone on the crumbling asphalt, pinned down by two big men in ski masks. Dominga shrank back against a tree, her eyes wide with terror as a third masked man yanked her purse off her shoulder.

Hez launched himself at one of the guys on top of Ed. The force of the impact knocked the guy off, and he and Hez wrestled on the asphalt.

Hez's opponent was bigger and managed to force him onto his back. Thick fingers wrapped around Hez's neck and started to squeeze. Black spots danced in his vision, and he knew he had only a few seconds of consciousness left. He flailed around for a weapon, and his hand closed on a rock. He smashed it on the guy's head with all his strength. The grip loosened and Hez broke free. He staggered to his feet, looking around for another weapon.

"Look out!" Dominga shouted.

Something crashed into the left side of Hez's skull and blackness took him.

The loan consolidation was everything Jess had been working for, but Savannah fiddled with her pen as she read it in the afternoon sunshine streaming through her office window. "This legalese makes my head hurt. I'm forwarding it to Hez before I sign it." She clicked the forward button and sent it off. His teaching day would be mostly over, and he should get to it quickly.

Jess had one elegant leg crossed over the other, and her taupe heel swinging back and forth was a sure sign of her exasperation. "Savannah, this is a great deal." She leaned forward in her chair to touch a manicured nail to the interest rate percentage. "We should finalize it while we can. I worked hard on getting this put together. Not only does it consolidate all our debt where we can concentrate on paying it down, but it will save us money. With our precarious financial situation, we need every penny."

Savannah wasn't going to let herself be bullied. "Hez won't take long to get back to me."

Sirens screamed past outside, and she went to the window. Several police cars and an ambulance tore past her building and vanished toward the edge of campus.

Her door flew open and the old security guard, Oscar Pickwick, burst in. His cap was askew and his face pale. "The police just called! There was an attack at the old track—it's Professor Webster! There's an ambulance on the way."

Professor Webster.

Savannah ran past Jess and dashed out the building. She raced toward the old track, and her labored lungs screamed for oxygen as she pushed herself to go faster.

A cluster of officers and bystanders thronged the edge of

the cracked and weedy asphalt oval, and fear clutched her by the throat.

Augusta Richards grabbed her arm as Savannah forced herself through the crowd. Augusta, with her tall, lanky figure, exuded confidence in her role as a Pelican Harbor detective. Her brown eyes held sympathy. "You can't go in there, Savannah. It's a crime scene."

Crime scene.

Savannah's terror ramped up a hundredfold, and she shook off Augusta's restraining grip. "Let me go—I have to see Hez." She reached the track. Dominga stood by a tree talking to a police officer. Savannah's gaze skipped to Ed, who sat on the cracked asphalt. She could smell a coppery scent in the air. Blood trickled down his cheek, and an EMT was working on a cut on his head while another officer stood talking to him and jotting down notes.

Where was Hez? He had to be here. Then she spotted him on the grass beside the track. His breathing didn't look right, and he was pale and sweaty. Paramedics positioned a gurney into place and began to lift him onto it.

"Hez!" She started forward, and Augusta put a hand on her arm.

"The paramedics need to be able to help him," Augusta said.

The attendants got him situated on the gurney, and Savannah caught a glimpse of his open eyes. The blankness in his face sent ice down her spine. His pupils were enormous, and very little of the blue in his eyes could be seen. He grunted and his arms twitched, then his legs. He was having a seizure.

"Help him!" Sobs shook Savannah. "I have to be with him."

What if he died? What if the harshness between them this morning was their last spoken exchange?

Augusta tugged her back. "Stay calm. The paramedics know what they're doing."

The seizure ended, and the two paramedics rushed with the gurney toward the waiting ambulance. Savannah stood out of the way and touched his arm as they passed. "Is he going to be okay? I'm his wife. Can I ride to the hospital with him?"

The paramedic in front, a blonde woman in her twenties, gave Savannah a sharp glance before giving a reluctant nod. "You'll have to stay out of our way."

"I will." Savannah followed them to the ambulance and climbed into the back behind Hez and the paramedics. She tucked herself into a corner by the door where she could see his face. They secured him, and the driver headed toward the hospital with sirens blaring. The strident sound added to the nightmarish fog surrounding her. "He—he has a hematoma. Could it be bleeding again?"

Before the paramedics could respond, Hez stiffened and started grunting.

"He's seizing again," the female paramedic announced. Another crew member nodded and helped her keep Hez secure.

Savannah wanted to cover her eyes and not watch him twitch and groan again, but if watching and praying for him while he went through it was the only way she could be with him, she'd do it. It seemed to go on forever, and by the time it was over, her jaw hurt from clenching. They reached the hospital, and she hopped down and went to stand out of the way while they got him out of the ambulance and into the ER.

"Wait here," the nurse told her. "We're taking him straight in for a CT scan. I'll come get you when he's in a room."

Savannah nodded and found a seat by the window. The receptionist handed her a form to fill out his medical history. Her eyes blurred as she answered the questions, and when she was finished, she couldn't remember exactly what she put in the boxes. Hopefully it was accurate.

The time ticked by painfully slowly, and an hour after they took him back, the nurse finally came out. Savannah leaped to her feet to go with her, but she shook her head. "He's in surgery, Mrs. Webster."

Savannah's stomach bottomed out. "Surgery?"

"He's undergoing an emergency craniotomy to relieve the pressure on the brain. The doctor will speak to you when it's over."

"What's happened?"

"The doctor will explain it all."

"He's going to be okay, isn't he?"

The nurse hesitated. "Dr. Moore is doing everything he can, and he's an excellent surgeon so your husband is in good hands."

Savannah recognized the woman's cautious tone, and her vision blurred. Hez might die. Had he been shot? What had caused the seizures? The lack of information added to her fear. She got a cup of coffee from the coffee station, but it was so burnt that it was nearly undrinkable. She forced it down anyway to have something in her hands.

All she could do was pray and hope.

CHAPTER 19

SAVANNAH GLANCED AT HER WATCH FOR THE THIRD TIME IN fifteen minutes. It had been over four hours, but it felt like four days. The sky outside was dark now, and the soft sounds of janitors cleaning the area filtered through her head. Jess and Simon had brought Savannah's purse and stayed a few minutes, but they'd left as Simon became more worried and agitated. Jess had texted her twice since, but Savannah had no updates.

All she had was growing fear after she looked up online what a craniotomy entailed. Hez was back there right now having a piece of bone removed from his skull. She still didn't know what had happened even though she'd sent a panicked text to Nora.

A man in his fifties wearing scrubs stepped into the room. "Mrs. Webster?"

She shot to her feet and rushed to him. "I'm Mrs. Webster," she said by instinct. "How is he?"

"Holding his own. He was struck in exactly the wrong place, at the site of an already existing hematoma. It caused more bleeding in his brain, and we had to drain it. He's stable in recovery, and we'll watch him overnight to make sure the bleeding doesn't start again."

"What about the seizures?"

"He had another one just before the surgery, but so far there's been no recurrence."

She closed her eyes and exhaled. "Thank God. And thank you, Dr. Moore. Can I see him?"

His smile was warm but tired. "Yes, once he's in the ICU. That won't be for another hour or two. A nurse will let you know. There's time for you to grab some dinner from the cafeteria. We have your phone number and will call you."

The last thing she wanted was to eat, but she nodded and thanked him again before she returned to her seat. More waiting. It was going to be a long night. Her eyes burned, and her heart ached at the memory of the distance between them when they last spoke. And most of it stemmed from her fear of trusting what he'd told her. What was wrong with her? She didn't want to carry that fear all her life, but she didn't know how to let go of it. She buried her face into her hands and sighed.

"There you are."

She looked up at the sound of Nora's voice. Tears stung her eyes at the sympathy on her friend's face, and she stumbled to her feet to fall into Nora's embrace. "I'm so glad you're here."

"Have you been alone this whole time?"

Savannah shook her head. "Jess and Simon were here for a few minutes."

Nora released her and held up a blue thermos. "I brought you some herbal tea. Caffeine is the last thing you need when you're already stressed. Have you eaten?"

Savannah shook her head. "I wasn't hungry."

Nora settled beside her. "I'll brave the cafeteria with you. Maybe there's something edible. Even yogurt would help. How are you doing? I've been praying for you and Hez both."

"We need those prayers. I'm scared of so many things right now. Scared he'll die, scared he'll have brain damage, and scared I'm going to let my mom's situation poison my relationship with him."

Nora poured a mug of tea for her and pressed it into Savannah's hands. "Here, drink this and we'll talk."

Savannah took a sip. The aroma of lavender reached her nose before the honey in it hit her tongue. She sighed. "It's wonderful." She savored the sweetness of another sip. "Are there any suspects?"

"No."

Savannah frowned at the short answer and the way Nora didn't meet her gaze. Even the calming tea couldn't stop the spike in her adrenaline. Savannah studied her friend's downcast face. "Do you think your family might be involved? Is that why you're acting so strange?"

Nora set the thermos on the floor by her feet. "With the Willard family, you never know. I have a picture from a family reunion a few years ago on my fireplace mantel. Everyone is gathered under an enormous oak tree. Some of them are in the light, but a lot are in the shadows and their faces can't be seen. I'm not even sure who some of them are, both in the picture and in their morals as well."

Was that a tacit admission Nora thought one of them did this? "My family is a mess too."

Nora's expression hardened, and she took Savannah's hand. "I love them, Savannah, but if I find out one of them did this, I will tell Augusta immediately. It might hurt, but it's the right thing to do. I won't let them get away with hurting you or your family. I pray for them all the time, and I know they're in God's hands. I derive a lot of peace from that."

Savannah clung to her friend's hand. She'd told Hez that Nora wouldn't betray her, but the confirmation she was right felt as sweet as the honey in her tea. "I've been sitting here praying for Hez. And while I might not have full peace, at least I have certainty."

"Certainty about what?"

She lifted her chin. "I'm never letting Hez go, no matter what. I'm not going to let my doubts and fears run my life. My time with Hez is precious. Our days are numbered, and I want to spend mine with him."

A floorboard squeaked in the hall outside Jess's bedroom.

She jolted fully awake. She had been dozing fitfully, haunted by dreams while asleep and memories while awake.

She reached over to her nightstand and slid open the drawer. Her fingers closed on the butt of her SIG Sauer P365.

The bedroom door opened slowly.

"Mom?"

She let go of the gun and quickly shut the drawer. "What is it, Simon?"

He appeared in the doorway, his small shape dimly lit by the winter moonlight. He hugged his thin chest through the oversized TGU T-shirt he wore to bed. "I can't sleep."

She sighed. "Neither can I."

He shifted his weight from foot to foot. "Am I too old to sleep in your bed?"

Her heart warmed. "No, of course not." She patted the space next to her in the queen-sized bed. "Hop in."

He got in, burrowed under the down comforter, and snuggled up to her. His feet were little lumps of ice, but she didn't mind. He put his head on her shoulder. "Are the men who hurt Uncle Hez going to come after us?"

That was one of the questions that had kept her awake, but she hid her fears. "No, we're safe."

He moved back a little so he could look at her. "How do you know, Mom? They kidnapped me when you were in jail, and then they tried to kill me and Uncle Hez and Aunt Savannah out on the water."

She squeezed him tighter at the memory. "I know, honey, but one of the men from the boat is dead and the other is in jail. And they only went after you because you went after them first. You ran away and tried to catch the bad guys on your own. Never do that again, okay?"

He was silent for a long moment. Then he nodded. "Okay."

"We'll leave bad-guy catching to trained professional adults, like police, right?"

"And Uncle Hez. He does really cool stuff at the Justice Chamber. I want to be like him when I grow up." He paused and looked up at her again. "Will he be okay?"

She decided to play it straight with him. "I don't know. The very best doctors are treating him right now, but we won't know anything until tomorrow. We should try to get some sleep tonight, and maybe we can visit in the morning if the doctors say it's all right."

"Okay." He rolled over and curled up with his back touching her. That was how he always slept when night terrors drove him into bed with her, ever since he was a toddler. Five minutes later, he was snoring quietly.

Jess lay awake, staring at her shadowy ceiling. Simon's words echoed in her head. He wanted to be like Uncle Hez and fight bad guys. Bad guys like her.

She was doing the right thing, wasn't she? Her mother deserved the justice she never received in life. So did Mimi Willard and all the others victimized by the Legares over the decades. TGU was the monument to that injustice, and Pierre Legare was the parasitic paragon of the Legare bloodline. It would be entirely fair to destroy them—and irresponsible not to. Otherwise, they'd just keep hurting people forever.

The well-rehearsed arguments rolled through her mind, but she couldn't shake the feeling that they wouldn't persuade the little boy sleeping beside her. She imagined the skepticism in those intelligent blue eyes. He wouldn't see a noble Fury meting out justice. He'd just see someone who was helping the men who attacked the uncle he idolized.

Simon's eyes weren't the only ones needling her conscience. She'd felt another set of eyes watching her, especially since she came back to TGU. That gaze was so real that she sometimes instinctively glanced over her shoulder. But she knew the eyes weren't anywhere nearby.

They were in a little church in northern Italy. She went on an art tour of the area in college, and she saw dozens of churches. They all had crucifixes, of course. On some, Jesus looked up to heaven with a beatific expression on his face. On others, he hung his head and seemed almost unconscious. But on one medieval crucifix he stared straight at her with enormous brown eyes, which seemed to follow her as she walked around the church. His gaze unnerved Jess, and she left the church after only a few minutes. But those eyes never stopped following her.

She closed her eyes and tried to force herself to stop picturing hypothetical debates with shrewd boys and wooden Messiahs. She focused on relaxing her muscles one by one. It would be out of her hands soon. The moment Savannah signed the loan documents, the final countdown would begin.

And none of them would be able to do anything to stop it.

CHAPTER 20

IN THE ICU SAVANNAH BLOCKED OUT THE WHOOSH OF THE compression devices on Hez's legs and prayed for him as she clung to his hand. He looked like he'd been in a car accident. Half of his head had been shaved, and a white gauze bandage covered the incision. It was nearly dawn, and she hadn't slept a wink, but her tired lids fluttered as she watched the rhythmic up and down of his chest.

She must have dozed off for a few seconds, and she bolted upright with her heart pounding. She blinked the blur out of her vision and focused on his face again. His glassy eyes were open and wonderfully blue, not the black of the dilated pupils he'd had before. "Hez, you're awake." She scooted closer to the bed. "How do you feel?"

He licked peeling lips. "Like I was hit by a truck. Was I hit by a truck?"

"You had a brain bleed, and the doctor had to drain it."

He gave her a lopsided smile. "Seeing your beautiful face makes me forget all about the way my head is pounding."

She touched her hair, disheveled after spending the night slouching in a hospital chair. "I think you're delusional. I haven't so much as run a comb through my hair, and I'm sure my eyes are swollen from crying."

His fingers tightened on her hand. "I'm sorry I scared you. Did an accident cause the brain bleed?" His lids fluttered as if he was having difficulty keeping them open.

The doctor had warned her that he might not remember what had happened. "Not exactly." Hez didn't need to know more than that. She was sure Nora would update her if the news changed, and right now, he needed to rest without worrying about what was happening at the Justice Chamber.

The doctor swooped in, accompanied by a nurse. The doctor removed the stethoscope slung around his neck. "Someone's awake in here. Let's see how you're doing." He gestured for Savannah to move out of the way, and she retreated to a corner of the room and watched Dr. Moore check Hez's pulse and then his pupils before taking him through a battery of cognitive tests. Hez remembered his name, could identify how many fingers the doctor held up, and was able to answer simple math questions.

Dr. Moore tested the muscle strength in his arms and legs and seemed satisfied. "What do you remember, Mr. Webster?"

Hez's forehead wrinkled, and he glanced at Savannah. "I was at your office, right? I—I can't remember exactly why." The confusion in his voice held a trace of panic as well.

"Perfectly normal. Those memories may or may not come back. If your condition stays stable, we'll move you to a room on the neurological ward later today, so try to get some rest. Your recovery is really remarkable."

Savannah followed the doctor out of the room. "So no brain damage?"

"He seems very coherent and present. It's possible he might still suffer some side effects. We'll monitor his blood pressure closely, and we'll be on the lookout for blood clots, seizures, or infection. Muscle weakness too. But let's not borrow trouble. Right now he looks good."

She thanked him and went back into Hez's room. His eyes were closed, but he opened them at the squeak of her chair on the floor as she settled next to him. He blinked several times, and she could see him mentally processing what he knew and didn't know.

She took his hand again. "I only went to talk to the doctor because I thought you might have brain damage. Your first words were that I looked beautiful, and we both know I look awful. But he reassured me and said you're in great shape considering what you went through yesterday."

"You always look beautiful." Hez reached out an unsteady hand and snagged a strand of her hair to run through his fingers. "I love you."

Her eyes burned, and she swallowed past the lump in her throat. "I thought I lost you," she whispered. "That kind of fear has a way of showing you the truly important things. I'm not going to let my fear control me any longer, Hez. When you're recovered, I want us to get married. Like right away. As soon as you can totter down the aisle and say your vows."

His eyes sparkled, and his grip on her hand tightened. "Like right now? I can manage that much." He tried to sit up and winced.

She nudged him back against the stack of pillows that elevated his head to help with swelling. "Not quite yet."

"I might need to lean on you a bit, but we could get it done."

He patted his hips. "I've been carrying a ring around in my pocket for days, but I seem to have misplaced my pants."

A choked chuckle escaped her throat, and she couldn't decide if the moisture blurring her vision was from joy or the release of terror. Maybe both. "I saw you fiddling with something in your pocket several times recently. It was the ring?" And the first time she'd noticed it was just before she'd found the empty wine bottle in the trash. If not for her suspicions, she'd likely have that ring on her finger right now.

His smile faltered and he nodded. She knew he was remembering that aborted proposal as well, and she could have kicked herself. Right after taking down Beckett, things had seemed so straightforward and perfect. They'd plan a quick wedding and resume their life together, but things hadn't worked out that way, and it was all her fault.

She realized Hez had spoken and she hadn't heard a word. "I'm sorry?"

"The ring. What happened to it?" His brows furrowed as he tried to focus. "Where did it go? Can you search for it?"

"That can be arranged. The nurse probably has your personal belongings in a locker somewhere. I'll see what I can find." She stood and leaned over to kiss him. "But not quite yet."

Hez lay back in bed and let his mind drift. Not that he had much choice. Between the pain meds and the aftereffects of his injury and surgery, he couldn't focus on anything. He also had virtually no energy. If his bed hadn't been set in a raised position, he doubted he'd be able to sit up for more than a few seconds without tiring. When they moved him into a private room, the neurologist told him to rest and get plenty of sleep if he could. Hez had no trouble following the doctor's orders.

While he was awake, his thoughts kept floating back to Savannah. She'd assured him that she'd found the ring and that it was now on the counter of his condo next to his wallet. When would he give it to her, and how? Maybe a dinner cruise on Bon Secour Bay, with the proposal timed to happen as the sun set, turning the water into a sheet of gold. Or maybe he would take her back to the scene of their first date, Schwarzburg Stadium. Will Dixon played quarterback for the TGU Gators, so he might be able to get them into the Schwarz on a weekday. Or would it be better to do it during a game with the proposal up on the scoreboard? But that would mean waiting until the next football season, which was seven months away. Still, that would be fun. He closed his eyes and pictured the scene.

A door squeak woke him. He opened his eyes to see Ed, Toni, and Dominga in the doorway. Dominga carried an enormous card that said *A BIG Get Well from All of Us*, and Toni held a bag with the Petit Charms logo. Hez's stomach rumbled as the familiar scent of fresh beignets reached him. The women both looked uninjured, but Ed had two black eyes and a healing cut on his forehead.

"Sorry to wake you, Professor Webster." Ed started to close the door. "We can come back later."

"No, no." Hez gestured them in with a lazy sweep of his hand. "I could use some visitors. And some beignets. The food here is terrible, even for a hospital."

"We also brought you a card." Dominga walked in and handed it to him. "I think your entire legal writing class signed it, and a bunch of other people too."

Hez opened the card. The inside was completely covered with hundreds of handwritten messages. He didn't even recognize all the names. His eyes blurred and he swiped at them. The pain meds must be making him emotional. He cleared his throat. "Thanks. So how are things going?"

"Okay." Ed's eyes widened as his gaze went to the side of Hez's head. "Uh, how do you feel?"

Hez had a similar reaction when he saw himself in the bathroom mirror. The left half of his head was bald, bruised, and had a seam. It looked like an enormous well-used softball. "Better than you look, Ed."

Ed grinned. "I'm sure the other guys don't look great either. Two of them weren't moving too well when they ran away."

"Ran away." Hez processed the information. "So they all escaped?"

Ed nodded. "I'm afraid so. They got all our phones and took off before the cops arrived. And they all wore ski masks, so the security cameras didn't get anything useful."

Their phones. Hez knew that should mean something. Maybe it would come to him. "That's too bad, but I'm glad you three are all right. Toni, I have a dim memory of something happening to your car. Is that right?"

"It is." She handed him the bag of beignets. "Someone smashed in the window and took my phone. Probably the same guys who attacked you."

He took a bite of beignet and chewed slowly. "Mmm, thanks. Is your insurance covering it?"

She rolled her eyes. "They should, but they're giving me a hard time. Ms. Legare is letting me borrow her car in the meantime. She's been a huge help."

Hez didn't need to be at the top of his mental game to guess why. "Are you working on something involving the Pierre Legare Trust?"

"Yep. The trust, Ellison Abernathy's estate, and Beckett Harrison's estate own a vacant lot behind a gas station outside Nova Cambridge, and they've been leasing it to the university for fifty thousand dollars per year. Since Abernathy signed the lease for TGU and was also a partial owner of the lot, he had an obvious conflict of interest. I think we can get the lease voided and maybe even recoup some of the past payments."

So Pierre's trust would take another hit. No wonder Jess was being a huge help. Hez nodded, which was a mistake. Despite the meds, a twinge of pain ran across his skull from left to right, and he carefully leaned his head back on the pillow. "Could you write up a memo?"

"I already am. Ms. Legare asked for one yesterday." Toni bit her lip. "That's okay, isn't it?"

Of course Jess already asked for a memo. "Sure. The university is our client, so it's fine to do stuff for the officers. Just run it past me first—if I'm not in the hospital, that is. I'll give her a call—" And then he finally connected the dots. "Our phones. Did they only take our phones? Why?"

"I think your hunch was right, Professor," Toni said. "The smugglers must have figured out that the tip came through the Justice Chamber, so they stole our phones to search our call and text histories."

Hez didn't remember having that hunch or telling Toni

about it. Should that worry him? "Do we know if they found anything?" He turned to Ed. "Have you heard from our source inside the smuggling operation?"

Ed's expression turned grim. "I have. He's okay for now, but he's scared. Fortunately, he used a burner phone to contact me, but he thinks the smugglers will catch him sooner or later. They've put out the word that they'll kill the traitor and his whole family. He begged us to catch them first. He sounded pretty desperate."

"I'm sure he is." Hez closed his eyes and suddenly felt very tired. He forced them open again. "I'll need to think about what to do." Unfortunately, thinking wasn't his strong suit right now.

CHAPTER 21

BOO RADLEY GAVE CODY AND MARLEY A DISDAINFUL GLANCE before lumbering over to slide his nine-foot body into the pond. The tupelo trees and moss-covered oaks lining the water shook their leaves in the stiff breeze. "Stay." Savannah tugged on Cody's leash when he lunged. "That gator would swallow you in one bite." Hez's dog believed he was armor-coated and invincible, so walking him was always . . . interesting.

Dominga had joined her to walk the dogs, and Marley, always a perfect gentleman, trotted leisurely at her heels. "Have you talked to Professor Webster—I mean, the other Professor Webster—this afternoon?" she asked. "Ed, Toni, and I were there yesterday. He looks pretty terrible."

Savannah guided Cody toward the statue of TGU founder Joseph Willard. "Everything was turning black and blue this morning when I was there. He's going to look a little like Frankenstein's monster for a while until his hair grows back to cover that scar, but if that's the only effect he has from brain surgery, I'll take it."

"I'm not even sore today, but it would have been much worse if he hadn't shown up." Dominga held up her phone. "I finally got a new phone too."

Cody's short legs stiffened, and he growled ferociously at the statue. Savannah couldn't budge him an inch. "It's a statue, Cody, you weirdo." She picked him up and carried him past the offending object before putting him in the grass. "Hez will be laid up awhile, and I'm not going to stand by and watch anyone else get attacked. Would you help me, Dominga?"

Her student had always been one of her favorites, and she had a quick brain and great insight. Plus, Jess was working with Toni to keep the Justice Chamber's investigations going on the financial front while Hez was out of commission. It made perfect sense for Savannah to do the same on the smuggling front.

Dominga's dark eyes lit, and she gave an enthusiastic nod. "I'd love to!"

"We've tried targeting the source of the artifacts in Mexico, and we've studied the provenance letters from TGU. Neither avenue has gotten us very far. What if we try catching them when they sell the artifacts?"

"I think you're on to something. During my research I found some of the websites where the smugglers are offering the artifacts for sale. Their scam is good—very good. They have great pictures of the artifacts for sale as well as PDFs of what appear to be legitimate provenance documents. The descriptions say they represent a private seller and invite offers. From what we could tell, most of the artifacts are bought by legitimate dealers and galleries. They resell them in a more public forum."

Cody started to eat a decaying piece of hamburger a student had tossed away, and Savannah quickly yanked him back as she tried to temper her excitement at the idea that sprang to life at the details Dominga shared about the sales. "Maybe we could impersonate a dealer or gallery owner and offer a very high bid for an artifact! We could catch them when they deliver the item."

Dominga's expression gave nothing away as she thought about it for a moment. "We'll need to set up a fake company. And it has to look legit to fool these guys. They aren't dummies. It would be great if we could get someone good enough to put software on the fake company's website that lets us collect data about anyone who checks us out."

Savannah's excitement spiraled into dismay when Cody gagged, swallowed, and licked his lips. She envisioned a night spent cleaning up dog vomit. And worse. She turned back to Dominga. "I think Hez knows a guy who might be able to help. I'll give him a call."

Dominga glanced at her phone. "I have class in five minutes. Think you can handle both dogs by yourself?"

"Marley is never a problem. It's Hez's demon dog that's a challenge, but I'll be fine. I'll let you know what I find out." She reached the bench overlooking the pond and settled onto it holding both leashes. Marley lay down with his head on his paws, watching the ducks gliding on the water. Cody gave an indignant sniff and circled her ankles several times, wrapping the leash around them.

"Cody, you're a menace." Savannah extricated herself and pulled out her phone to place a call to Hez's hospital room. She'd ordered a phone for pickup from his carrier, which would be easier for him when he got it. Getting to the hospital phone required him to sit up and reach.

"Hello?" His deep voice sounded a little groggy.

"Were you napping?"

"Savannah." His voice gentled. "I was just thinking about you."

"Sure you were. With your eyes closed, right?" she teased. From the tender note in his voice, she didn't doubt what he told her. Her thoughts continually went to that velvet box she'd found in the pocket of his pants and had taken to his condo. She'd wanted to peek at it, but of course she didn't. Her heart still hurt at how her suspicions had kept him from proposing that night.

He yawned on the other end of the line. "I got off the pain pills right away and am on Tylenol. I don't want to run the risk of getting hooked on them. My head is pounding, but hearing your voice makes me feel better. What are you doing?"

"I'm walking your crazy dog." She told him about Cody's behavior.

"He's fun all right."

"I don't know if that's the proper adjective for him." She chuckled. "Dominga and I have a plan, but I need a little help. What's the name of that computer genius friend of yours—the one who helped you defend Jess?"

"Why?" The caution in his voice came through loud and clear.

If it were possible to keep the plan to herself, she would—if only to keep his blood pressure in check—but she had no choice. "I have a plan, and I think it might work." She proceeded to tell him what she and Dominga had discussed.

"Savannah, I don't want you in danger! Look what happened to me."

"And I'm not going to stand by and let it happen again. I can't lose you, Hez. I just can't. There's very little danger to this. It will take some time anyway, and I'll confer with you every step of the way."

A long silence ensued before he gave a heavy sigh. "Fine. Got a pen?"

She dug a pen and notepad out of her purse. "I'm ready." She jotted down the name Bruno Rubinelli as well as the email and phone number he gave her. "Sounds like a mob enforcer."

Hez chuckled. "Bruno is more dangerous than any enforcer, so tread carefully. If you make him mad, you'll find your Social Security number up on a billboard in Times Square or somewhere else equally public."

She dropped her pad and pen back into her purse. "I'd better get out of here. Cody is staring at Boo Radley like he's daring him to come closer. I have to referee." She ended the call in time to pick up Cody and run with him in her arms and Marley on her heels before the gator took up the dog's challenge.

Hez wanted to look as professional as possible for his meeting with Hope, and he couldn't do that wearing a hospital gown and a five-day beard. He didn't bother trying to make his hair presentable—it would be months before that was possible. His cousin Blake had suggested that he shave the other side of his head and wear a Mohawk for the rest of the semester.

In addition to unhelpful hairstyle advice, Blake had also provided clothing from Hez's condo and some toiletries, so

Hez looked and felt basically presentable. He still tired quickly and his head throbbed if he moved suddenly, but he felt almost normal. Most important, his brain fog seemed to be lifting. He needed to be as sharp as possible by the time Hope walked through his door.

Hope wasn't just an old friend visiting him in the hospital. She was the prosecutor he had persuaded to get the warrant that led to that embarrassing roadblock a week ago. Coming up empty in a significant operation like that must have been humiliating for her, and it would make perfect sense for her to blame him. He would if he were in her place. So how did he convince her to give him a second chance? Because if he couldn't do that, the Justice Chamber investigation wouldn't get very far.

A crisp rap on his door announced Hope's arrival. "Come in," he called.

She opened the door and entered. She wore a conservative navy suit, and her hair was pulled back. "Good to see you, Hez. How are you feeling?"

"As good as can be expected under the circumstances. Better actually." He glanced over her attire. "Please tell me you just came from the initial appearance for the guys who put me in the hospital."

She shook her head. "I wish." She perched on the chair beside his bed. "I did just come from court though, and the hearing would have interested you. It was a scheduling conference for Deke Willard's murder case."

Hez arched an eyebrow. "Murder? Of Beckett Harrison?"

She nodded. "We got the indictment last week, thanks to a jailhouse snitch, who is now in protective custody, of course.

He wore a wire and got Deke to confess to calling the hit on Harrison and making it look like a suicide. The guy couldn't help bragging."

"They never can." Hez held out his fist. "Congratulations!"

She smiled and bumped her fist against his. "Thanks. Deke's lawyer is already sniffing around for a plea bargain."

"So your boss will get his murder conviction after all—though probably not the way he wanted it."

She sighed. "A win is a win, but I'm sure he would have preferred something splashier."

Hez kept his tone casual. "Maybe we can give it to him."

Her brows went up. "Oh? How can we do that?"

"By bringing down that smuggling ring. We've got a couple of promising new angles, but we'll need your help."

She groaned. "That's what you said last time. It didn't turn out well."

"I know, but this time will be different. Really." That sounded pathetic, so he hurried on. "We're approaching the smuggling pipeline from a couple of different angles." He told her about Savannah's idea and Ed's renewed contact with his source. "I don't think we'll need another roadblock or anything like that."

She drummed her fingers on the chair's padded vinyl armrest. "Are you going to need another warrant?"

"Um, maybe."

She took a deep breath and blew it out slowly. "I won't be able to get one based on the same anonymous source who was wrong last time."

"I'm not sure he was wrong. We know there's a mole in the PHPD. What if that's not the only one?"

She gave a quick nod, like she'd already considered the

possibility. "Could be, but it won't help me get a warrant. I'll need enough supporting evidence to show probable cause, and the bar will be higher this time because of what happened last week."

"I understand. What will you need?"

"I probably have to talk to the source myself."

Hez chewed his lower lip. He'd been afraid she would say that. Was Ed's source desperate enough to reveal himself? Or would he cut off all contact and go into hiding? And even if he was willing to talk to Hope, would he even survive long enough to make a statement?

"I'll see what we can do."

CHAPTER 22

SAVANNAH STEADIED HEZ AS HE WALKED SLOWLY TO THE bench by the small pond in the hospital exercise area. She inhaled the spicy scent of the white rhododendrons wafting from along the concrete path. "Their flowers are gorgeous."

He sank onto the bench with a sigh of relief. "I'd rather look at you than the flowers."

Even injured, he took time to make her feel loved and desirable. She let him tug her down beside him. "Are you exhausted?"

"The doctor says my strength will come back the more I walk. This was a good idea to come down here even if I feel like I just ran a marathon." He squeezed her fingers. "Any update from Bruno?"

She relished his strong grip. A couple of days ago he barely had the strength to hold her hand. "The fake website and company are all set up, and we're primed to make an offer when a smuggled artifact is posted. Bruno was fast. Now it's in Hope's court."

"She stopped by yesterday. They've concluded Beckett didn't commit suicide."

She shuddered at the mental images that flooded her head. "He was murdered?"

He winced before fumbling in his pocket for sunglasses and slipping them on. "That sun is brutal. Hope said they've got a prison snitch who will testify Deke Willard called the hit."

She tensed at the unsettling news. "More confirmation there are bigger fish to catch."

"Once we get what Hope needs for another warrant, we can spring a trap that hits the smugglers from multiple sides at once. Your idea was a good one." He glanced down at his phone. "What time are Jess and Simon coming?"

"Any minute. She's bringing you a po'boy for lunch."

"Did I ever tell you how much I like your sister?"

She nudged him with her elbow. "That's your stomach talking."

"Uncle Hez!"

Savannah turned at the sound of Simon's excited voice. Carrying a paper bag from Little New Orleans, her nephew raced down the walk ahead of his mother. Jess looked like a model in her heels and blue dress, but the fake smile on her face told Savannah she'd rather be anywhere but here.

Simon skidded to a stop in front of Hez, who reached up to pull him down onto his knee. "Thanks for coming to see me, Simon. Have you been staying out of trouble?"

Simon nodded. "I've been helping Mom and Toni. We haven't found any clues yet, but we're working on it. When Mom brought me in before, you were slurring your words, but you sound like yourself today." His gaze settled on Hez's incision. "Are you always going to have the scar?"

Hez exchanged an amused smile with Savannah. "My hair will grow back and cover it."

"That's too bad." Simon eased off Hez's knee and squeezed between him and Savannah, then handed Hez the bag of food. "There's one for me and Aunt Savannah too. Mom didn't want one. She likes the one with onions and she didn't want her breath to stink before her meeting."

"Simon, do you need to repeat everything?" Jess muttered on her way to the bench on the other side of the walk.

Savannah hid a smile. "Thank you both. Your uncle Hez is getting tired of hospital food, but he gets out tomorrow."

Simon was already unwrapping his po'boy and didn't answer. Savannah's mouth watered at the scent of blackened shrimp in the sandwich Hez handed her, and she realized she hadn't eaten yet today. Lunch would be a good excuse to avoid telling Jess about her plan. Her sister was even more protective than Hez and would demand that Savannah stay out of the detective business. Silence settled around them as they dug into their food.

Jess sat on the bench on the other side of the path and set her bag down beside her feet. She watched the ducks dive for food before clearing her throat. "I hate to bring up business, but it's important. Did you sign that loan paperwork yet, Savannah?"

Savannah took her time with her last bite of food. The strident tone of her sister's voice was unmistakable. Savannah took a sip of her sweet tea and balled up her sandwich wrapper. "Hez hasn't had a chance to look over the papers."

Jess's lips pressed together and she shot a pointed glance at Hez. "Is that really necessary? It's all very straightforward."

He nodded. "It would be foolish for Savannah to sign them without a lawyer checking out the fine print to make sure the financiers' attorneys haven't hidden any questionable clauses."

Jess reached into the bag at her feet. "You could just skim them to make sure. I brought them along for you to see." She withdrew a sheaf of papers and rose to hand them to Hez.

He didn't take them. "It'll have to wait a few days, Jess. I still have a splitting headache, and my eyes want to jump around when I try to read."

"Don't be a wimp! Just get it done. The financiers are getting frustrated with the delay."

Don't be a wimp? Her sister was way out of line. Savannah saw the indecision on Hez's face and leaped up to step between him and her sister. "Jess, he told you it's going to have to wait until he's physically capable of doing it."

Jess's hand containing the papers dropped back to her side. "But they may pull out of the deal! I've worked hard on this, Savannah, and you're about to waste all my efforts. Worse, it leaves TGU in a terrible position. It would take him fifteen minutes or less to skim these."

"He needs to do more than a light read. Jess, he just had brain surgery. I'm not going to put up with you pushing him. Put those away for now. He has a copy, and he'll look it over when he's able." Her counselor would be proud of her for standing up to her sister. Savannah glanced at Hez and saw his color had gone paler. "Now I'd better get him inside to rest. Thanks for coming to see him."

She saw the defeat in Jess's eyes as she guided Hez back toward the hospital. It was about time her sister learned who was in charge here.

The gorgeous day matched Savannah's excitement at finally taking Hez home from the hospital in Mobile. She was so thankful to have him beside her in the car and on the mend. She'd been happy to grant his request to take the scenic route to Pelican Harbor down Highway 98. They both loved the drive through Fairhope and Point Clear. She always slowed to take in the view of a house she'd loved since childhood, but she was so focused on Hez's condition she missed seeing it today.

She turned onto the bridge over the inlet between Mobile Bay and Weeks Bay and inhaled the salty air pouring in their open windows. Hez had his eyes closed and his face turned to the sunshine. "Don't think you're going to go home to plunge right into work, mister. The doctor said you have to take it easy."

He opened his eyes and turned toward her. "I'll do my best. I could certainly get used to having a personal chauffeur for the next three months, especially one as easy on the eyes as you."

"Just be grateful it was a few seizures and not an epilepsy diagnosis. They would have made you suffer through my driving you around for six months." The neurologist had told him he couldn't drive for at least ninety days because he'd had seizures, and Savannah knew the loss of independence must bother him. "And thanks for the compliment, but you'll probably have to get used to Uber. I have a day job, remember? Besides, you'll be able to relax in that cozy condo most days."

"True. The law school is letting me teach my classes online for the rest of the semester, so I'll have a chance to answer the tsunami of emails in my inbox."

"One of those is from me. I emailed you the loan papers Jess wants me to sign. Don't let her push you into reading them before you're ready, though."

"I'm sure they're fine, but I'll take a look." He yawned. "Maybe not today, though."

"The first day home from the hospital is exhausting, so I'd suggest taking a nap when I get you to the condo."

"I'm sure Cody will be ready to have one with me. He's there, isn't he?"

"I asked Jess to drop him off this morning so he'd be waiting for you. He's been so mopey he didn't even want to challenge Boo Radley to a fight last night on our walk."

"I can't wait to see him." He glanced back out his open window and gestured toward a park ahead near the Fairhope Tea Plantation. "It's so gorgeous out. Do you mind stopping to take in some fresh air? I'm tired of being cooped up."

She nodded and pulled into a small parking lot. "I love this spot." Oak trees towered over masses of rhododendrons and azaleas, and as usual, the place was deserted. The beautiful spot was one of those mostly unknown treasures in the area. "The last time we were here was about a month before Ella died."

She smiled as the memories flooded back, each one tender and wonderful. Ella loved the swings here, and they'd had the park all to themselves. Hez had carved their three names in a tree, and they'd eaten s'mores until they'd all had stomachaches. They'd taken Ella home covered in mud, and she'd fallen asleep in the bathtub.

His eyes glistened with moisture. "I pushed her on the swing until my arms about fell off. I like to remember that day. I think it was the last perfect day in my memory."

She reached across to take his hand. "It won't be the last."

"I hope not." He released her hand and opened his door to clamber out. "Let's see if our initials are still in the tree."

When she joined him at the front of the car, he tucked her hand into the crook of his arm. "I think it's this way."

"It's there." She pointed to the big oak next to a rambling thicket of bushes. "I love the smell of the air after a rain even if it's as muddy as a swamp. It's like everything is new." She pressed her fingers tighter on his arm. "Seems appropriate, don't you think?"

"Sure does." His voice was hoarse, and he stopped when they reached the tree. She touched their initials in the bark before he started to crouch as he glanced toward a nearby blackberry bush.

She followed his gaze and saw a glint of something metal. The flash was followed by a clicking sound. A gun? "Get down!" Before he could drop to the ground, she leaped on him. Her weight pushed his face into mud, and he came up sputtering with goo dripping from his chin.

"Are you okay?" Adrenaline made her voice shake, and she kept her hand on his back as she stared at the bush. Was there one shooter or more than one? How did they get to safety? She couldn't lose him. She jerked her head slightly toward the bush. "There's someone there with a gun."

Hez pushed up against the press of her hand. "I'm fine, honey. It's not what you think."

The bush shivered, but not from the wind. A figure with dark hair stood from behind the leaves. She blinked. "Blake?"

Carrying a camera with a high-powered lens, Blake stepped from behind the bush. "Sorry to scare you." He was trying not to smile, but a grin kept peeking through. When he glanced at Hez, they both chuckled.

"What are you doing here?" She turned and checked Hez's incision. It had been spared the onslaught of mud and no blood oozed out. "What's going on?"

Hez wiped red mud from his cheeks. "I asked him to come. He's supposed to be taking pictures of me proposing. This wasn't quite how I imagined it playing out." Hez gestured for Blake to come closer.

Blake reached them and turned the camera around to bump through a series of pictures. There was a perfect shot of them walking through dappled sunlight with her hand on his arm and another of them looking toward their names in the tree bark. The next one showed Hez starting to go down on one knee while Savannah stared at the camera with sheer terror on her face. When the last picture flipped into view, it was of Hez face down in the mud with Savannah on top of him.

Laughter bubbled up in her throat. "It looks like we were about to go head-to-head in a mud fight." Her smile faded. "I did it again, huh? Ruined a proposal? You're going to get tired of trying."

"Third time's the charm?" He sank onto one knee and pulled out the velvet box while Blake took a few steps back and raised the camera. "We've had rough spots, my love—horrible, agonizing experiences—but one thing has never changed. I love you—I always have and I always will. I love the sound of your laughter and the way your mind works. I love hearing you talk to the dog first thing in the morning like he's a person. I love the little line between your eyes when you're concentrating, and I love how your eyes reflect your mood."

He reached out to curl a lock of her hair around his finger. "I love the way your hair glows red in the sunshine. I'm a better man when I'm with you, Savannah. I hope you know that. I want us to experience all of our tomorrows together."

When he opened the lid of the box, she gasped at the sight of a halo of rubies around a familiar diamond. "It's beautiful." She stared into his hopeful blue eyes, and her chest expanded with the strength of the love she felt for this man.

"Will you marry me again—this time forever? I won't fail you again, babe."

Joy overwhelmed her, and she could barely breathe, let alone speak, so she managed a nod before she could force out a trembling, "I will."

Hez plucked the ring from the box and slipped it onto her finger. It fit perfectly, and she flung herself into his arms. They toppled over together, right smack in the middle of a mud puddle.

Hez held her and laughed in her ear. "Life will always be an adventure with you, but I'm ready."

CHAPTER 23

IT FINALLY HAPPENED.

The realization hit Hez as he drifted into wakefulness. He and Savannah were actually getting married again. The ring was out of his pocket and on her finger. It was official.

He stretched and rolled over, relishing the sensation of being in his own bed for the first time in a week. Better yet, he'd slept through the night without having anyone come in and check on him—except for his dog. Cody had been overjoyed when Hez arrived home yesterday evening and had been very clingy ever since. Cody was a rescue and feared being abandoned again, so he hadn't taken Hez's weeklong absence particularly well.

Hez rolled out of bed and walked into the kitchen. Sunlight streamed in through the windows, creating warm, bright spots on the hardwood floor. He stood in one while he made coffee. He inhaled deeply, savoring the rich aroma of brewing coffee as he poured himself a bowl of granola and sliced a banana on top of it, all while his emotionally needy dog kept trying to trip him. It was wonderful to be back in his own space again.

It wouldn't be his space for much longer, though. He pictured Savannah walking out of the bedroom, lured by the scent of fresh coffee. The sunlight would bring out her first-thing-in-the-morning beauty: the gold flecks in her sleepy green eyes, the highlights in her auburn hair, her perfect zero-makeup skin. She'd slip into his arms, still warm from the bed.

Would they stay in his condo? Probably not. Savannah's cottage was just off campus, so it would be more convenient for them both. But her place wasn't much bigger than his, and hopefully they'd need room for a nursery soon. He smiled at that thought and carried his breakfast into his home office to do a little virtual house hunting.

He turned on his computer—and was greeted by a notification that he had 536 unread emails. He sighed and took a swig of coffee. Maybe he could look at houses while he took a break later in the day.

Since Hez's surgery and in-hospital recovery had gone well, his hospital discharge instructions had been mostly limited to incision care and avoiding driving or strenuous activity. However, the neurologist had warned that he might have problems with his vision and ability to focus for long periods. An oversized monitor and the large-font option on his computer solved the vision issue. The big, steaming TGU mug next to his keyboard helped with his focus.

The first mug powered him through an initial pass as he culled spam, notices of meetings that happened while he was in the hospital, perky announcements about campus recycling day, and the sort of things even his foggy brain could handle. By the time he went back to the kitchen for a refill, his inbox was down to 253 and he felt pretty productive. But his ears were ringing and his vision was blurry. It was probably time for a break, but he couldn't bring himself to stop now.

COLLEEN COBLE AND RICK ACKER

He finished his breakfast and half his second mug as he triaged the remaining emails. He flagged the ones that could wait until he was back in the office in a week or so when he could think more clearly, starred the ones he needed to deal with before then, and put exclamation points on the handful he really should get to today. Fortunately, most of those didn't require much work.

Hez drained the last of his coffee and took his dishes to the sink. Cody had been asleep under the desk, but he woke as soon as Hez moved and trailed him into the kitchen, his nails clicking on the floor. He even tried to follow Hez into the bathroom and sat outside, whimpering and scratching the door until his owner reappeared. The poor dog really was convinced that Hez could vanish without warning again if he let him out of his sight.

Despite the heavy dose of caffeine, Hez yawned as he sat in front of his computer again. He shook his head. Despite a good night's sleep and having worked for barely an hour, he felt a nap coming on. He decided to knock one last item off his to-do list. Then he could find a sunny spot on a comfy couch and browse real estate listings until he drifted off.

He opened the email from Savannah with the attached loan documents she'd asked him to look over. It had arrived in his inbox at almost the same moment he was attacked. Was that a coincidence? Or was someone trying to stop the loan from going through? He couldn't be sure, but that just made him more determined to read the documents before he did anything else.

Hez wasn't a corporate lawyer, but he could see why Jess was eager to close the loan. TGU currently had over two dozen loans from eleven different lenders, each with its own terms and payment schedule—and none of those looked as good as this one. The interest rate was lower than any of the other loans, there was no prepayment penalty, and TGU could make payments either monthly or annually. Not bad. Not bad at all. The numbers and letters danced a bit in his vision, and he blinked before continuing.

Hez had never heard of the lender, Hornbrook Finance, LLC, but that didn't mean much. New York was full of serious financial firms that no one outside of Wall Street knew anything about. After a little googling, Hez was satisfied that Hornbrook was a serious company. The founder, James Hornbrook, had left Goldman Sachs a decade ago to found his own firm. Jess had also worked at Goldman, which was presumably how she knew him. Hornbrook had over $3 billion under management, so he would have no trouble making the loan to TGU. Besides, he had a dog in one of his publicity pictures—a magnificent cream-colored golden retriever—which boosted Hez's view of him.

Hez could feel the tug of his overstuffed sofa in the sunlit living room, but he forced himself to read—or at least skim— the dozens of pages of boilerplate terms. Even blown up to sixteen-point font, they made his vision blur. These turgid, complex clauses had all been written by Hornbrook's lawyers, of course, so they favored the lender. Hez was pretty sure this was all standard language that Hornbrook included in all deals and that he wouldn't be willing to negotiate. Still, Hez owed it to Savannah and TGU to have at least a general idea of what these documents said.

He sat back and rubbed his eyes. Cody took the opportunity to jump onto his lap, lost his balance, and tumbled back to the floor. Hez laughed and leaned over to scratch his dog's huge, scraggly ears. Cody gave a doggy grin and panted, alerting Hez to the fact that no one had given his dog a brushing chew while he was gone.

Hez coughed and waved his hand in front of his face. "Whew! What did Savannah let you eat?" He got up and walked over to the dog closet. "Actually, don't tell me. I don't want to know."

Cody's grin widened at the sight of the bag of brushing chews. He ran over to his bowl and wagged his tail in anticipation. Hez dropped two chews in the bowl for good measure. Then it was back to work while Cody gnawed on his treats.

Hez stared at the screen for a long moment. Should he call it a day? He'd put in two hours, and his brain was starting to feel like oatmeal. His discharge instructions said he should try to go for at least one walk per day. Maybe he should take Cody for a short trip to the beach and then let that nap take him. He could give the loan documents a fresh look tomorrow.

But would tomorrow be too late? He remembered the urgency—almost fear—in Jess's face when she pressured him to look over the documents two days ago. Was there something she wasn't telling them? Were their enemies putting some secret pressure on Hornbrook that only she knew about?

He sighed and forced himself through the remaining pages. He wasn't retaining much, but there probably wasn't much worth retaining. Twenty minutes later, he reached the end. Finally.

He created a reply to Savannah's email and typed, "These look fine." He paused for a moment, then added, "Nice work by Jess."

Then he hit Send.

Savannah hurried through the bustling administration building, making a beeline for Jess's office. She rapped her knuckles
on the door, then pushed it open. "I have what you've been
waiting for."

Jess looked up from the computer, and her gaze fell to the
papers in Savannah's hand. "You signed the loan papers?"

"I did. Hez said they looked fine." She had called him as
soon as she got his email, happy for an excuse to hear his
voice. "He was impressed you got such a great interest rate and
terms." Savannah slid the papers across the desk and watched
Jess snatch them up.

"Oh, I did." Jess held up the papers in a triumphant gesture.
"This will make my upcoming trip to New York City much
less stressful. I was so worried we would lose out on this outstanding deal. Let me shoot the financiers an email to let them
know I'll upload the signed documents in a few minutes."

"You're going to New York?"

Jess didn't look up as she tapped away at her keyboard. "It
just came up." She pushed back from her computer when she
was done. "That reminds me—can you watch Simon for a few
days? I leave on Tuesday. I know that's only four days out, and
I'm sorry for the short notice."

Savannah hesitated. Her nephew would have to be kept in
the dark about her plans to trap the smugglers. Simon tended
to rush in without thought of his own safety.

Jess eyed her when she didn't reply. "I know you're busier
now that you're president, but Simon is self-sufficient. He

announced a few weeks ago that only babies get walked to the bus stop, so he goes by himself now. And I haven't even had to help him with any homework. I've been slammed here in the office, and he's even started cooking dinner for both of us. It's just warming up freezer meals, but he's great at it. He won't be a bother."

"Of course he won't. Of course he can stay. I was thinking through my week, but it will be fine. I love having him around." Savannah tucked a lock of hair behind her ear, and her ring caught the sunshine and glowed when she dropped her hand back to her side.

Jess's eyes homed in on the dazzling light. "Let me see. And I want to hear the full story now that we have a little time."

Savannah held out the ring for her sister to admire. "Isn't it gorgeous? You'll never believe how he proposed." She launched into the story of how she tackled him into the mud.

Jess's lips curved in a genuine smile. "I wish I'd seen that."

"Blake got pictures, and I'll share them with you when I get them. We're going to have a big engagement dinner for friends and family. I'll make sure it's at a good time for you."

A frown settled on Jess's face. "What family will be there?"

There weren't many Legare family members around, but Savannah knew Jess was asking about her father. "I'll invite my dad, but he may not come. I'm not his favorite person right now. There's really only you and Dad around, so it will be mostly friends. And Hez's family. Would you be my maid of honor? I'd like to announce it at the dinner. I know you haven't always been a fan of Hez's, but I think you're getting over it. And I want you to be happy for me."

Jess held her hand to her mouth, and her eyes went luminous

with moisture. She came around the end of the desk and folded Savannah into a tight hug. "I want you to be happy and safe," she murmured against Savannah's ear. She stepped back and dabbed at her eyes. "Sorry for being so emotional. Things have been so hard, and I'm thrilled to know life will be better for you. You're getting everything you've ever wanted. President of TGU, Hez back in your life, a close community of friends and people who love you."

"And a nephew I adore," Savannah added.

"That too."

"He'd be a great ring bearer." Her glance sank to the ring on her finger again. Though they hadn't talked about it yet, she knew Hez would welcome the thought of a baby. She pictured Simon and their child playing and laughing together someday. The future looked so bright that it felt like tempting fate.

CHAPTER 24

HEZ SAT BY HIMSELF AT A TABLE TUCKED INTO A CORNER at Petit Charms, watching the coffee shop's door. While he waited, he sipped milky chicory coffee and took careful bites from a piping hot apple-filled beignet from the heaping plate in front of him. Winter rain streamed down the window, and it felt good to be warm and inside, especially since Cody had insisted on an unreasonably long business walk half an hour ago.

Hez would have gotten his order to go and enjoyed it in the comfort of his apartment upstairs, but Ed had asked to talk in person, and he'd been vague about the subject. The risk of bugs went unspoken between them, so Hez suggested meeting for beignets and coffee. The odds that someone hid microphones here were slim, and the rain and restaurant noise would mask their conversation.

Ed walked into Petit Charms, collapsing a dripping umbrella as he pushed through the glass double doors. He glanced around the dining area, and Hez waved him over. The waiter came by with a coffeepot as Ed settled into his seat. Hez pointed at the plate of beignets in front of him. "Dig in. I got the apple ones."

"Awesome, thanks!" Ed took a long sip of his coffee, holding the blue mug with both hands. "And thanks for meeting with me. I know you're supposed to take it easy."

Hez smiled and pointed to the ceiling. "Nothing easier than taking a walk down one flight of stairs, and I'm always looking for an excuse to eat here. What's up?"

Ed set his mug on the red-painted tabletop. "Remember Hernando Morales?"

"Sure. He's the guy the Coast Guard caught fishing off the Gulf Coast last year and charged with drug smuggling. I haven't heard from him since we got those charges dismissed." Hez always suspected there was more to that story than Hernando admitted, but the government hadn't been able to prove it. "What about him?"

Ed cleared his throat. "He, uh, wasn't fishing."

"Oh, really? What was he doing?"

Ed took a beignet and picked at it. "Smuggling looted artifacts from Mexico."

Hez nodded slowly. "That explains why the feds were convinced he was smuggling, but they were never able to find the drugs." He paused. "Why am I just hearing about this now?"

"Because I just confirmed it a couple of weeks ago." Ed lowered his voice. "Hernando is our source inside the smuggling organization."

"Really? How did that happen?"

Ed grinned. "I called his mom. We had her number in the case file, so I gave her a ring and explained that the man who got her son out of an American jail needed help catching some criminals looting Mexico's proud heritage. I said Hernando might have gotten mixed up with the wrong crowd and might know something about what was going on. Maybe he could do the right thing and repay a debt of honor at the same time? She thanked me for the call and said she would talk to him. Two days later, he called me. He said he'd help, but he made me promise not to tell a soul—not even you. Sorry."

"But you just told me," Hez observed. "Did he change his mind?"

Ed finished his beignet and took another. "Yeah. When I told him the DA couldn't get another warrant without his name and some other corroborating information, he agreed. He didn't like it, but he's pretty desperate. These guys almost caught him after they stole my phone."

"They got his number from your call history?"

"Yeah. Fortunately, it was a burner phone. Still, the smugglers somehow managed to figure out the store where he bought it, and now they're checking out every person who bought a phone from that store."

Hez frowned. "Maybe they have a local cop on their payroll."

"Could be. Anyway, he says they'll find him soon. He's living on borrowed time—and so are his mom, wife, and baby daughter."

Hez took a sip of his coffee. "Does he know who's receiving the shipments in the U.S.?"

Ed shook his head. "This organization is very compartmentalized. Now that the feds know his name and face, he can't come to America anymore. His current job is to pick up the artifacts at illegal digs and take them to a trucking company in Mexico City. He doesn't even know the real name of his contact at the trucking company."

"When he used to come here, who did he meet with?"

Ed shrugged muscular shoulders. "He didn't know that either. His job was to pick up packages from a ship offshore and bring them to a beach in Pelican State Park and hide them in the seagrass ten feet behind a broken bench. Someone else would pick them up from there. Once he got caught by the Coast Guard, he had to switch to the Mexican part of the operation, of course."

Hez ate the last bite of his beignet, chewing slowly as he thought. "Well, we can go to Hope now, and this should be enough for her to get a warrant—but the police won't be able to execute it until another shipment comes through. They might be able to make a referral to Mexican authorities, but that's it."

Ed nodded. "That's what I figured. He says he's supposed to deliver another shipment to Mexico City tomorrow. He thinks that means it will leave the following day and cross the border the day after that."

Hez drummed his fingers on the wooden tabletop. "So we have three days to get our act together. And we have to get it right this time—we won't get a third chance."

Monday morning, Savannah sat with Hez, Ed, and Dominga at a back table in University Grounds. The noise of steam wands frothing milk and the din of student chatter would drown out their private conversation. It was ten o'clock and the coffee shop was abuzz with excited voices discussing Sunday night's basketball game. She spotted Will Dixon's dark head two tables over with a couple of the cheerleaders and the team's star center. He waved to them, and Savannah returned the greeting.

She inhaled the rich aroma of espresso before taking a sip of her peppermint mocha. "You have an update, Dominga?"

Dominga nodded and tucked a strand of long black hair behind her ear before she logged in to her laptop. "The smugglers posted another article for sale late last night. The auction ends in an hour, and it will be available for delivery in New York City in three days." She turned her computer around to show Savannah and Hez. Ed leaned in close to her side, and a blush ran up her neck.

Ed glanced at Dominga. "We thought about calling last night, but it was after midnight when I dropped her off from the game, and we thought that might be too late."

Savannah hid a smile at the realization they were dating. She set her mocha down on the table and gasped as she studied the artifact, which would have been used by Incan priests. "This silver appliqué is really rare and looks authentic. Let's make sure we win, and I'll book a flight right away." Her thoughts ran through what she could wear to impersonate the buyer.

Hez's hand came down on hers. "It's way too dangerous for you to go, Savannah. Let's call Hope and let her send an officer to impersonate the buyer. The smugglers might recognize you, and the whole plan could blow up in your face."

She frowned and shook her head in spite of his worried expression. "And that's exactly why it needs to be me. Our target is connected with TGU, and if he recognizes me, I'll recognize him and the arrest can happen instantly. Besides, a random officer couldn't impersonate a buyer realistically. I know artifacts. I'll be able to discuss types of art and time periods. But this smuggler is smart. He'll recognize a fake in ten seconds and bolt before we can spring the trap."

Hez fell silent, and his fingers played with the ring on her hand for a long moment. "You're right, but I don't have to like it. Who else do we know in the history department we can trust?"

"No one. It has to be me. I can wear a wire like you did last time."

"We were nearly killed last time."

He had a point, but she wasn't going to let anyone dissuade her. Her gaze wandered to Will again, and the sight of Simon's favorite person reminded her of her promise to her sister. "Jess asked me to watch Simon for a couple of days while she attends to some business. Could you take him?"

"I'm always happy to have our awesome nephew. We can order pizza, play video games, and he can help keep me calm while you walk into the lion's den." He grimaced. "I really wish there was someone else who could do this."

Dominga turned the laptop back around to face her and Ed, who didn't move his chair away. "How much should I bid?"

The artifact was exquisite and should command a high price. "Can you see existing bids?"

Dominga squinted. "The high bid right now is just over twenty thousand."

Savannah took another sip of her mocha. "Let's double that."

Dominga nodded and tapped at the keyboard. "Now we wait a few minutes. I wouldn't mind a beignet."

Ed jumped up. "I'll get some." He strode off to the counter and got in the pastry line.

Hez still had his hand on Savannah's, and she could feel his unease. She turned her palm up and laced her fingers with his. "I'll be fine. I'm sure the meeting place will be public, and they wouldn't dare to try anything where they'd be caught."

"I hope you're right," he muttered.

She studied the healing incision on his head. The shaved area gave him a rakish, dangerous appearance, and for the first time since his injury, her thoughts wandered to that wine bottle in his trash. She desperately wanted to believe his assertion that someone had planted it, but the best she could hope for was that he'd had a blackout. And now that the blood was drained off, maybe it would never happen again.

They sipped their coffee and ate beignets while they waited for the auction to end. At eleven o'clock Dominga's computer dinged, and she pumped her fist. "Yes! We won, and there's an email." She read out loud the directions to meet at Mad Dog & Beans at two on Thursday. "There will be a reservation in the name of Priest."

Savannah's pulse accelerated. She toyed with her bracelet, pulled out her phone, and opened her travel app. "I'll fly in on Wednesday night, and I'll go to the restaurant early so I can watch for the smuggler's arrival in case it's someone I know."

Dominga was still working on her laptop. "I've got the IP address from Bruno's tracking program." She looked up with worried dark eyes. "It's very close to us. Either right here in Nova Cambridge or at TGU."

The reality was a punch to the gut. Though it was exactly what Savannah had suspected, she'd held out a smidgeon of hope that the auctioneer wasn't someone she knew. But who? And why would they do something like this to TGU?

CHAPTER 25

HEZ TOOK A DEEP BREATH AND WALKED INTO THE BALDWIN County District Attorney's Office, an unassuming one-story beige building in Bay Minette. Hope greeted him in the reception area and took him back to her office. She looked as polished and professional as ever, but he caught the stress in her tight smile and tense shoulders. And she could probably see the same taut nerves in him.

Two days ago, he and Ed had met with her here. She'd been very interested, and the three of them called Hernando from her office for an impromptu interview. After that, she thanked them and shooed them out, saying she would have a lot going on. That was the last Hez had heard from her. He understood, of course—he'd been in her shoes plenty of times. But that didn't make the radio silence any easier to bear, especially with Savannah now on her way to New York. So in the Uber on the way home from the airport, Hez had called Hope and asked if he could buy her a cup of coffee. She'd replied that she couldn't leave her office right now, but he was welcome to stop by. And here he was.

Her office was a utilitarian box with a view of the sidewalk outside, but she had added some personal touches—shells and

COLLEEN COBLE AND RICK ACKER

a jar of sea glass from her regular beach trips, family photos, and a blown-glass vase her uncle had made. Her desk bore a brass paperweight inscribed with *Drake's Dragon Slayers* and a depiction of a heroic knight killing a dragon. It was a "morale-boosting" gift from her boss that always had to be on display, especially if reporters might be stopping by.

Hez lowered himself into one of her government-issue office chairs. "What's the word?"

"Busy," she replied without hesitation. "The word is definitely *busy*. We've been scrambling nonstop, but things are going well so far. We interviewed Hernando again and got our warrant the same day we met with you."

"Wow, that's great. I had no idea."

She gave an apologetic smile. "Sorry I didn't loop you in. He was willing to talk to us directly and time was of the essence."

Hez arched an eyebrow. "And there may be a security leak somewhere on my side of the fence."

She shrugged. "The fewer people who know, the better."

"I get it. I would've done the same thing. Are you planning another roadblock? Don't tell me if you'd rather not."

"I trust you personally. Just don't tell anyone else."

He nodded. "Of course."

"Okay." She got up, shut the door, and returned to her seat. "The plan is no roadblock this time. We managed to get a tiny GPS tracker to Hernando before he dropped off the looted artifact. He hid it in the piece, so we've been tracking the smugglers' route. We know every place they stopped, and we have an ID on every vehicle they've used. Once the artifact reaches its destination, we and our partners can wrap up the whole operation in simultaneous raids across the U.S. and Mexico."

"That's terrific! I'm sure Drake will be thrilled."

She smiled and pointed at the brass paperweight. "I polished that just in case we have press in the office in the next day or two."

He chuckled—and then stopped when he did the mental math. "Next day or two. So the raids would happen as soon as the smugglers hand the artifact to Savannah?"

Hope pressed her lips together and nodded. "That's the plan. We want to arrest her contact in the restaurant where they're meeting. And once that happens, the other raids have to happen immediately, of course."

Hez's heart rate spiked. "Wait, so you're saying she'll be in the middle of a police raid?"

"Our New York colleagues will brief her before she goes in and will do everything they can to keep her safe. They'll also give her the option to back out."

"That's unacceptable! They can arrest the smuggler on the street after they leave the restaurant."

Hope grimaced. "I don't like it either, but the New York team was adamant. They're worried about bystander casualties and the target escaping if they do it on the street. They insist that it's much safer for everyone if they do a preplanned operation in the restaurant."

"It's not safer for Savannah."

She sighed. "No, it's not. But she'll have a choice and people walking by on the street won't."

Hez knew what she'd choose, of course. She'd march straight

into the lion's den without hesitation. He offered up the first of a steady stream of silent prayers. He loved Savannah's courage—except right now.

The hustle and bustle of New York City always surprised Savannah. Though she'd been here a handful of times, she always forgot how many people it held. The streets and sidewalks teemed with a kaleidoscope of humanity, all seemingly hurrying in different directions. But it wasn't the chaos of the city that caused her heart to race as she sat in the back of the taxi and tensed as the driver navigated the insane traffic—it was knowing how much depended on her performance today. If the smuggler spotted the wire tucked into her silk blouse or any of the police watching her every move, all bets were off and she would have failed.

This could all spool out perfectly, or she could end up shot and dying on the floor. She wasn't afraid of heaven, but Ella's death had nearly destroyed Hez, and losing Savannah would finish the job.

Her thoughts ran through who might walk in that door. She hoped to recognize the smuggler, but she couldn't imagine anyone she knew doing this to TGU.

She watched the map on her phone, then leaned forward when the restaurant was still a few blocks away. "I'd like to be dropped here." If the smuggler was already there and watching, she wanted to be able to do the same. She handed over cash, then scrambled out into a cold, blustery February wind that sent icy fingers down her neck.

She zipped up her inadequate coat and hurried down Pine Street. The scents of car exhaust, grilling meat, and hot asphalt from a street repair assaulted her nose. The sounds of car horns, jackhammers, and dozens of people talking at once crowded into her ears. Her steps slowed as she turned onto Pearl and neared the restaurant. She looked around, scanning for anyone familiar.

A man, collar up against the wind, sheltered in the doorway of a storefront opposite the restaurant. She glanced at him and froze. Wasn't that Graham Warner, Nora's new romantic interest? Could he be the one meeting her? She ducked out of sight into a deli with her heart pounding. Though she hadn't seen any police officers, they had to be here somewhere.

She paused by the door and whispered into the hidden wire, "I saw someone I recognized—Graham Warner, the university bookstore manager. He's six-two with blond hair. Khaki slacks, white shirt, and navy blazer. He seems to be scouting out people like I am."

"We see him," a voice said from the tiny microphone hidden in her hair near her ear.

Once her panic dissipated, she ducked back out into the wind and hurried down the sidewalk without looking at Graham again. Would he abort the meeting once he recognized her? Probably, but she needed to get to the restaurant.

She entered Mad Dog & Beans ten minutes ahead of the meeting time and glanced around as she waited to be seated. It was nearly two o'clock and the place wasn't busy. She mentioned the reservation for Priest and asked for a back table. The hostess beckoned for her to follow, and Savannah wound her way through the seated patrons to a table in the corner. She'd been too nervous to eat breakfast, and the aromas of Mexican spices and cheese made her stomach rumble.

She shrugged out of her coat and draped it on the back of her chair, then ordered coffee along with chips and salsa and settled down to wait. With her back to the wall, she watched the entrance to the restaurant. Did Nora's association with Graham implicate her in the scheme too?

Savannah battled a wave of nausea. Her best friend couldn't be working against her—she wouldn't believe it without proof. She tried to formulate a prayer for strength and wisdom, but all she could come up with was a single word: *Help!*

It was still five minutes before the planned time to meet. Would Graham come in or stay out there watching? They'd only met once, so maybe he hadn't recognized her.

A petite woman dressed in a smart navy suit stopped at the hostess stand. Savannah's view was blocked by the tall hostess, and she couldn't see the woman's face. The hostess turned and started leading the woman in Savannah's direction.

Savannah bit back a gasp and rose to her feet when she finally saw the woman's face. "Jess?"

CHAPTER 26

JESS'S BRAIN REFUSED TO FUNCTION. SHE STARED INTO her sister's wide green eyes. Jess was supposed to meet a new buyer, an art dealer named Hannah Rickard. It should have been a routine transaction. Jess would sit down, take the artifact and provenance documents out of her purse, and put them on the table. Rickard would examine the artifact and documents and, once she was satisfied, authorize a wire transfer to a Swiss bank account. As soon as the transfer was confirmed, Jess would leave.

So why was Savannah standing where Rickard should have been?

Savannah gasped and pushed her auburn hair out of her face. "Jess, what are you doing here?"

Her sister's voice broke Jess out of her trance. "I—I was about to ask you the same thing. I'm having a late lunch before meeting with our bankers. What about you? Why are you in New York?"

"You—you have to get out of here!" Savannah's gaze darted to the front of the restaurant. "A smuggler is going to walk in any second, and then there will be a police raid."

Icy talons gripped Jess's heart. "What are you talking about? Savannah, I—"

Savannah grabbed Jess's arm with surprising strength and propelled her toward the back of the restaurant. "Go, go, go! He'll see you! You can get out through the back. I'll explain when we're back in Nova Cambridge."

Jess half ran through the restaurant, ignoring the curious stares of the scattered diners. She pushed through the kitchen doors, where a phalanx of SWAT-equipped police waited. She hesitated for an instant, but one of them stepped out of the way and jerked an impatient thumb over his shoulder. She rushed past and somehow found an exit.

She ended up on a narrow street—hardly more than an alley—flanked by tall brick buildings on either side. She stumbled along the sidewalk, still reeling from shock. The burner phone she'd bought for the trip buzzed with a text: *Raids everywhere. Destroy everything.*

Raids everywhere? The cold claws in Jess's chest tightened. Savannah must be part of a coordinated sting aimed at taking down the entire operation. But how was that possible? They had been very careful to separate all the components of the smuggling operation. The diggers in Mexico didn't know the Mexican truckers, the Mexican truckers didn't know the American truckers, and the American truckers didn't know her. At each stage the artifacts were left at prearranged drop spots so none of the people involved ever saw each other. So how had law enforcement managed to put all the pieces together?

The artifact. It was the only thing that connected them all. She pulled it out of her purse. It was a beautiful, fragile silver appliqué in a glass-fronted wood case. It should have netted tens of thousands of dollars. She looked both ways to make sure no one was watching, gritted her teeth, and smashed the case on the edge of a metal garbage can. The appliqué fell out of the shattered case—and so did a black metal object about the size of a quarter. A bug. Of course.

Sweat beaded Jess's forehead. She crushed the bug under her heel and dumped the appliqué and broken case into the trash. She pulled the provenance documents out of her purse and shoved them into another can half a block away. Then she walked away as quickly as she could without drawing attention.

As the blocks and minutes slipped past, she gradually relaxed. The familiar crowds pressed in around her in a comforting flow of humanity. Her panic subsided and her thoughts calmed. She'd worn gloves the entire time, so there wouldn't be any fingerprints on the artifact or case, even if the police found them. Also, the police and Savannah had another suspect in mind—that much was clear from their reactions in the restaurant. If they had any hint that Jess was involved in the smuggling, they wouldn't have shooed her out the back door without even searching her.

Savannah. Jess recalled the shock on her sister's face—the wide-eyed, open-mouthed bewilderment. The thought that Jess might somehow be involved had plainly never even crossed Savannah's mind. Savannah wasn't dumb, but she loved and trusted Jess. She believed Jess's lies and looked for traitors everywhere else. How long could that last, especially after today?

A cold, wet gust off the East River caught Jess's open jacket and chilled her to the bone. She shivered and hugged herself. She suddenly felt very exposed, and not just to the elements. Time to get out of here. She hurried back to her hotel, feeling unseen eyes on her back the whole way.

COLLEEN COBLE AND RICK ACKER

Savannah stood on the busy street with an undercover officer as people hurried past them. Her ears were frozen by the wind, and she wished she had worn gloves. "I was in a panic to get Jess out of here. What about Graham?"

The officer's nose was red from the cold. "We lost track of him when things went south inside. We'll find him, though. Thanks for your help, Ms. Webster."

When he rejoined his team, Savannah turned and walked toward her hotel. She could have called an Uber, but it was a busy time of day, and she didn't want to wait for a car to arrive when she could be tucked in her warm room in a few minutes. A sea of people parted around her going the other direction as she scrolled through her text messages with cold hands. She had half a dozen from Hez. The tone of his comments became more and more alarmed.

She pulled out her Bluetooth earpiece and called him, then dropped her phone in her purse before stuffing her hands in the pockets of her coat. "The smuggler never showed up, so it was a nonevent." Her stomach rumbled. "I didn't even get to eat."

"I'm thankful no shots were fired there." Hez's deep voice in her ear held relief. "I had a preliminary report from Hope, and it couldn't have gone better. The coordinated sting hit simultaneously in three places—Mexico, Texas, and just outside Pelican Harbor. Over a dozen smugglers are in custody, but not without shoot-outs in all of the locations. I was afraid the same happened there."

She ducked around the corner and started the last two blocks to her hotel with the full force of the wind in her face. "Anyone hurt?"

"Several smugglers were killed and a few others were injured." He paused. "Two Willards were among the casualties, and several more were arrested."

Nora's family. Savannah prayed it wasn't anyone close to her friend. "Do they have any idea of the group's hierarchy? Did they catch the kingpin?"

"Hope didn't say. Hernando and his family are in protective custody in Mexico too, and I'm glad they're safe. She thinks they got enough evidence to prosecute everyone."

"Except whoever was supposed to show up today. The smuggler never showed, but that wasn't the only surprise. On the way in I saw Nora's boyfriend, Graham Warner. That seemed suspicious, so I let the police know. They were closing in on him, but Jess showed up in the restaurant."

"Jess?" His volume went up a notch. "How odd."

"Right? That's what I thought. I was shocked and so was she. I hurried her out through the back door, but the ruckus had to have tipped off the courier. I could have kicked myself for not telling her what was going on. She wandered in at exactly the wrong moment. I'll bet Graham saw her and got cold feet." Hez didn't answer right away, so she yanked out her phone to see if the connection had been lost. "You there, Hez?"

"I'm here." Another long pause followed. "That's odd about Jess. When are you getting home?"

"Tomorrow." Hez sounded a little off. Was he holding back something about the sting?

Savannah reached the hotel and hurried through the door

into the welcome warmth of the lobby. Her heels clicked on the marble floor to the elevator. She stepped inside and pushed the button to go to the third floor.

"I miss you." His voice was soft.

She smiled as the elevator dinged at her floor and the doors opened. "I miss you too. How's it going with Simon?"

"We've been having a great time playing video games, though I admit I let him stay up until eleven last night. He was dead to the world when his head hit the pillow. Me too."

"Nephews are meant to be spoiled. How are the headaches? Are you doing too much?" At least with Simon there, he likely wasn't drinking.

"The pain is better, and I'm not falling asleep at three in the afternoon. My team is making sure I'm not working too much. Did Jess say when she was getting back?"

That odd tone again. "We didn't have time to talk, but I'm sure she'll be back tomorrow night like she planned. My flight is early tomorrow, and I can't wait to see you. Oh, and let's have dinner tomorrow to celebrate taking down the smuggling ring. I'll come over and make something special."

"You sure you want to come here? I can meet you at your cottage."

She couldn't hide the smile in her voice. "You have the better kitchen, as well as that romantic balcony."

"That's a plan I can get behind. Get some rest, babe. I love you."

"I love you too. Follow your own advice and don't stay up until eleven tonight."

"I'll tell Simon I'm following orders."

She smiled as they said goodbye, then slipped out of her

coat. When she got home she'd figure out what was bugging him. Did he know something about Graham that she didn't? But no, he had seemed fine until she mentioned Jess.

Her thoughts flicked back to the moment Jess had seen her. The color had leached out of her face, and she'd gone so white that Savannah thought she might pass out. Ending up in the same restaurant in a city the size of New York had been strange.

It didn't mean anything, though. Coincidences happened.

CHAPTER 27

THE INSTANT HEZ ENDED THE CALL WITH SAVANNAH, THE door to his home office burst open. Simon rushed in, face flushed with excitement. "Was Aunt Savannah in a police raid?"

Hez swiveled his chair to face his nephew. "I thought you were supposed to be doing homework."

"I'm almost done. Besides, I can't concentrate with you talking so loud."

Hez leaned back and crossed his arms. "I was speaking in a normal tone and the door was shut. Are you sure you weren't eavesdropping?"

Simon frowned. "I wasn't eavesdropping! I walked by to go to the bathroom, and I heard 'police raid' and 'smugglers.'"

Hez chuckled. "I'll remember this the next time you say you didn't hear me tell you to quit gaming and get back to work."

Simon rolled his eyes. "Okay, okay. Now tell me about the police raid! Is Aunt Savannah all right?"

"She's fine. There were actually three police raids, but she wasn't in any of them. You know those smugglers the Justice Chamber has been investigating? The police hit them in three simultaneous raids in Mexico, in Texas, and just outside Pelican Harbor. They arrested over a dozen people."

"Get out!" Simon's eyes went round with awe. "Our Justice Chamber did that?"

Hez smiled and nodded. "Our Justice Chamber did that. We had a lot of help, of course, but it wouldn't have happened without us." He gave one of Simon's narrow shoulders a light punch. "Congrats."

"Nice!" Simon beamed. "I can't wait to tell Mom. I heard you mention her name. Was she involved?"

Hez had been asking himself that exact question, though not in the way Simon meant it. "Exactly how long did it take you to walk past the door on the way to the bathroom, Simon? Should we get you checked for pediatric arthritis?"

Simon reddened and gave a sheepish grin. "I'm not sure what that is, but maybe I, uh, forgot to walk for a little while. Sorry, Uncle Hez."

Hez tousled his nephew's blond hair. "Thanks for being honest. Don't worry about it—but don't let it happen again."

"No, sir," Simon said, trying a little too obviously to be sincere. "But, um, what about my mom?"

"She wasn't working with the Justice Chamber on this. She just happened to be in New York on other business, and she and Aunt Savannah ran into each other. I'm sure she'll want to hear all about it when she's back—and you'll want to be done with your paper on the Civil War so you'll have plenty of time to talk about it, right?"

Simon bobbed his head. "Right." He started to walk back toward the living room, then stopped after a few steps and turned. "Thank you for making me part of the Justice Chamber."

Warmth glowed in Hez's chest. "Thanks for joining. You've been a great help."

Simon grinned and sat in front of his laptop. Hez closed the door, and the warm feeling vanished as a cold wind blew through his heart. He pulled up his work email and hunted through it. He ignored dozens of items he'd ordinarily read as soon as they came in: excited emails from the Justice Chamber members forwarding news articles about the raids, two new real estate listings in Pelican Harbor, and an email from Toni titled "More car problems."

There it was: the email from Savannah with the loan documents. He opened the attachments and started going through them again, line by line. He focused on the boilerplate this time, not the splashy headline terms like the interest rate. He reread a handful of buried terms three times to make sure he understood them. Then he logged onto Westlaw and spent an hour doing online legal research. Sweat prickled his brow as he worked, and he could feel his heart rate rising.

When he finished, he sat back and stared at the screen. Could he be wrong? He wasn't a corporate finance specialist, and he was still recovering from brain surgery—but the answer seemed clear. Clear, but crazy. Why would Jess agree to this? It made no sense. But then, it also made no sense that she appeared at the exact time and place where Savannah was supposed to meet the smugglers' courier.

He picked up his phone to call Savannah, but then he put it back down. She wouldn't know anything about how the details of the loan documents worked. That was supposed to have been his job—and he was supposed to have done it before he told her to sign the loan. He winced at the memory. If he called her and told her what he thought he'd found, she'd just be worried and upset.

No, he needed to talk to the other Legare sister. Hez didn't relish the thought, but she understood this loan much better than he did. If there was an innocent explanation for what he'd found, she would know it. If there wasn't—well, he'd want to hear Jess's story before he went to Savannah.

He picked up his phone again, braced himself, and dialed Jess's number. She didn't answer, and he hung up when the call went to voice mail. He texted her: *Call me ASAP! I think we have a serious problem.*

He put down his phone and shook his head. For the first time in his life, he wanted Jess to prove him wrong about something.

———

God had sent a gorgeous pink-tinged sunset for Ella's birthday. The solace of the little Gothic garden around the family plot encircled Savannah. She traced the verse on the black granite headstone above the engraved picture of their little girl. *For where your treasure is, there your heart will be also.* Their beloved treasure, their darling Ella, was in heaven, but they'd see her again someday.

She took a deep breath of the sweet scent of blooming camellia and released the tension she still held from the long flight home from New York today. The clasp of Hez's hand around hers anchored her as they stood looking at their baby's final resting place. "The sunset reminds me of how much she loved her pink pony, that one Blake got her when she was born."

"I remember." Hez pulled her down with him onto the bench

COLLEEN COBLE AND RICK ACKER

by the headstone, then slipped his arm around her to press a kiss against her hair. "I can't wrap my head around the fact she would have been six today. She would have been going to school and learning to read."

The grief in his voice hollowed out her chest, and her eyes welled with tears. "I found an old video and listened to her little voice over and over again. I know you've seen it. It's the one where she's dressed like a princess and she's lost her tiara. You're helping her find it, and she won't let anyone but you put it back on her head."

A choked sob erupted from his chest, and she listened to his ragged breathing for a long moment. "She's safe in heaven now." She watched a hummingbird hover over a pink blossom. "I'm so glad you're with me this year. Grief shared is so much easier to bear."

"I should have been here all along. I'm so sorry I drove you off." His voice wobbled.

She lifted her head and straightened so she could gaze into his eyes. "It was for the best. We grew during that time apart, both of us. A lot has changed in the past year, all good. We're back together, we both have jobs we love, and we have a nephew. Next year will bring even more great changes. We'll be married, and we might even have a baby on the way." She rested her hand on her flat stomach and imagined a baby's flutter there. "And TGU will be in great shape with the smugglers gone and better finances thanks to that new loan. Even Jess is starting to come around where you're concerned. I think she might actually like you."

His lips smiled but his eyes stayed somber. "That last part is debatable." He cleared his throat. "And about the smugglers—we still don't have them all. The courier got away, and I'm not convinced we've got the leader."

She studied his expression. What was he keeping from her? Before she could probe a little deeper, her phone sounded with a message. She dug it out of her purse and frowned. "Nora needs to talk to me. You think she's heard about the raids?"

"News like that has probably raced through law enforcement."

"I should have told her and not let her be blindsided."

"You were staying quiet like we were told. She'll understand." He glanced at his watch. "I'm going to check out the new AA group here in town. I've been meaning to go but haven't, and I think it's time."

Was he battling with the desire to drink? Remembering their daughter's birthday might have resurrected those old demons. "Let's walk down together. I'll have Nora meet me at the pond."

He rose and took her hand, and they walked through over-grown wildflowers and sprawling trees sprinkled among pillared crypts and ornate headstones of stained and decaying marble. They picked their way down the oyster-shell path toward TGU. The view from up here never failed to soothe her. With the sunset glimmering color on the buildings and the water, she couldn't see the maintenance that needed to be done. They'd soon have money to do it.

Hez kissed her goodbye and hurried off to catch an Uber while she walked briskly to Tupelo Pond. She spotted Nora waiting by the bench and lifted a hand in greeting. Nora's strained expression and lack of greeting told Savannah all she needed to know—her friend knew.

Nora shot her an accusing stare. "Elliot Drake has been all over the news bragging about how he led the effort to take down an international artifact smuggling ring. The media somehow got old family photos showing the Willard family, and I'm in some of the pictures." She pulled out her phone and swiped through the images. "Look."

Savannah studied the old pictures. One of them showed a young Little Joe, barely out of his teens. He had his arms around Nora and another cousin. They stood smiling on the beach at Pelican State Park, and they looked impossibly young, happy, and wholesome. What turned Little Joe into the glaring thug with the ugly Punisher tattoo on his shoulder?

Savannah handed Nora's phone back. "At least your face is blurred."

Nora huffed and dropped it in her purse. "Like that matters. Everyone knows it's me. Officers are looking at me like they think I should have known. The past twenty-four hours have been horrible. You were part of the raids that wrecked my family, weren't you? Don't try to deny it."

Savannah barely managed not to look away from the hurt on her friend's face. "I-I'm not supposed to talk about it, Nora. I'm so sorry I couldn't tell you."

Nora took off her glasses and wiped tears from her eyes. "Two of my cousins are dead, including Little Joe. Another cousin is in the hospital and likely heading to prison. Uncle David was arrested and so were some other relatives. Was the Justice Chamber behind this?"

"Sort of, but I'm not supposed to talk about it."

Nora's brown eyes pinned Savannah in place. "You were in New York. Were you working with the NYPD?"

"I . . . I . . ." Savannah couldn't lie. "Yes."

"Graham was taken in for questioning." Nora raked her

hand through her thick brown hair. "He's never even had a speeding ticket, but they badgered him for two hours. He was on a trip to visit publishers and he had proof, but the police refused to believe him. He probably needs an attorney, which he can't afford. Would you know anything about why the best man I've ever met was picked up? He told me he saw you there, so I want the truth."

Her friend needed at least a heads-up that Graham might be involved. "I hate to have to say this, but, well, I have reason to believe he might not be who you think he is, Nora. Be careful."

Nora's mouth dropped open, and her eyes filled with tears. "I can't believe my best friend would do this." A sob broke from her chest, and she turned and ran back toward the parking lot.

Savannah wanted to go after her, but what could she say?

CHAPTER 28

THE LOAN DOCUMENTS SAT IN A NEAT STACK ON HEZ'S desk. Annotated yellow sticky notes stuck out in random spots, like weeds sprouting from a sheer cliff. His temperamental office printer had been busy for over an hour and had quit in protest several times. It would have been much faster to use the copy room printer, but he didn't want to risk someone seeing one of these documents before he had a chance to talk to Jess.

Jess hadn't responded to his text, but she must have seen it by now. He sent it almost thirty-six hours ago, and she'd gotten back to Nova Cambridge yesterday evening. She hadn't even asked him what was so urgent, which presumably meant she knew or she was ignoring him. Most likely both.

Well, she wouldn't be able to ignore him much longer. Her office was just a few doors down from his, and he made a point of walking past every fifteen minutes this morning. He glanced at his watch. Time for another lap.

He picked up the stack of papers and headed into the hall. Her light was on and her door was ajar. He stopped and glanced in. She sat in front of her computer, her petite frame erect and her eyes fixed on the screen in front of her.

He knocked with his free hand. "Morning, Jess. We need to talk."

She didn't look away from the monitor. "Not now. I have a meeting to get ready for."

He pushed the door open and walked in. "Sorry, it has to be now." He sat in one of her office chairs. "Whatever your meeting is about, this is more important."

She gave a sharp sigh and turned toward him, her mouth pressed in a thin line. "I don't care who pays for it. I'll get a rental if I need one. Now get out."

Hez blinked. "What are you talking about?"

"My car, of course." Jess turned back to her monitor. "Toni found all the tires slashed and the paint scratched when she came out of a witness interview on Tuesday. She said she told you and asked you how to get the damage fixed."

So that's what Toni's email was about. Hez had been too focused on the loan issue to clear out his inbox. "Sorry, I haven't had a chance to go through my emails. There's been an urgent matter that I—"

"Read it and we can talk after my meeting. I'm pretty sure Pierre did it. See if you can find a way to stick him with the repair bill."

"You think Pierre vandalized your car?"

She rolled her eyes. "Of course. Toni was interviewing a witness who had dirt on another one of his trust-fund scams. You're way behind on this, aren't you? Seriously, go read your email. I have other things to do."

"I—"

She flicked a glance at him and started typing. "And figure out what I'm going to drive in the meantime. Is the Justice

Chamber going to rent me a car or pay my Uber bills while mine is in the shop?"

"I, uh, I'm not sure. Let me—" He stopped.

She's trying to distract me.

He should have seen it immediately, despite his post-craniotomy brain fog. There was no way she really thought he barged into her office to talk about her car, especially when he was carrying a stack of loan documents. She was playing for time and trying to sidetrack him—and he'd been letting her do it.

He reached into his pocket and took out his key ring. He detached the fob for his Audi A3 and put it on Jess's desk. "Drive mine. I can't drive for another two and a half months thanks to this." He tapped his left temple. "It's been sitting in the faculty lot since the day I was attacked. Now, I'd really like to get your input on what I found in these loan documents before I talk to Savannah."

Jess stopped typing. "You approved the loan. Savannah signed it. It's a done deal."

"And we may need to undo it. There's a very serious problem buried in these documents." He held up the stack. "There are three provisions scattered throughout that, read together, make this a demand note secured by all of TGU's assets."

She licked her lips. "I don't know what you mean."

He doubted that with the way she evaded his gaze. "Hornbrook can demand full payment of the loan at any time and the university has to pay every penny in twenty-four hours. If we don't, they can grab everything."

She arched an eyebrow. "If there's a problem, why did you recommend signing the loan?"

"Because these provisions are very obscure." He paused. "It's almost like they were deliberately hidden. Do you want me to walk through each clause and explain how they work together?"

She waved a perfectly manicured hand as if shooing away an annoying insect. "This is standard language in high-end business loans. The interest rate and other terms are good. Don't worry about it."

Hez shook his head, causing a warning twinge from the left side of his skull. "It is not standard. I researched that. And even if it were, it's crazy. This is like having a clause in your mortgage that says the bank can demand the full amount anytime they want and take your house away if you can't pay it all in twenty-four hours. No one would take that loan, no matter how good the interest rate."

She gave him a placating smile, but a cold and calculating look glinted in her hazel eyes. "I don't want to sound condescending, Hez, but you're not a banker or a Wall Street lawyer. You're very good at what you do—I know that from firsthand experience—but this just isn't your area of expertise. It's mine. Trust me on this, okay?"

Hez pressed his lips together for a moment. "I wish I could, Jess. I really do. But I can't put TGU at this kind of risk. I'll have to tell Savannah about this. I'll recommend that we go to Hornbrook and try to renegotiate these clauses. If they won't agree, we'll have to refinance the loan again, even if we're forced to give up the terrific interest rate you got."

He started to get up, but Jess held up her hand. "Wait." She stood, walked around her desk with quick, precise steps, and shut the door. She resumed her seat and looked him in the eye. "If you call Hornbrook and try to renegotiate, they'll immediately call the loan. They'll do the same thing if you try to refinance with someone else."

Hez's heart rate spiked. "What? You knew that and you still agreed to these terms? Why?"

"That's irrelevant." She leaned forward, every muscle taut. "What matters is that you do nothing about this. Absolutely nothing. Do you understand?"

"No. Why should I just leave this alone? It's a bomb that could go off any second."

"Because you love Savannah." She took a deep breath. "And so do I."

His pulse roared in his ears. "What . . . what do you mean?"

"You said this is a bomb. Well, we need to get her outside the blast radius before it goes off. I'll help." She talked fast, the words pouring out as she tried to persuade him. "I have connections. I can arrange a position for her at a prestigious university or a big museum. It would be perfect for her. I'll even help you set up a legal clinic. Famous universities and museums tend to be in big cities. There's lots of need for legal clinics in places like that, right?"

The pieces clicked into place. "You arranged for her to be denied tenure, didn't you? That would have forced us to leave, but Pierre messed up your plans by getting her into the president's chair." He gave a grim smile. "That didn't work out well for either you or him, did it?"

She was silent for a heartbeat. "We're getting off topic, Hez. I need you to tell me that you're going to help me get Savannah out of here by the end of the semester. I can hold Hornbrook off that long, but no longer."

"Why are you doing this, Jess?" He paused. "You have a secret deal with Hornbrook, don't you? What's your cut going to be when they foreclose on TGU and turn it into a casino or something?"

Her face reddened and tight lines appeared at the corners of her mouth. "You think this is about money? If all I cared about was money, I would have stayed in New York."

Anger flared in his chest. "What do you care about more than money?"

Her response was instant. "Family."

"Oh? And isn't Savannah family?"

"Yes, and she's the only reason that bomb hasn't gone off yet."

There was a tentative knock on the door, and it opened slightly. Jess's secretary poked her head in. "I'm sorry to interrupt, but, um, everyone is waiting for you in the meeting, Ms. Legare."

Jess looked up. "Tell them I'm on my way."

The secretary nodded and shut the door.

Jess stood and picked up a notepad and pen. "If you care about Savannah, you'll get her out of here. And you'll do it fast." She walked out without waiting for his response.

Hez followed her into the hall and retraced his steps to his office, moving like a sleepwalker. The magnitude of her betrayal stunned him. She must have been planning this for years, probably since she first set foot on campus. Maybe even before. Why? She said it was for family, but what family did she have other than Simon and Savannah?

Savannah. How was he going to tell her about Jess's treachery? It would devastate her. And what if Jess was right that the best thing he could do was get Savannah away before the university imploded? Every fiber of his being resisted giving up without a fight and running away, but he had to consider Savannah's best interests too. He hadn't done that often enough in the past.

Dear God, what am I going to do?

The breeze from Bon Secour Bay lifted Savannah's hair and swirled the scent of water and seafood with it as she walked toward Hez's condo with a carton of buttermilk. The streets were crowded with residents and tourists in town for the gumbo festival, and she'd had to park several blocks away. She spotted groups along the waterfront setting up tasting tables. The chef of the winning dish would take home a Best Gumbo ribbon as well as a weekend at Bayfront Inn along with a full-course meal for two at Billy's Seafood.

The catfish she'd promised Hez needed to marinate at least two hours in buttermilk and hot sauce, and she was later than she'd planned due to the challenge of finding parking. She stepped around a couple arguing in the middle of the side-walk and speed-walked down the side of Hez's brick build-ing to the iron steps leading to the condo. She hurried up the stairs, reached for her key, and twisted it in the keyhole, but the door wasn't locked. Hez was always careful about security, especially since he didn't own the condo, but maybe his head injury had let the routine lapse.

She pushed inside and gaped to see Jess, still in her skirt and heels, standing in the kitchen near the sink. "Jess? What are you doing here?"

Jess whirled and went pale. Her hand shot to her throat. "Savannah, you scared the life out of me. What are you doing sneaking in like that?"

"Sneaking? Hez is my fiancé, so it's hardly unusual for me to stop by. Your presence here, however, is the real shocker. How'd you get in?"

Jess didn't look at her as she reached for her purse on its side on the counter. "I came by to pick up some paperwork Hez left for me."

Savannah glanced around the kitchen and dining table. "What paperwork? I don't see anything."

"It's in my purse."

Savannah eyed the medium bag now slung over her sister's shoulder and unease trickled down her spine. "What paperwork did he have? I can call Hez and make sure you get what you need."

Jess pressed her lips together and shook her head. "I don't have time for this, Savannah. I needed the paperwork for a meeting, and I've got it, but I'm late now." She brushed past Savannah and exited, shutting the door behind her.

What on earth had just happened? Savannah should have pressed Jess on how she got in. Savannah rubbed her head. Her sister's peculiarities weren't important right now. A romantic evening with Hez stretched in front of her, and she didn't have time to worry about Jess's behavior when she needed to prepare dinner. Hez would be home in half an hour.

Her sister's scent still lingered as Savannah stepped into the kitchen and dropped her large purse onto the table before moving toward the fridge. Her gaze swept the room and landed on the cabinet under the sink. The door stood ajar, and she peeked in Hez's trash bin. Her gut clenched at the bottle resting on top of plastic and cardboard. With a trembling hand she reached in and removed the empty bottle of Mondavi cabernet sauvignon. Just like last time.

Could . . . could Jess have put it there? She had seemed flustered and evasive, and she never explained how she got into Hez's locked condo. Did she steal his key? Savannah suddenly wanted to throw up.

She set the glass container on the counter and pressed her fingers to her eyes so she didn't have to look at it. She'd been so quick to believe the worst of Hez even when he protested his innocence. He'd been convinced all along the first wine bottle had been planted, and this appeared to be proof he was right and Savannah was wrong.

Savannah didn't want to believe her sister would be so devious, but Jess was used to getting what she wanted, and she'd never warmed to Hez being part of their family.

If Jess had done this, it was utterly despicable.

Savannah opened her eyes and put the bottle in her large bag where Hez wouldn't find it. She needed to think this through before she told him about it after dinner. Maybe the two of them could figure out Jess's motive.

CHAPTER 29

JESS WALKED ALONG THE DESERTED SIDEWALK ON THE EAST side of campus, trapped in a waking nightmare. The cooing doves in the tupelo trees, bright afternoon sun, and gentle breeze all felt unreal. The hints of the coming spring and fresh life did not touch the cold, dark ruins in her heart.

Just over twenty-four hours ago, everything had seemed perfect. Savannah had finally signed the loan, the smuggling operation was humming along nicely, and Jess was headed to her favorite city for a quick trip to sell an artifact at a very good price. And to top it off, Hez's Justice Chamber minions were doing a marvelous job of aggravating Pierre and chipping away at his sleazy trust fund. On their most recent call, Punisher had even complimented Jess on the flawless execution of her plan.

Then the avalanche began. It started small, like avalanches often did. As Jess was walking to Mad Dog for her meeting with the artifact buyer, Toni had texted to say the tires on Jess's car—which Toni was still borrowing—had been slashed. She was very apologetic that she hadn't returned the car earlier. She said she'd make sure the tires were replaced ASAP and that she'd talk to Hez about how to handle the repairs. Jess had taken it in stride. She didn't drive much, and the more distractions Hez had on his plate, the better.

After that, the disasters cascaded one after another, crashing down on Jess like boulders. She still didn't understand how Savannah came to be sitting where the buyer should have been. Then the raids hit every part of the smuggling operation, followed by the news that Little Joe and Tommy were dead. Jess was still reeling from the disastrous blow at the meeting with Hez, and now Savannah had walked in while Jess was planting the bottle in Hez's trash.

The worst part was that Jess knew the avalanche would only grow more massive. Hez would probably tell Savannah the truth about the loan. He couldn't do anything about it—the documents were airtight—but he would try. And the instant he tried, James Hornbrook would pull the trigger, which he'd been itching to do ever since the ink on Savannah's signature was dry. Savannah's career would be destroyed, and she wouldn't understand why. She would look at Jess with uncomprehending pain and grief—and then cut her out of her life.

Jess's eyes blurred and she stopped in the middle of an empty stretch of sidewalk. She took a deep breath, held it for a few seconds, and blew it out slowly, like her New York therapist had taught her. She found a green-patinaed bronze bench, sat down, and held her head in her hands.

The wine bottle had been her last-ditch gambit to save both Savannah and their relationship. Jess knew her sister was coming over to make dinner, so she would find the bottle just like she did before. Jess would comfort her sister again, putting a compassionate arm around her while she cried and worried. Then Jess would tactfully suggest that the demands on both

Hez and Savannah were too much. They needed time to heal. The two of them should go someplace quiet and peaceful—and Jess would help. She'd make some calls and find the perfect spot for Savannah to take a relaxing research sabbatical and keep a closer eye on Hez. Jess could even be acting president while Savannah was gone. But then Savannah arrived half an hour earlier than Jess expected.

Jess could still feel Savannah's eyes on her as she'd hurried out of Hez's condo. Her sister's face had held the same shock Jess saw in New York, but this time with undertones of suspicion and accusation. Once Savannah found the bottle, those undertones would harden and deepen—and become permanent.

Savannah's eyes weren't the only ones drilling into Jess's soul. The dead eyes of Little Joe and Tommy stared at her too, silently blaming her for their deaths. And then there were those old, inescapable painted eyes of Jesus, of course.

The sensation of being watched got so strong that Jess lifted her head from her hands—and discovered that someone really was looking at her. A dove perched on the other end of the bench and stared at her with a single eye, as bright and perfect as a tiny black pearl.

Jess smiled. She was happy to have uncritical company, even if it was only a bird. The doves around campus had become semi-tame, though she'd never seen one this unafraid of humans. It must be very bold. Or hungry.

"I don't have anything for you," she warned the bird.

The dove ruffled its feathers but didn't fly away.

"You like this place?" Jess swept her arm at the empty field of brilliant green grass around them. "It'll be gone soon."

She chuckled and shook her head. "Here I am, chatting with

a bird like one of those crazy ladies in Central Park. I guess I don't have anyone else I can talk to."

The dove eyed her expectantly.

"Are you asking why I did this? It really is about family. Family and justice. If I wanted more money, I really would have stayed on Wall Street." She did some quick mental math. "I gave up at least three million in salary and bonuses so I could come down here and right old wrongs. And money isn't all I sacrificed. I got my hands dirty with smuggling to help grease the wheels of the operation. I went to jail for crimes I didn't commit—and I may go there again for things I did do. I even killed a man." She paused and shook her head again. "Was it worth it?"

Her movement made the rickety bench wobble slightly, and the dove spread its wings. Jess suddenly realized she didn't want it to leave. "Hold on a sec!" She opened her purse and fished out a protein bar. She unwrapped it, broke off a piece, and tossed it on the sidewalk in front of the bench. "Here you go."

The dove hopped down and pecked at the food.

"The family part hasn't worked out so well, has it? Mimi is burying two more boys and dealing with another stain on the Willard name. And Savannah . . ." Jess's voice trailed off. "Well, at least I still have Simon."

Her heart froze, and she caught a glimpse of another boulder hurtling down to crush her. How long would she have her son? Simon was intelligent and inquisitive. How long before he figured out the truth? And how would he react? He loved TGU, Savannah, and Hez, and he was so proud to be part of the Justice Chamber. Would he understand and accept his mother's explanation for why she destroyed the university and betrayed his aunt and uncle? Or would he stare at her with that stunned, who-are-you expression she saw in Savannah's face half an hour ago? "Secrets never lie buried, do they? They always rise to the surface like stones in a New England field."

She sighed and tossed another crumb to the dove. "This place was stolen by Legares, you know." She gestured to the distant brick-and-stone buildings, their hues warmed by the rich yellow of the afternoon sun. "All of it. And a Legare destroyed my mother. She's buried on that hill. They're parasites, sucking the life out of everything they touch. Especially Pierre. Thanks to him, TGU is just a sick shell of what it once was—what it should still be. Destroying it will be a mercy killing. And taking him down at the same time will be long-overdue justice. And yet . . . and yet . . ."

The dove watched her with that piercing obsidian eye, waiting for her to go on. Or for another piece of her protein bar.

She broke off another hunk and dropped it in front of the hungry bird. Laughter from a distant group of students drifted on the breeze. "Will they think what's about to happen is mercy and justice? Will anyone? And will they ever be able to forgive me?"

She tossed the last bit of protein bar to the dove. It ignored the offering and continued to watch her. In its gaze she felt the weight of all the other eyes on her. "Justice and mercy," she whispered. "And forgiveness. That's all I want."

The dove cocked its head, then spread its wings and flew away into the bright blue sky.

⎯⎯⎯

The aromas of andouille sausage, shrimp, Cajun spices, and peppers from the gumbo festival mingled with the sweet scent of beignets frying in Petit Charms below Hez's balcony. But Savannah could barely choke down any of the catfish, hush puppies, or mac and cheese she'd spent hours preparing. Not with the questions swirling inside.

How did she tell the man she loved that her sister was so determined to keep them apart that she had sabotaged their relationship?

Savannah couldn't get the memory of Jess standing in the kitchen out of her head. Had she planted any other kind of bomb in the condo that would eventually show up? What else had she done in the past seven months to try to keep them apart?

Hez speared a piece of fish. "Jesse's Restaurant called to confirm tomorrow's engagement party. They had a cancellation for the Café Room. I nabbed it." The noise of a band down by the water escalated and he glanced over the balcony.

He'd been as distracted tonight as she was. She mustered a smile. "That's great news! It's my favorite." She cleared her throat. "Jess is helping plan the party. I'll let her know."

"It should be perfect. Have you heard whether Nora is coming?"

Savannah's smile wilted, and she shook her head. "She's not even answering my texts."

He gave her his full attention at that news. "I'm sorry, babe. As more of the truth comes out, I hope she'll come around."

"Me too." She slipped a piece of fish to Cody, who had been watching her hopefully, and he gobbled it down. Should she just jump into what she'd found out this afternoon? She set her fork on her plate and reached across the table to take his hand. "Hez, I-I'm sorry for doubting you about the drinking. I should have known you wouldn't lie to me. We've had our problems, but lack of truthfulness was never one of them."

A questioning frown settled on his forehead, but she rushed on before he could say anything. "This afternoon I found Jess in your kitchen, and there was another wine bottle in your trash bin. The cabinet door was open. I'm pretty sure she planted it."

His eyes widened. "Wow. I . . . I didn't even consider the possibility that she could be the culprit—though I should have."

"I know her better than anyone, and I never dreamed she might do something like this."

His hand tightened around hers, and his expression sharpened. "Jess has had her own agenda all this time, Savannah. She's duped us both. I did something I should have done in the first place and read the fine print on that loan more closely. I couldn't believe what it contained."

Savannah listened to what her sister had done. "Are you sure, Hez? I can't believe she would do something that would hurt me. Anything Jess has done has been because she thought she knew best."

He hesitated and his eyes filled with compassion. "She admitted it."

Savannah bit back a gasp. "But why? I don't understand. I need to talk to her."

Hez ran his thumb over her hand in a soothing motion. "Don't do anything until I can figure out a strategy that has a chance of success. She said this was about family."

That could only mean one thing—Jess's deep-seated hatred of Pierre Legare.

"She hates Dad so much she's willing to destroy the Legare name and legacy? And what about me? If TGU is gone, so is my job. I can't believe she would be willing to hurt me in the process of taking down Dad." Her voice wobbled, and she swallowed down the pain before her eyes welled up with tears.

"We've never talked about her parentage, and maybe we should."

Savannah exhaled and clung tighter to Hez's hand. "It's an ugly story, Hez, very ugly. I can barely stand to think about it, which is why I've never told you. Michael Willard is Jess's biological father. I was a child, so I may not have all the details right, but the way I heard it was that Dad stole money from Michael's mother, Helen. Michael decided if Dad took something from his family, he'd take something from Dad. So he took Mom."

Hez's thumb stopped its soothing rhythm. "He took her? Kidnapped her, you mean?"

"No, no. He seduced her, and she left Dad. She took me with her, but I was just a baby so I don't remember anything until later. I always sort of knew Mom was miserable and Dad never let her forget something she'd done, but I didn't really understand until I got older. Mom never talked about it, but I put the pieces together from what Dad had said and rumors I'd heard. When Jess was born, Dad knew she wasn't his daughter and Michael knew too. He sent Jess gifts for birthdays and Christmases, but he didn't have visitation rights and kept his distance."

"And all this time Jess never felt like she belonged anywhere."

"Exactly. I felt so sorry for her—the only true innocent in the whole sordid saga. None of this was her fault, but she suffered so much." Savannah bit down hard on her lower lip. "Maybe my pity blinded me to some hard truths about Jess."

"I don't want to ruin our special night, but once the dinner is over tomorrow, we need to have a hard conversation with Jess. I know how much you love your sister, so I'll take the lead on this."

Savannah sat up straighter and lifted her chin. "I love you for trying to spare me the pain, but I've avoided dealing with difficult family situations all my life. They're layered and convoluted, and it always seemed impossible to navigate them, but this is my problem, Hez. My avoidance of facing this kind of thing was one of the reasons our marriage failed the first time. Jess is my sister. I'll make her tell me to my face what she's done and why."

Until today she'd assumed Jess reciprocated her fierce love, but Savannah had clearly been wrong. And that opened a wound inside so deep that she didn't know if it would ever heal.

CHAPTER 30

THE SKY OUTSIDE WAS BRIGHT AND CLOUDLESS, BUT JESS could feel the storm coming. It had been building ever since she left Hez's condo yesterday. The air felt more charged and breathless with every hour that passed. Everything was coming to a head.

Savannah and Hez had hardly spoken to Jess, but their body language was eloquent. Neither of them made eye contact when they passed her in the hall. They stopped talking whenever she was near. The few times today she had to go into one of their offices, they wore tight little smiles and practically held their breath until she left.

When would the storm break? Jess half expected to be called into Savannah's office at any moment and summarily fired, with that old security guard escorting her out. Or maybe Savannah would have Hez do the dirty work for her. And what would happen tonight? Would Savannah still introduce Jess as her maid of honor? Or would she pull her aside before dinner started to tell her there had been a change of plans?

Not knowing was agony. Jess couldn't even be sure Savannah had found the bottle and realized that her sister planted it or that Hez had told her about the loan. Hez also hadn't given any hint of whether he would listen to Jess about taking Savannah away and not fighting Hornbrook. If he didn't, wedding plans would be the least of their concerns.

By four o'clock, Jess couldn't take it anymore. She needed to leave soon to get herself and Simon ready for the dinner, and she wasn't going to walk into that engagement party at Jesse's Restaurant with no idea what was going on. Hez wasn't in his office, so she walked over to the Justice Chamber in Connor Hall.

Fortunately, he was there and he was alone. He sat behind that ancient little desk with the plaque hanging on the wall behind him: *"But let justice roll on like a river, righteousness like a never-failing stream!"* She shivered, probably from the draft leaking through the Gothic window.

She shut the door. "Are you going to take my advice about the loan and Savannah?"

His eyes were hard. "I don't see why I should. You don't exactly have the university's best interests at heart."

"But I do have Savannah's."

He raised his brows and folded his arms, but he said nothing.

She kept her voice even. "Did you tell her about the loan?"

"Yes, and she told me about the bottles." His voice was stony and grim.

The blow made her close her eyes. It had to have seemed like the ultimate betrayal to Savannah. "What are you going to do?"

"The three of us need to have a long talk, Jess. But not tonight. This evening is a celebration, and I don't want you ruining it."

"Of course not. I want Savannah to be happy—you must know that."

"Must I?"

"Absolutely!" Heat rose in her chest. "I love my sister!"

He leaned forward. "Then act like it!"

She put her hands on her hips. "What do you want me to do?"

"For starters, help us get out of this loan. Savannah's not going on some cushy research sabbatical while the university implodes. You know her better than that. She'll stay here and fight. And I'll be by her side. If you love her, you will be too."

It was true. Savannah never backed down from a battle if she was convinced she was right. She would stay at TGU until the bitter end. Something deep in Jess refused to abandon her sister, no matter what the cost. She licked her lips. "If . . . if you wind up meeting with Hornbrook, be careful what you say. He has hidden cameras and microphones all over his office."

Surprise crept into his face and his voice softened just a little. "Thanks for the tip. Is there anything else I should know?"

She sighed. "Just that it really will be impossible to get out of that loan. Hornbrook had LeBoeuf & Bingham draft the documents. You're familiar with them?"

Hez made a face like he'd just bitten a lemon. "They're very good at what they do." He looked at his watch. "I've got some paperwork I have to send out before I leave to get ready for tonight. We'll talk tomorrow." He paused. "You've got some big decisions to make."

She nodded. "We all do. See you tonight."

She left the Justice Chamber and walked to the parking lot, the late-afternoon sun warming the back of her black leather jacket. She almost looked forward to the conversation with Savannah and Hez tomorrow. The truth was finally out and they could talk about it. No more lies and evasions. They knew what she did, and now she could tell them why. It wouldn't be an easy conversation, but it would be honest.

How would the conversation end? Jess still wanted justice, of course. She wasn't going to give up on airing all the Legare dirty laundry and making Pierre pay for his crimes, but did that have to mean destroying TGU? She used to detest the place, but she was beginning to see it through the eyes of her sister and son. They adored the traditions, the crumbling ivy-covered buildings, the students, the greedy doves, and even Boo Radley. On cue, the fat old bull gator roared from Tupelo Pond.

Jess smiled—and in that instant she knew what she needed to do. She couldn't keep fighting this war, not with Savannah on the other side. She couldn't just quit either. Her place was with her sister, but how could she get there? She was about to cross some very powerful and dangerous men. What would they do to her? To Simon?

She felt the eyes of the wooden Messiah on her again as she reached Hez's Audi. This time, though, the eyes held hope rather than accusation. Maybe there was a way to make things right, even if she couldn't see it. Maybe he could.

She got in and pressed the ignition. Brilliant light and over-whelming sound enveloped her.

Though she was nearly out of time, Savannah paused in her rush to finish her day to admire her engagement ring glowing in the late-afternoon sunlight. Tonight should have been as perfect as her ring, but she wasn't sure what to say to Jess after the discovery of everything her sister had done to ruin TGU and Pierre. The depth of her sister's desire for revenge was impossible for Savannah to understand, but she had no choice but to deal with it. How did she even begin to unravel what had been done?

A deep boom sounded from somewhere outside, and she turned that way in time to see several panes of glass hurtle from their window grilles.

She instinctively cowered back as the flying glass knocked over her family pictures and broke into dozens of pieces on her desk. Her ears still rang from the blast or whatever it was, and she rushed to the window. The parking lot was on the other side of her little garden, and she nearly cried out.

Hez's car was in flames.

Some kind of explosion had left it a twisted carcass that was almost unrecognizable.

She was barely aware of turning and running out the door for the exit. *Please, God* echoed over and over in a silent prayer that Hez was all right. But how could he have survived that kind of devastating blast? She couldn't think beyond the fear compressing her chest. This couldn't be happening.

She had to get to Hez, but though she ran as fast as she could, it felt like her feet moved through mud with the seconds ticking by like minutes. Maybe he'd been blown clear. They could deal with a broken bone or two. Surely that was all it was. But as she neared the car, her breath caught in her throat.

No one could have walked away from that inferno unscathed.

She peered through the flames but didn't see anyone in the burning wreckage. A flash of blue on the green grass caught her eye, and she turned to see a figure there. It was a female in a skirt, and Savannah slammed her eyes shut. The woman had lost most of one leg and blood was everywhere, flowing out onto the grass and staining the mud and the skirt with red.

Savannah's first instinct was to drop to her knees to help, but the certainty settled in her chest that the woman would be beyond human assistance. She sank to her knees amid a strong coppery stench but wasn't sure where to apply pressure to stop the massive amount of bleeding. But she could pray, so she did.

"Savannah, help me."

Savannah's head swiveled toward the woman's blonde hair.

Her brain refused to believe it was her sister's hazel eyes peering at her through tangled, singed blonde hair.

"Jess." Her sister's name felt wrenched from her. "Oh, Jess." A massive amount of blood poured from everywhere. Savannah needed a tourniquet for the badly damaged leg, but she had nothing, not even a belt.

She grasped both hands around Jess's thigh and tried to apply enough pressure to stop the hemorrhaging, but the flow didn't falter.

Jess grabbed Savannah's arm. "I'm s-sorry. F-for everything." Her teeth chattered and she struggled to speak.

Her sister was going into shock, and Savannah had no help to offer. The wail of a siren came from somewhere. "The ambulance is on its way. Hang on, Jess. You'll be okay." It was a lie. The paramedics would never arrive in time, not with the way the color was gone from Jess's face. This couldn't be happening.

"Liar," Jess whispered. "Sorry, so sorry. Forgive."

"I forgive you, Jess." Savannah gripped her sister's hands

with both of her bloody ones. "Of course I forgive you. Hang on, help is coming."

"Simon. Promise."

"I'll take care of him until you're better. You know I will. Hang on, Jess. Don't leave me, please don't leave me." When Jess's lips moved with no sound, Savannah slipped her arm under Jess's head. "Save your strength. The ambulance is nearly here."

Jess gasped as she looked at something past Savannah's shoulder. "He's here. He came." She coughed, blood bubbling from her blue lips. "I don't deserve, but . . . he forgives."

Savannah turned to look behind her, but no one was there.

"His eyes . . . they've always watched." Wonder crept across Jess's face.

"Who, Jess?" But Savannah knew Jess was glimpsing someone not of this world.

"His eyes . . . his eyes." The expression of wonder still on her face, Jess expelled a long breath, her lids closing partially. Then her body fell slack and lifeless.

"Jess?" Savannah clutched her tighter as no more breaths came from her sister. "No! Jess, please, no."

The siren's wail was a shriek, but it was late, too late. Savannah clutched her sister's body to her chest and keened, rocking her sister back and forth in her arms. "Oh, Jess."

Then Hez was there on the grass beside her, murmuring her name and enfolding her in his arms. "I've got you, babe."

"She's dead. Jess is dead." She finally released her sister to turn and bury her face in Hez's chest. "Jesus came for her."

CHAPTER 31

THERE WAS NO SIREN WAILING IN AUGUSTA'S POLICE CAR, but Savannah heard the ghostly shriek in her head as she sat in the back of the vehicle. Even wrapped in Hez's arms, she was cold, so cold. How did she adjust to life without her sister? A thousand memories churned in her head: teaching Jess to swim, helping her pick out a dress for her first dance, staying up late cramming for Spanish class.

Where did it all go wrong? When had that smiling little girl turned into the woman consumed with revenge? If Savannah could go back in time to the moment it had started, maybe she could have stopped it. But life wasn't like that. One wrong step led to the next and the next until there seemed to be no way of turning around. If only she had one more day to change what had happened.

Hez pressed his lips against the side of her hair. "We're here, babe. Augusta has been waiting a few minutes, so we'd better let her get back to work."

Augusta turned toward them from the front seat. "Take your time. I'm so sorry, Savannah." Her warm brown eyes held a wealth of sympathy.

Savannah blinked. She hadn't realized the car had stopped.

She lifted her head and saw Jess's mansion. Jess had been so proud of her home and how beautiful she'd made it. She'd never brew coffee in that beautiful kitchen again, would never tend the flower bed or watch the leaves shimmer in the wind. Fresh tears sprang to Savannah's eyes, but she blinked them back. She had to be strong for Simon.

She opened her door. "Thanks for delivering us, Augusta."

"It was the least I could do. I'll let you know when we're sure your car hasn't been sabotaged in any way."

Savannah nodded and stepped out onto the pavement. The police car pulled away, and she clung to Hez's hand to walk to the house. The scent of Jess's roses was the stench of death, and Savannah decided in that instant that she didn't want any roses at the funeral. She shuddered at how familiar this all was. It had been just like this when Ella died. The sirens with their flashing lights and the grim paramedics who moved with methodical precision instead of the urgency she felt inside. That thick fog of grief and shock blurring everything was the strongest déjà vu she'd ever experienced. She'd never thought to be in a place like this again.

The door opened, and Simon dashed out as she and Hez approached. His blue eyes widened as he took in her appearance. "You were in an accident and that's why the police brought you home?"

Savannah glanced down at her bloody clothing. She should have stopped to change. This would be a picture in his head he'd never forget. She wet her lips. "I—I don't know how to tell you, Simon. Your mother was in a terrible accident. Sh-she didn't make it." Her voice wobbled, and she bit down on her lip to keep the sobs in.

She opened her arms, but he froze on the sidewalk and stared at her. She waited for him to speak, but he continued to stand with his arms hanging at his sides. The boy had only her and Hez now. Tears welled again, and this time she couldn't stop them. She took two steps and folded him in her arms, but he still said nothing and his arms didn't lift to hug her back.

Finally movement started in the form of trembling that shook him from his shoulders to his knees. "M-Mom."

Hez came alongside them and put his arms around both of them. "We're here, Simon. We won't leave you."

Savannah spoke against the side of his face. "I promised your mom I'd take care of you, and I will. Your uncle Hez and I love you very much, and we'll get through this together somehow." She pressed her lips against his hair and inhaled the aroma of boy.

"Mom," he whispered. The word held a fountain of grief he couldn't release yet.

Savannah's geyser of tears felt unstoppable. Only God could get them through this, and she knew he would. He'd proven his steadfastness when she lost Ella, and she clung to the knowledge that he would help them now.

Hez woke to the aroma of fresh coffee. He lifted his head off Savannah's sofa—and instantly regretted it. He'd fallen asleep with her curled up against him, exhausted from grief. He'd been in an awkward half-sitting position when her ragged breathing finally gave way to soft snores, and he hadn't wanted to wake her by moving. Sleep had taken him a few minutes later, and he'd apparently slept through the entire night without changing position.

He levered himself into a sitting position and then stood, discovering a dozen more cramped muscles in the process. Pins and needles shot through his numb right foot as he staggered into the kitchen, lurching like a zombie from an old horror movie.

Savannah turned toward him as he entered. She gave him a warm smile, but her eyes were red and puffy. "You look like a man who could use some coffee."

She poured him a mug, which he gratefully accepted. "Very astute observation." He took a long sip, savoring the smooth taste and rich smell. "Aah. Captain Davy's?"

"Of course. Sleep well?"

"Yeah." He rubbed his neck. "Waking up was the problem."

"Me too. I dreamed about our wedding, and then I woke up and realized Jess wouldn't be my maid of honor." Tears pooled in her eyes.

He put down his mug and took her in his arms. "I know, babe. Those 'oh, yeah' moments are the worst. They always got me with Ella too. I'd see a butterfly or a puppy and I'd be about to point it out—until I remembered. Just last month, I found a Cheerio under the passenger seat of my car, and it hit me all over again."

"Your car . . ." Her voice dissolved into sobs, and she buried her face in his chest. He kissed the top of her head and held her.

He wasn't going to make the same mistake he made after Ella had died. He and Savannah should have experienced the pain together, talked it through, held each other, taken long walks, packed up Ella's toys together, and so on. Instead, he hid from his guilt and grief by burying himself in work and numbing the agony with booze and pills. The woman in his arms deserved—needed—so much more.

Her breathing became even, and then she suddenly tensed. She looked up at him. "Your car. Were they trying to kill you?"

"Maybe." He released her and picked up his mug. "I talked to Hope last night while you were with Simon. She's not sure who the target was. It might have been me. The bomb was in my car, after all. But I'm not driving, which the killer would have known if I was being watched. I let Jess borrow my car after her tires were slashed, and the killer might have seen her driving it. So she might have been the target all along. Hope thought it might even have been you."

Savannah's eyes widened. "Me? Why would they put a bomb in your car to kill me?"

He took a sip of his now-lukewarm brew. "Because your car was in the president's reserved spot, which is right next to the building and in clear view of a security camera, while I park with the rabble in the staff lot."

Savannah's lips twitched with the ghost of a smile. "That's right. Ellison Abernathy's Cadillac got keyed two years ago, allegedly by a female adjunct professor whose contract wasn't renewed after she rejected his advances. He was furious and insisted that his car be kept safe from 'terrorists and vandals' in the future. So he got a special spot and a new security camera. But that doesn't explain why the killer would think I'd be driving your car."

"Unless the killer realized I wouldn't be driving it and that we probably wouldn't just leave it sitting in the staff lot for three months. There was a good chance you'd eventually drive it over to my condo, where it would be out of the elements."

"I guess that makes sense." A crease appeared between her brows. "Are we safe here?"

He shook his head. "Probably not. Did you notice the police car outside?"

"No." She stepped to the kitchen window and scanned the street. "Has it been there all night?"

"Yep." He finished his mug and poured a fresh one. "Hope sent them. State police, since we still have to worry about the mole in the Pelican Harbor department."

"How long are they going to stay?"

"Hope didn't say, but they can't be our personal security indefinitely. This isn't a permanent solution."

"Should I get a new security system?"

"You could, but there's only so much you can do here." He swept his hand in a wide arc that encompassed her cozy little cottage. "You've got a ground-level stand-alone house with two doors, windows in every room, and outside parking."

"What do you suggest?"

He cleared his throat. "You'd be much safer someplace like, well, my condo. Jane is getting the locks changed as we speak, it already has good security, and your car would be in a locked garage that's hooked into the building security system. Plus, it's on one of the main streets with a regular police presence."

"Are you sure you don't mind us barging into your small space before you're ready? I'll have Simon too. And my dog. It will be a very full condo."

He smiled and pulled her close again. "I'd love it, to be

honest. I've been counting down the days until the wedding anyway. I miss having you around—finding you in the kitchen first thing in the morning, talking over sweet tea at the end of the day, and all the little moments in between. It'll be great to have Simon too. He's a terrific kid, and he gives me an excuse to play my old video games."

She nuzzled against him. "I've missed it too."

CHAPTER 32

STEPPING INTO JESS'S HOUSE STILL ECHOING WITH THE silence of her absence was one of the hardest things Savannah had ever done. Her sister's perfume still lingered in the air, and next to Savannah, Simon teared up and clung to her hand. "You okay?" she asked.

"Yeah."

She and Hez exchanged a concerned glance. How did they help their nephew process all this when it was more than she could take in herself?

When Simon headed toward his room, Hez pulled her into an embrace. "We'll get through this."

She gave a wordless nod into his chest before she swallowed hard and pulled away. "See if you can find anything in her office that might point to the killer."

He pressed a kiss on top of her head. "I'll just be down the hall if you need me. Hope said they aren't treating it as a crime scene for now, but if I find anything, I'll call her. She doesn't want us to remove any potential evidence."

Savannah nodded and waited until his footsteps faded before forcing herself upstairs to check on Simon. Her job today was to go through Jess's bedroom, but the thought of poking through her sister's personal things felt like more than she could bear right now. She needed to adjust to being here first. This had to be so hard for Simon.

She found her nephew sitting on the edge of his bed. He stared blankly at the wall with its pictures of Will Dixon playing football. She entered the room and stopped by his bed. "Hey, buddy. Need some help?"

He didn't respond at first, and it wasn't until she touched his shoulder that he seemed to realize she was there. He shook his head wordlessly.

"I can pack for you."

He stared at his hands and shook his head again. She'd talked to one of the counselors at the college and he'd told her to expect this kind of withdrawn behavior, but Savannah had thought their close relationship would weather the tragedy. Now she realized moving forward would be harder than she'd hoped. She squeezed his shoulder and backed out of the room. He needed to process his grief in his own way.

She went down the stairs and had started toward Jess's bedroom when Hez called her from the office. The delay was more than welcome, and she hurried to join him. The impersonal space in the office let her catch her breath. She found Hez rummaging through a leather bag in Jess's favorite taupe color. "Find something?"

"I think so." He pointed at two passports and a leather wallet beside the bag. "Have a look. She bought fake IDs."

Savannah frowned and opened the top passport. Though the woman in the picture had red hair, it was clearly Jess. "Susan Jones." The other passport was Simon with matching red hair and a fake name of Shaun Jones. "She probably had them done digitally. Simon would have mentioned dyeing his hair for a picture."

"She had the money to get them done right. Look here." He opened the bag wide to show a burner phone, a package of red hair dye, and a gun. "The pistol's loaded and ready to go. This was her escape bag. She clearly knew she was in danger and might need to run quickly."

A chill went down Savannah's back. "Her desire for revenge was so strong. No wonder she'd kept Simon hidden away. Things spiraled out of control, and I don't think she fully understood how things were closing in on her. She thought she was prepared." What must it have been like for Jess to live in constant fear for her life—and her son's life? Savannah wanted to know how this all started. Could there be information in the old journals she'd found?

She glimpsed the shine of something silver in the bottom of the bag and reached inside to lift out a necklace caught in the seam along the back. Her pulse kicked at the heart-shaped locket that dangled from her fingers. "I haven't seen this in years."

"You recognize it?"

"Our mom gave it to her for her fifth birthday. It was Jess's first piece of real jewelry, and she loved it. She didn't take it off for years. It had two pictures of her with Mom." She fumbled with the clasp and opened it. A photo of Savannah and Jess together smiled back at her on the left side and one of Simon was on the right.

Her sister hadn't intended to go anywhere without Savannah and Simon close to her heart.

Hez forced himself through the end of his mandatory—and overdue—online HR training. With a sigh of relief, he took a swig from the mug of lukewarm coffee on his office desk. As a lawyer he understood why institutions required this sort of thing, but that didn't make it any less painful.

Now he could finally make the call he'd been itching to make all morning. He picked up his phone and dialed Hope's number. She answered on the first ring. "Hi, Hez. I was just about to call you."

"Do you have news?"

"Some. Thanks for telling us what you found at Jess Legare's house. We sent in evidence techs, and they processed her home with a focus on her office."

Hez nodded. "Makes sense. Have they found a safe yet?"

"A safe?" Hope's voice sharpened. "No. Did she have one?"

"I'm guessing she did. Her house was burglarized at least once while she was in jail last year."

"True, but wouldn't that have been the place for those fake passports and other items you found in her desk?"

"Yes—unless she didn't think she'd have time to go to a safe and open it if she needed to run."

Hope was silent for a moment. "That couldn't have been an easy way to live, especially with her son."

"No." Hez took a deep breath and blew it out slowly. Jess had made her own choices, but he still pitied her. And he especially pitied Simon. Would the poor kid ever really recover from being orphaned at ten? What would happen when he eventually learned the full truth about his mother?

Hez pushed those unanswerable questions aside and focused on the topic at hand. "Did your techs find anything interesting so far?"

"I hate to say it, but we have pretty clear evidence that she was involved in the artifact-smuggling ring. Her laptop contained images of looted items and PDFs of forged provenance documents. We also found TGU history department letterhead in her printer. Since she's not in the history department, there was only one reason for her to have that."

"She was forging provenance documents." Hez stared out his office window, barely registering the sweeping view of the campus. "So her appearance at the meeting with Savannah wasn't a coincidence. That's not a shock—I've suspected it since I heard she walked into that restaurant in New York, and any doubt vanished after we learned about her other activities. Still, it's not great news. Do you think Jess's murder was tied to the smuggling?"

"It's possible, assuming she was the target. She had relatives in the smuggling ring, but this wouldn't be the first time one family member killed another over a criminal enterprise. Maybe they had a dispute about money. Or maybe they suspected Jess was working with us."

Hez replayed the memory of his last conversation with Jess. Had she been on the brink of switching sides? If so, had her criminal cohorts found out in time to plant a bomb in Hez's Audi? "That's an interesting thought. I—" He heard a noise behind him and turned. Savannah stood in his doorway, face white. She clutched a document in her hand. "I have to go."

As soon as he ended the call, Savannah held out the document to him. Her hand shook. "It's a certified letter from Hornbrook. They're demanding full payment within twenty-four hours."

He took the letter from her and read it, which only took a few seconds. "I'm disgusted, but not surprised. Now that Jess is dead, there's no reason to wait."

Savannah's eyes widened. "Do you think Hornbrook killed her?"

He shrugged. "I have no idea—and neither does Hope. I was just talking to her when you walked in." He decided to hold off on telling her about the new evidence of Jess's involvement in the smuggling. They had more immediate problems. "I'm sure she and her team will get to the bottom of it." He held up the letter. "In the meantime, we need to deal with this."

"How can we?"

"We really only have one option: bankruptcy."

She gasped. "Won't that destroy the university?"

"It might. But it's also the only way to save it. I know that might sound a little crazy."

A little color returned to her cheeks, and she gave him a faint smile. "Maybe a little, but I trust you."

"Thanks. So you authorize me to file a bankruptcy petition on the university's behalf?"

She swallowed hard. "Yes."

CHAPTER 33

THE HITS JUST KEPT COMING.

Savannah stepped into a pool of warm March sunshine on the steps of the administration building and assessed the reporters waiting to interrogate her on the bankruptcy proceedings Hez had filed yesterday. The last thing she wanted today was to talk to the media camping out in the parking lot. Not while she was still reeling from Jess's death. Her sister wasn't even laid to rest yet, and Savannah somehow had to maintain her composure even while being peppered with questions.

A nearby reporter tucked her dark hair behind her ear and thrust her mic toward Savannah. "Is it true Tupelo Grove University has filed for bankruptcy?"

Savannah needed to project an air of confidence and control, so she squared her shoulders and lifted her chin. "Yes, it is, but it's a temporary measure we're taking to ensure TGU is around for a long time. I know this news feels devastating for many of you." She connected gazes with several students and professors she recognized. "Remember this—I'm here for you. The Tupelo Grove board is here for you, and we plan to come out of this stronger and in a better position to have an impact in today's world." It was a lame statement, but she had no real assurances for them.

The crowd grew as she spoke, and she estimated fifty people were gathered in the parking lot now. Knowledge of the impromptu news conference was spreading through the campus, and it was a good thing she could address those affected directly. Maybe she could quell the speculation and give them a little more time to figure things out.

Hez stood close to her left elbow in his gray power suit, and while she was grateful for his support, it might not have come to this if he'd actually read the loan papers. She shot up a quick prayer that he could pull a legal rabbit out of his hat for the university she loved so much. Without a miracle TGU would suffer permanent and irreparable damage. By summer it could be defunct.

The hopeful expressions on the faces around her increased the load on her shoulders. She had no answers, nor did Hez. Not really.

A bearded reporter in his twenties shouldered his way closer to her. "I've been talking to students and faculty all morning. Most of them are terrified they won't be able to graduate when they're so close. Others are fearful their degrees will be worthless. Professors are concerned their jobs and pensions could vanish. What do you want to say to them?"

"I don't believe any of those things to be true. Don't rush to transfer to another school or to apply for other teaching jobs." She swept her hand toward the crowd of students and faculty. "While my family has led TGU, you have made the school what it is, and together we are going to turn this around. These circumstances are temporary. This trial will make us better—stronger."

The man's dark eyes narrowed. "You admit your family has led the school to disaster? What caused the bankruptcy? There was no warning, nothing to prepare any of the students or faculty for this catastrophic news."

She couldn't tell the truth here, not without throwing Hez and Jess under the bus. "I'm working to find out what happened and will fix it."

The female reporter stepped in front of the belligerent male. "Is there any connection between the university's bankruptcy and the CFO's murder?" She barked the question with a predatory gleam in her brown eyes.

Savannah could feel the crowd's interest sharpen. Scandal had a way of heightening everything, and she was helpless to keep Jess out of the spotlight when Savannah herself didn't know who had killed her sister or why. A memory of Jess's face in those final moments surged back, and Savannah struggled to keep the tears at bay. She didn't want to lie, and she couldn't think of a single thing to say.

Hez stepped forward. "The university can't speak to an ongoing police investigation, of course, but I can definitely tell you there's no allegation of wrongdoing by the university." His hand settled on Savannah's shoulder. "I hope all of you will respect the privacy of Ms. Webster and her family as they try to navigate this tremendous loss. Ms. Legare was much loved by the students and faculty as well, and we all are suffering from the overwhelming tragedy."

Savannah envied the way he was so cool under pressure. His DA experience helped him stay in control when besieged like this. Maybe she wouldn't have to answer anything more. The warm press of his fingers on her shoulder calmed her agitation.

When another reporter started to speak, Hez subtly nudged Savannah toward the door. "The university appreciates your interest and your patience. We will keep the media and the public informed on future developments." He steered her toward the entrance to the administration building.

Savannah let out the breath she'd been holding and glanced back as she hurried toward the haven awaiting her inside. Her calm deserted her when she spotted Helen Willard turning away toward the parked vehicles. One of her grandsons steadied her with his hand on her elbow. Though the Willard family matriarch appeared like an arthritic old lady, Savannah suspected Helen wielded more power than any of them knew. Helen had no love for the Legare family, and neither did her grandsons.

What had been Jess's relationship with the Willards? Could they have wanted her dead?

Hez found a package waiting for him in his office when he got back from the impromptu press conference. He groaned when he saw the address label. It was from LeBoeuf & Bingham. He tore it open and pulled out a thick stack of paper. It was a motion for relief from the bankruptcy stay with a tabbed supporting affidavit and various other related filings.

Savannah stuck her head in his door. "I heard you groan. What's up?"

He pointed to the pile on his desk. "Hornbrook's lawyers just filed a motion to lift the bankruptcy stay."

She gave him a blank look. "What does that mean?"

He sighed and leaned back in his chair. "It means they're asking the bankruptcy judge to let them seize all of TGU's assets even though we're in bankruptcy."

Her face went pale. "Can they do that?"

"They can ask. It's up to the judge whether to grant the motion."

"Do you think she'll grant it?"

Hez shrugged. "I haven't read a single word of the motion yet, let alone done any research. I'm not surprised that they filed something like this, just that they did it so fast. I haven't even served the bankruptcy petition on them yet."

"Huh. Are big firms always that fast?"

"Nope. I had hoped we'd have at least a few days, maybe even a couple of weeks." The realization hit him. "They must have figured that we would file bankruptcy, and they were ready for it."

"Oh." Savannah's shoulders sagged. "Can you beat their motion?"

He rubbed his eyes. "I'll need to read it before I can answer that."

"Got it." She gave him a small smile. "I'll take the hint and get out of your hair."

"What's left of it." He grinned and rubbed his head, which he'd trimmed down to a buzz cut so it was all the same length as his surgical site.

He bent his head and turned his focus to Hornbrook's motion. It was well written, organized, clear, and to the point.

Hez went on Westlaw and checked the legal citations in the motion. Those were all accurate. He researched every legal argument he could think of to beat the motion—and hit a brick wall each time. Jess's final words were proving prophetic: it really did look impossible to get out of this loan, even through bankruptcy.

His mind went back to that last meeting with his ex-sister-in-law. She had been as icy as ever until the end—almost. Had there been the hint of a thaw? She had warned him about Hornbrook's surveillance system. She didn't have to do that. And Savannah seemed certain that Jesus came for Jess. Had that been just wishful thinking brought on by stress? Maybe—

His phone buzzed, interrupting his train of thought. The screen showed an incoming call from Martine Dubois. He hesitated for a heartbeat. "Hey, Martine. What's up?"

"Hey, Hez. It's good to hear your voice. I saw the news about you almost being killed in an attack." Genuine concern filled her tone. "How are you?"

"I've got a new scar and a bad haircut, but otherwise I'm fine."

"I'm very glad to hear it. Are you back at work?"

He shifted uneasily in his chair. "Yes. Why do you ask?"

"I also saw that TGU filed bankruptcy. Are you handling that?"

He winced. "Don't tell me you're on the other side."

She gave a musical laugh. "No, no. We're on the same side this time. I have a client who has information related to the bankruptcy. I've been instructed to share that information with Tupelo Grove University's lawyer. Would that be you?"

He leaned forward. "It would indeed. What's the information?"

"My client is very security conscious, so my instructions are to say nothing further by phone. We need to meet in person somewhere we can't be overheard."

He stared into space and thought. This could be legitimate, but it could also be an ambush. If it was an ambush, though, Martine wouldn't be involved. They were friends. More important, she had an excellent sense for self-preservation and she was very good at reading people. If someone ambushed him while they were together, she'd be in danger too.

"Hez?"

"I'm here. Let's meet on the beach down by the boardwalk. The noise from the surf will keep our conversation private." And it was a public place with few spots for an assassin to hide. "How about two o'clock?"

"Perfect." There was a smile in her voice. "I look forward to it."

Hez tensed as he ended the call. Savannah wouldn't like him meeting Martine alone.

CHAPTER 34

SAVANNAH KNELT BESIDE THE BUDDING AZALEAS IN THE
garden outside her office and methodically pulled new weeds.
Another few weeks, and the bushes would explode with blossoms. She dropped the weeds into the bag she'd brought out
before settling on the bench beside Hez. Bees hummed around
them, and if not for her grief, she might have enjoyed the
warm sun on her face. But Jess's death had faded the colors of
life to a dull sepia.

Hez pulled her against his side, and she leaned into his
embrace. The familiar scent of his skin—a sage soap that
blended perfectly with his spicy cologne—made her move
closer. He pressed a kiss on the side of her head, and his
sympathetic presence was enough to lift a few of the gray
clouds in her heart. Her eyes blurred, and she swallowed
down the lump forming in her throat at the thought that Jess
would never see the shrub's white blossoms burst forth from
their buds. Savannah would never hear Jess's voice again and
would never coax another smile from her.

Hez trailed his fingers along the skin of her bare arm, and
his touch brought her out of her thoughts. She tucked her hair
behind her ear and straightened. He'd texted her for a reason,

and she needed to rouse enough from her stupor of pain to help figure out their situation. "So what's your update? Have you come up with a Hail Mary pass for TGU?"

"I don't know yet. I got a call from Martine."

She tensed at the woman's name but managed to control her expression. "She had an idea?"

"She has a client with information on the bankruptcy. He's skittish so he wants to meet privately."

"Privately? What if it's an ambush?"

He fingered his scar. "Her client is wise to be security conscious. He's putting himself in danger by helping us. She says we're on the same team, and I believe her."

Savannah pressed her lips together. "I hope that's true."

"We don't have many options. If we don't find something that will help us, we'll lose the stay motion. Hornbrook will seize TGU, and it will be all over."

All over. This couldn't be the end of the university her family had poured its life into for decades. She exhaled. "Okay, I get it. We have to try." She turned his head toward her so his gaze locked with hers. "Promise me you'll be careful." She gently traced the healing incision on his head. "You can't take another blow to the head, Hez. And I can't b-bear the thought of losing you too."

Her eyes flooded with moisture and she bit her lip, trying to gain control. Hez needed to attend that meeting focused and ready. She couldn't send him off to slay dragons while he was worried about her.

He leaned in for a lingering kiss. "You know I will. It's in a public place, so there's little danger."

She could think of all kinds of danger. A sniper, an attack

out of nowhere. The cunning ways of their enemy had taken a heavy toll, but he didn't want to see it. Jess had been in a public lot, yet they'd managed to set a bomb without detection.

His phone sounded, and he drew it from his pocket. "It's Hope." He answered it and put the phone to his ear for a moment. "Savannah is right here. Let me turn on speakerphone so we can both hear the news." He touched the screen. "Go ahead, Hope, we're both listening."

"Savannah, did you know Jess had a safe in her office?" Hope sounded energized.

"No, she never showed me anything like that."

"It was built into the back of her closet, and we found the key to open it. In addition to a copy of her will, we found several thousand dollars in cash."

"Her will?"

"She left everything to you in trust for Simon and named you as his guardian."

Savannah closed her eyes. She hadn't thought through this kind of thing, but it made sense Jess would want her to care for Simon. But what about Simon's father? Erik Andersen had vanished and the police suspected foul play, but they had never found his body. If anything would make him reappear, it was money. He would move heaven and earth to get the boy if it meant he would be in control of Jess's estate. Savannah knew her sister well enough to be certain she'd left behind a substantial amount of money and investments.

"Are you guys still there?" Hope asked.

"Sorry, yes. Just a little stunned. I would never let him go anywhere else." Savannah wanted to stand and pace, but she didn't think her legs would hold her.

Hez's arm tightened around her. "I'll help you figure it out, babe. I'll get probate opened to get the will processed."

"I've read the will, and everything is in a trust," Hope said. "The house, her personal property, all her investments and cash. She left nothing out."

"That's helpful," Hez said. "The trust will likely be automatic, and Savannah would have become the successor trustee the instant Jess died. Anything in that trust would pass to you, Savannah. That makes one thing easy anyway."

"The crime techs should be done soon, and I'll release all of it to you, Savannah. You can have most of the house's contents immediately. Her phone and laptop are in the process of being imaged and will probably be done by end of day. I'll text you when you can have them."

Savannah sagged against Hez as she realized all she needed to do. Jess's beautiful house would need to be sold. Savannah would have to oversee financial records, investments, bank accounts—everything. But she had a university to save too, and even that task by itself seemed impossible. Simon wasn't a burden but a blessing—but the other things would take more time and focus than she had to spare.

Hez's deep voice rumbled against her ear. "Thanks for everything, Hope."

Savannah straightened. "Yes, thank you, Hope."

"My pleasure."

The call ended, and Hez put his phone away. "There's another probate proceeding I'll start immediately—adoption." He paused. "Do you think Erik Andersen is still alive?"

"I thought about him. The DNA tests on the blood drops found in his home showed that it was his, but that doesn't prove he's dead. I'm so afraid he's going to show up and fight for Simon."

Hez's jaw flexed. "He has to get past me to reach our boy. I'll fight him with everything I've got."

His words bolstered Savannah's courage. He truly loved Simon just like she did. And while Hez was a formidable attorney, would the law see the issue his way?

"Erik is—or at least was—Simon's father," Hez continued. "I've never handled an adoption case, but I know birth parents have strong rights in Alabama. Also, Erik has been denied contact with him for all of his life. A court might see that as unfair. And while we both know he was up to his elbows in the criminal activity involving TGU, he hasn't been convicted of anything."

"And hopefully he won't want to show up and face criminal proceedings."

"Hopefully." Hez tugged at his lower lip for a moment, then shrugged. "Let's not borrow tomorrow's trouble."

Dread curled in Savannah's stomach. Her sister had hidden away a whole other life—her son. What other secrets might be uncovered as they probed deeper into Jess's life? She turned toward Hez. "Let's look at those old journals." She led him inside to her office where she'd stashed them on a high shelf.

He got all three of them down and carried them to where she sat at the desk. "What are we looking for?"

"I need to understand why she did this. I think my great-grandfather, Luc, was gone by the time Jess was born. Let me look at his journal." She reached for the thickest, most well-worn one and opened it. "I know some of the early history, of course.

Joseph Willard founded the university and hired Louis Legare to teach. No one trusted Joseph from the very beginning. They called him a carpetbagger, and he was, even according to Helen Willard. He went to Mexico and came back with the Willard Treasure. A fire started during a burlesque show, and its aftermath turned up unpaid taxes that drove him out of town. My ancestors took over."

"So after founding the college, the Willards felt pushed out and excluded all these years."

She nodded. All the older history wasn't what she was looking for. What corrupted Jess? She flipped through Grandpa Andre's journal. The late 1990s were probably Jess's most formative years. Her finger jabbed an entry. "Listen to this."

> *Pierre is a fine president, though perhaps too focused on prestige projects at the expense of the mundane practicalities of running a university. I wish he would spend a bit more time with his daughters. Since Marie's death he completely shuns young Jess, and while perhaps understandable, it's not her fault. She's a sweet child, desperate for approval and love from him. She came to me on Sunday afternoon and sat by my feet in the rocker on the porch. She asked why Pierre hated her so much. My son had actually shoved her and told her he hated her. What could I say? It's not my place to explain something so complex. I hugged her and assured her of my love, but I could tell it was small comfort. I will have a talk with Pierre about it.*

Tears rolled down Savannah's cheeks as she saw Jess's pain in this short entry. That poor lost little girl. Dad was the one at fault, and he didn't care at all how much damage he'd done.

Hez scanned Pelican Harbor's picturesque boardwalk and waterfront, looking for people who might want to kill him. He leaned against the Bayfront Inn's clapboard exterior. The rambling old building started life as a mansion before being converted into a bed-and-breakfast two decades ago, and its harbor-facing side had convenient nooks between bay windows. Hez stood in one, which partially concealed him while offering a good view of the boardwalk and the beach beyond.

The mid-March sun warmed his face, and a gentle sea breeze carried the sounds of shouting and laughter from a group of swimsuit-clad TGU students playing beach volleyball. A few people strolled the boardwalk or sat at the wrought-iron tables outside Maria's restaurant. A vaguely familiar little old lady with a tiny dog smiled at him. No obvious assassins lurked among the beachgoers.

Martine appeared at the far end of the boardwalk. She wore designer sunglasses, but otherwise she wasn't dressed for the beach. She had on a formfitting cream suit and a navy blouse, and her heels knocked on the weathered wood as she approached.

Hez stepped out when she was about ten yards away. "Good afternoon, Martine."

She flashed a perfect smile. "Ah, there you are. Good to see you, Hez." She took off her sunglasses and her almond-shaped eyes examined his face. "I kinda like the scar and crew cut. They make you look a little dangerous and mysterious."

He ignored her comment and looked past her. "Where's your client?"

"Oh, my client isn't here. They're security conscious, remember?"

"Yes, which is why I'm here." Hez let a hint of annoyance into his voice. "I thought we were meeting on the boardwalk so they could give me information about Hornbrook."

"I have the information, but it'll be just the two of us." She sidled up to him and winked. "I hope that's okay."

His irritation grew. This sort of low-level flirting had been fun when they were unattached law students, but it got on his nerves now. At least Savannah didn't have to deal with it too. "What's the information?"

"Keep your voice down." She glanced around and a frown creased her smooth forehead. "More people are on the boardwalk than I expected."

He followed her gaze. A few people strolled around. None were within earshot right now, but it was true someone could walk past at any moment.

Martine slipped off her heels and put a hand on Hez's lower back, guiding him toward the beach. "Let's walk on the sand. It'll be more private, and I love how it feels when it's warm."

Hez kept his shoes on. "So what do you have for me?" he asked when they had walked a few paces.

"I assume you're familiar with that artifact-smuggling ring the police broke up a couple of weeks ago."

"You might say that. What about it?"

"It started in Mexico and ended in New York, right? The Mexican authorities wrapped up their end and American cops made arrests all the way from the border to the Big Apple. But the trail went cold there. No one was arrested at the retail end of the chain. Strange, don't you think?"

Hez kept a tight rein on his emotions. Was she going to tell him that Jess was the New York end of the smuggling route? Was that her secret information? "Go on."

"Most of the artifact buyers were Hornbrook Finance clients. James Hornbrook personally facilitated a number of sales. He even owns one or two of the smuggled artifacts."

"Seriously?" Hez stopped and stared down at her. "You have proof of this?"

She gave him a coy smile and tucked a strand of blonde hair behind her ear. "Yes."

"Where is it?"

She started walking again, forcing him to keep pace. "I can't give it to you, sorry."

"Why not?"

"The nature of the proof would put my client's identity at risk." She gave him a playful nudge with her elbow. "You're a clever guy. You'll find the evidence on your own. I have faith in you."

He tried to keep the exasperation out of his voice. "Can you at least give me a hint on where to find it? I—"

Martine stumbled against him. "Ow!"

He instinctively put an arm around her waist to steady her. "Are you okay?"

"I stepped on something." She lifted her right foot and

examined the sole. "No blood. It must've been a rock." She tried putting weight on it and winced. "Can you help me back to the boardwalk?"

He didn't have much choice. "Of course."

They turned around and recrossed the beach. She held on to his shoulder for support, and he kept his arm around her. He really hoped no one he or Savannah knew was watching.

They reached the boardwalk. She brushed the sand off her feet and slipped her heels back on. "Thanks. That feels better."

"Do you need help getting back to your car?"

"I'll be fine. Hez, I . . ." She paused and seemed to reconsider what she was about to say. She put on her sunglasses. "Good luck in court."

She turned and walked away without a trace of a limp.

CHAPTER 35

SAVANNAH CLUNG TO HEZ'S HAND AS THEY HEADED FOR the iron stairs to his condo. Her eyes burned, but she couldn't cry. The meeting with the funeral home had left her gutted. Only Hez's presence and her pastor's gentle support had gotten her through picking out Jess's casket and choosing the flowers for the funeral. She'd forgotten a funeral involved so many details, but she'd been in such a haze when Ella died that Hez's parents had handled many of the smaller things. This didn't seem real. How could she say goodbye to her baby sister? And how did she reconcile the way Jess had loved her and Simon with the way she'd betrayed them all?

The aroma of tomato sauce, garlic, and cheese rushed toward them when Hez opened the door. Will Dixon turned from stuffing the remains of pizza in the garbage. His normal smile was missing, and his dark eyes darted from her to Hez. "Simon didn't want to work on his homework, and I didn't want to push him." His Adam's apple bobbed. "Poor kid."

Hez whipped out his wallet and handed over cash. "Thanks for helping us out today, Will. It's going to take time." His worried glance lingered on Savannah. "For all of us."

259

Will stuffed the money in his pocket. "I'm here if he wants to talk. I can't imagine how hard it would be to lose my mom."

Savannah patted his forearm as she passed. "Thank you, Will." She walked into the living room and found Simon in the armchair. Cody snoozed under the chair with his head on Simon's bare left foot. Simon stared at the big-screen TV on the wall with a blank expression.

She approached and touched his shoulder, but he didn't move. "Hey, buddy. Looks like Will fed you pizza." The two pieces of pepperoni pizza on his plate on the coffee table were untouched.

He didn't shift his gaze from the screen. "Uh-huh."

How did Savannah help guide him through his grief when she didn't know how to navigate her own? So far she'd dealt with it by keeping busy, which meant she hadn't really faced it. Her grief was a tsunami waiting to engulf her, and she saw that same expression of impending doom in Simon's blue eyes. Even picking out a casket had been surreal, like some kind of nightmare that refused to be pushed away by the sunrise.

Hez joined her and took her hand. The strength of his grip reminded her she didn't have to do this alone. The two of them went to the leather sofa, and Savannah sagged against Hez. Was this even the right time to tell Simon what the future held? If only he would cry or scream. Anything that would break the blankness he'd wrapped around himself.

Hez cleared his throat, and she tensed. He reached for the remote and clicked off the TV. Simon blinked, but that was his only response. No objection, no question about why they'd turned off the show. Hez put the remote back on the table. "Um, Simon, there's something we wanted to talk to you about."

The boy's stare cleared just a bit, and he blinked again. "Okay."

Savannah's thoughts were a jumble, but she rushed to spill the important things. "You still have us, Simon. Your mom left everything to me to take care of you. We can never replace your mom." Her voice fell to a hoarse whisper. "We love you very much, and we are still your family too."

Hez leaned forward. "We both loved you from the first minute we saw you, buddy. We'll be here for you every step of the way, and that's a promise. I've already started the paperwork for adopting you so we're officially a family. Like Aunt Savannah said—"

Simon leaped to his feet and his rage eddied out in a wave that was almost visible. Cody whined and ducked deeper under the chair. "I don't want new parents! I want my mom, not anyone else. No one can replace her—not anyone! You should have talked to me first. How could you think I'd want to call anyone else Mom?" His gaze speared Hez. "Or Dad. It was me and Mom. We were our own family. It might not have looked like what other kids had, but it was good." Tears gathered on his lashes and rolled down his face. He stomped to the balcony door and slid it open to go out and stare toward Bon Secour Bay.

The tears Savannah thought she'd cried out already formed in her eyes too, and she rushed after him. "Simon, we only want what's best for you." She touched his arm and he jerked away.

His face was red and he balled his fists at his sides. "My mom is what was best for me, but no one can give me that." He ran past her back into the house and dropped to his knees by the chair.

COLLEEN COBLE AND RICK ACKER

She struggled to breathe past the monstrous lump in her throat as she watched him coax Cody out from under the chair. The dog crawled onto his lap, and Simon hugged him to his chest and buried his wet face in Cody's fur.

Marley, tail tucked between his legs, eased out onto the balcony. "Hey, boy," she said in a soft voice. He whined and nuzzled her hand.

Hez followed the dog out onto the balcony and folded her into an embrace. He said nothing, but his comforting arms were enough. "I thought maybe it would reassure him to know his mom made plans," she said against his chest. "But it was all wrong."

"It's going to take time, babe. He knows we love him. That's got to be reassuring on some level. It's a lot to take in. For all of us."

She wanted to ask about the meeting with Martine, but it felt very inconsequential right now with the grief raging through them all. Even losing TGU would not come close to this level of despair. She'd give everything she owned to hear her sister's voice one more time.

A gigantic form blocked the light from the hallway. Hez looked up from his worn plywood desk in the Justice Chamber, and his spirits lifted at the sight of his friend's grin. He rose and stuck out his hand. "Jimmy! Thanks for stopping by."

"Glad to. I had a hearing in Mobile, and I've been meaning to check out your new digs. So the timing of your call was perfect." Jimmy enveloped Hez's hand in one of his as he looked around. "You chose *this* over an office at Little & Associates?"

"This place keeps me humble. And it has the advantage of being a lot closer to Savannah."

A basso chuckle rumbled in Jimmy's chest. "Well, maybe so." His gaze lit on the plaque over Hez's desk. "*'Let justice roll on like a river, righteousness like a never-failing stream!'* I like it. But you've run into a beaver dam, haven't you?"

Hez nodded. "I'm afraid so. Any suggestions on how to get rid of it?"

"Grandpa used dynamite when beavers dammed up the stream on his place."

"Got any handy?"

"We'll see. I'll need to know more about the case."

Hez handed him a copy of Hornbrook's motion and the supporting documents. "Want some coffee?"

Jimmy eyed the thick stack of paper. "Yes. And make it strong and black." He took off the jacket of his two-thousand-dollar suit, hung it on a chair, and sat at the scarred old table.

Hez poured him a mug. "You're in luck. I just brewed a pot of dark roast."

Hez explained the case and answered questions as Jimmy flipped through motion papers and the loan documents. He absently rubbed his kinky black hair as he read. Toni arrived halfway through the conversation and took a seat at the table. She was five-seven or five-eight, but she looked like a little girl next to Jimmy.

When Hez finished, Jimmy leaned back and crossed his arms. "It seems that you, my friend, are well and truly stuck."

Toni's brow furrowed. "What about the tip Professor Webster

got concerning Hornbrook's connection to the smuggling? Won't that help?"

"Nope." Jimmy shook his head. "Hearsay."

Toni looked confused. "Hearsay? Sorry, I don't take Evidence until next year."

Hez poured himself coffee. "Hearsay is an out-of-court statement introduced to prove the truth of the matter asserted. It's generally inadmissible because the person who made the statement wasn't under oath and isn't available to be cross-examined. So my friend's statements to me aren't evidence the judge can consider. In fact, now that I think about it, this is *double* hearsay because she was repeating something someone else told her—also out of court and not subject to cross-examination. We don't even know who that person is."

"All sadly true," Jimmy said. "How about emergency discovery to Hornbrook to see if you can find some backup for these claims? The right judge might cut you some slack and continue the hearing to give you time to do a little digging. Who are you in front of?"

"Alice Sticklesby."

Jimmy rolled his eyes. "Ouch. She runs a very tight ship. Is she the one who made a lawyer stand in the corner for talking in the gallery?"

"That's her." Hez took a swig of his coffee. "I'm not counting on her cutting me any slack."

Jimmy drained his mug and Hez held out the carafe. Jimmy extended his mug, which Hez filled. "Thanks, Hez. You always have good coffee." He took a sip of the fresh brew. "You know, if Martine's client is right, all the strands of the spiderweb lead back to Hornbrook. The smuggling, the predatory loan, every-thing."

Toni leaned forward. "I've been thinking the same thing. The police raid in New York failed, but that must be because he somehow figured out it was coming."

Hez hadn't revealed Jess's true role—and he didn't want to—so he changed the subject slightly. "Are you saying he was behind the bomb, Jimmy?"

"I'm saying you'd best be very, very careful if you're going after him."

Hez turned, revealing the holster on his hip. "You know what a cautious fellow I am."

Jimmy smiled at the reference to *Raiders of the Lost Ark*, which they'd watched multiple times together. "That's a good first step. But a gun on your hip won't protect against another bomb in your car."

"I Uber now."

"You know what I mean. I think this guy plays for keeps. You need your eyes wide open."

Toni sat up straight. "Speaking of car bombs, I wonder if the bomb that killed Jess is tied to the failed New York police raid. She was the only known contact between Hornbrook and TGU, right? What if she came across evidence connecting him to the smuggling, and she was killed to keep her from sharing it?"

Jimmy drummed his fingers on the table for a moment. "That would make sense, but how do we prove it?"

An idea flashed into Hez's head. "I've got to make a couple of calls, but I think I just might be able to find us some dynamite."

Savannah had often passed Horton Funeral Home on the outskirts of Pelican Harbor, but this was the first time she'd been here. Multiple balconies with black railings accented the painted white brick with French flair. It was beautiful and terrifying.

A boulder lodged in her throat as she stared at the double entry doors. At least Jess would have a closed casket funeral, and Savannah wouldn't have to stare down into her baby sister's face. The funeral home had a time for family set aside for the first hour of visitation, but she, Hez, and Simon were the only ones here. Hez's aunt Jenna and cousin Blake planned to come a little later. But that was all. Such a tragic ending to Jess's bright future.

She turned off the engine, and Hez took her hand. "I know it's hard, babe. Do you need a minute?"

She glanced at the rearview mirror to take a peek at how Simon was faring. She could only see the top of his head as he stared down at his phone. His hand moved in a swirling motion, so she knew he was catching a Pokémon in his game. He probably didn't want to face the day any more than she did.

She shook her head. "Let's go on in. I want Simon to have some time to process it before people start to arrive." She opened her car door. "Time to go, Simon. Leave your phone in the car."

He gave a small nod, and she caught a glimpse of his face—misery etched in every pore of his expression. If only she could spare him this pain. She walked around to his side of the car. Hez got out and opened the door for the boy, and Simon clambered out in his new khaki slacks, white shirt, and navy blazer.

She took his hand. "You look very handsome."

His fingers closed around hers in a tight grip. "Thanks." His voice was barely audible, and his gaze stayed on the asphalt.

He let her keep his hand as they walked to the entry. A suited employee greeted them and opened the door. "Your sister is in the room on the right."

She nodded and took Hez's arm to steady her weak knees as they entered the big room. Faint music played from speakers around the space, and she recognized the tune of "Amazing Grace."

She pressed her trembling lips together when she spotted the casket. At Simon's almost inaudible gasp, she tightened her grip on his hand. "We'll get through this," she murmured to him. "Remember, your mom isn't in that casket." Hoping it would comfort him as much as it did her, Savannah had told him about Jess's last moments.

He nodded and yanked his gaze away. He pulled his hand free and started for the back row of chairs. Savannah let him go. They would have to move to the front row for the funeral, but he needed some alone time right now. No amount of words on her part could help him.

She caught a movement from the corner of her eye and turned to see four people enter. Nora was flanked by Helen Willard on one side and Michael Willard on the other. A younger woman with a curly brown bob and glasses trailed them. They headed toward the casket draped with flowers.

Hez nudged her. "What are they doing here so early?" he whispered.

The realization nearly made her buckle. "Th-they're family. Jess was a Willard at heart. They fostered that desire for revenge in her."

Nora turned from the casket and started for Savannah. Moisture glistened behind her glasses, and her lips trembled when Savannah stepped out to meet her. "I-I'm so sorry, Savannah. I'm doubly sorry my last words were hurtful. I started to call you several times, but it hurt too much, especially since I knew you'd probably be testifying against my family in the smuggling case. I should have done it anyway. I had no idea Jess was involved."

Savannah gaped. "Wait, what? Jess was involved in the smuggling operation?" Everything clicked into place. "That's why she was at the restaurant? She was supposed to hand off the artifact?"

Nora's brown eyes widened behind her glasses. "You didn't know? It was in the prosecution disclosure to my uncle's and cousins' legal team. I thought for sure Hope talked to Hez about it."

Savannah's jaw tightened. "He didn't tell me." She glanced around for him and found him sitting beside Simon with his hand on the boy's back. Why had he kept something so important from her? Did she even know her sister at all? Wasn't it enough that she'd tried to destroy TGU?

Nora touched her hand. "I'm sorry this is a shock, Savannah. Especially today of all days."

"It's all right. Hez should have told me." And a chat with him needed to happen as soon as this awful funeral was over. "I should go talk to Helen at least."

"Um, I'm not sure Mimi will talk to you. She's lost a lot the past few weeks, and she . . . well, she's processing some anger. More than some, to be honest. Michael too. They were both really proud of Jess, and they loved her very much." Nora cleared her throat. "They were hoping Jess would bring Simon to meet them, but she must not have gotten a chance."

Savannah knew Jess had slipped off sometimes while they were growing up to meet with her Willard relatives, but she never realized they were close. "Why am I learning all this about Jess now that she's dead? It's like Jess had a whole other life I knew nothing about. I—I can't wrap my head around all of it." She took a step back. She wasn't going to pull Simon into this, but she knew what she needed to do. "If Helen and Michael loved Jess that much, the least I can do is say hello."

"I'll come with you. I'd like to introduce you to my niece, Tammy."

Savannah nodded and pinned on a neutral expression as they approached the Willards, who had wandered into the adjoining room to watch the digital pictures on the screen. When she entered with Nora, Helen's expression soured. She spoke to Michael, whose face hardened. The younger woman, Tammy, rose from the seat where she'd been watching the picture presentation.

Nora spoke first. "Mimi, I'm sure you know Savannah, Jess's sister."

The reminder of the relationship didn't soften the older woman's hard brown eyes. "I notice you didn't have any pictures of Jess with her true family. Typical of the Legare arrogance."

The attack dried up Savannah's welcome, and she struggled to think of something to say to disarm the woman's hostility. She couldn't engage in an argument here in the funeral home. It would be too disrespectful of her sister. "I didn't find any pictures or I would have included them, Mrs. Willard. I'm sorry."

"You could have picked up the phone and called me," Michael put in. "She was my daughter, Savannah, not just your sister. She was a granddaughter, an aunt, a cousin. She had more relatives on our side than on yours, and she loved being with us." He fumbled out a picture from his shirt pocket and thrust it at her.

Her hand trembled as she took it. Surrounded by a dozen other people, Jess's smiling face turned toward the camera with a joyous expression Savannah hadn't seen in years. She stood next to Little Joe, whose shoulder didn't yet have that ugly Punisher tattoo. Savannah handed it back. "I'm so sorry. I didn't know."

"And I'd like to meet my *grandson*."

"We'll arrange that later, Michael, but not today. He's already reeling." And so was she. She turned and fled from their accusing stares. The bathroom could be her only haven now. She couldn't talk to Hez right now either, not when he'd kept important information from her. She locked the bathroom door behind her and buried her face in her hands.

CHAPTER 36

HEZ TOOK A DEEP BREATH AND CLICKED SUBMIT. THE BRIEF he just e-filed could decide the university's fate. He'd done his best, but would it be good enough?

He pulled up the brief and read it for the dozenth time—and of course he found a typo he'd somehow missed despite three rounds of proofreading. He sighed and closed his laptop.

Cody scratched at the door and yipped. Hez had shut his dog out of his home office—now doubling as Simon's bedroom— two hours ago because Cody insisted on being a lapdog while Hez was trying to focus on the brief during the precious hours while Simon was in school. "Okay, okay." Hez got up and walked to the door. "You've been patient—or as patient as you get anyway."

He opened the door and Cody started bouncing on his improbably springy little legs, crooked tail whipping the air. He settled down as Hez bent over and scratched those over-sized ears. "Hey, goblin! Miss me? Where'd you get those Great Dane ears, huh? Steal them from an elephant? And what about the tail—did you find that in a landfill? I don't even want to know where the brain came from."

Cody grinned and rolled over to present his belly for a rub.

Hez complied. "You're weird, but you're the best dog in the world. Don't tell Marley I said that."

Cody looked to his left and scrambled to his feet. Hez turned the same way and saw Savannah and Marley emerging from the main bedroom. Neither of them looked happy.

Hez straightened. "Hi, babe. What's up?"

"Are you still working on the brief? I don't want to distract you if you need to focus on it."

"I just filed it. Why?"

"Nora told me there's proof Jess was involved in the smuggling. Did you know about that?"

He thought for a moment. "Oh, yeah. Hope told me about that a couple of days ago. There were forged provenance documents on Jess's computer and history department letterhead in her printer."

Storm clouds gathered in Savannah's eyes. "Why didn't you say anything? Why did the Willards' lawyers find out about this before me?"

He was a little confused. "I didn't think it was a big deal. We already knew about Jess, right?"

Anger lines formed around her mouth. "I didn't know about this! I was devastated when I found out—especially since I was at her funeral."

"I'm sorry, but I figured you could fill in the blanks too—especially after her other betrayals."

Color crept into Savannah's cheeks and her voice shook a little as she spoke, but he could tell she was making an effort to control herself. "I gave her the benefit of the doubt. I don't always assume the worst about her."

He bristled at the accusation in her tone. Did she really think he should have given Jess the benefit of the doubt too? Her blind spot where her sister was concerned had landed them in this mess. "And we know how that turned out, don't we?" His words came out harsher than he intended.

Savannah turned white, and for an instant he thought she was going to lash out. Instead, her eyes filled and tears spilled down her cheeks. "She was my sister. I loved her."

Hez felt like a jerk. Of course Savannah loved Jess and couldn't be coldly rational about her, especially while she was still reeling from Jess's murder. He shouldn't have assumed that Savannah would connect the dots about Jess's involvement in the smuggling—and having Nora do it for her at the funeral must have been a slap in the face.

"I apologize for not telling you about the evidence against Jess." He stepped forward and took Savannah in his arms. "You were an incredible sister. I know this is hard, and I'm sorry for making it harder." He rested his head on top of her hair and held her close, hoping to heal some of the pain she was feeling.

She buried her face in his chest and clung to him as sobs shook her. All the love in the world couldn't hold back her torrent of grief.

Savannah's eyes burned from fatigue and grief as she approached her office door. Her father had been no comfort at the funeral. He showed up at the last minute and hadn't gone to the interment, claiming he had work to do. When he left she'd breathed a sigh of relief that she didn't have to deal with him. She wanted to focus her attention on Simon, who was as pale as a wraith and just as silent. He hadn't been able to focus in school yesterday, and the principal suggested he take today off. Savannah had left him sitting in the library by a window, watching Boo Radley glide through the turgid water of Tupelo Pond.

She greeted her assistant's sympathetic "Good morning" with a watery smile. "Do we have a lot on the schedule?"

"Not a busy morning, Ms. Webster."

Savannah nodded and went into her office. The click of the door shutting behind her steadied her resolve to do what she could for TGU. A small bag was in the middle of her desk beside a hot peppermint mocha. She picked up the bag to read the tag. *Here's a happy to tell you I love you. Nora.* The Deep South term for "gift" was usually something personal meant to bring happiness to the recipient, and Savannah smiled at her friend's thoughtfulness. The funeral had at least cleared the air and mended their friendship.

She settled in her chair and untied the pink ribbon before she lifted out a chocolate eclair and a silver bracelet. The bracelet's construction of small round beads and longer pieces puzzled her until she read the note in Nora's bold writing.

The bracelet spells out "best friend" in Morse code. Anytime you need me, I'll be by your side. I'm sorry I let other things come between us. I brought an eclair instead of a beignet to save you from a powdered sugar apocalypse on your blouse because I love you.

Savannah sniffled and swallowed past the thickness in her throat. Nora's friendship was something she never wanted to run the risk of losing again. She fastened the bracelet around her wrist and took a sip of the peppermint mocha before reading her morning reports. Her happy feelings vanished as the bad news began to pour in.

Almost a quarter of the incoming class had withdrawn and asked for their deposits back. She couldn't return their money because the university was in bankruptcy and funds were locked. Even Jane had called asking if she should transfer Will to Ole Miss, something he didn't want to do. Ed was scoping out places to go too. He'd asked Hez for a letter of recommendation for a potential employer yesterday. One of the incoming students was already threatening to start a class action lawsuit, and the student's father was a well-known attorney. Hundreds of students had already applied to transfer. She'd also heard most of the top faculty had begun circulating their résumés—and who could blame them? They all needed paychecks.

She rubbed her forehead. The situation had seemed overwhelming before this terrible list.

The door burst open, and Simon rushed in with a smile she hadn't seen in days. "Aunt Savannah, Boo Radley has a girlfriend! The students are calling her Pika. Get it? Together their names sound like peekaboo." He reached her desk and held out his phone. "I took pictures."

Her heart warmed as she scrolled through his pictures of the two gators bumped up against each other. He'd taken a video, and when it played, she heard Boo Radley bellowing his mating call while he slapped the water. She handed back Simon's phone. "I love these, Simon! Boo isn't alone any longer. Maybe he'll quit taunting Marley."

"Maybe. I'm going to go take more pictures."

She smiled as she watched him race back the way he'd

come, slamming the door behind him. At least something had momentarily lifted him out of his funk. She reached for her keyboard and mouse to check social media posts. Students would be all over the gator courtship. She pulled up the TGU account and chuckled at another cute picture of Pika and Boo.

She scanned the entries and spotted her name. There were dozens of ugly posts about her. Those who were trying to be kind said she was in over her head, which she knew to be true. But nasty posts far outweighed the nicer ones. Several accused her of being corrupt or criminally incompetent. One of the posts said she should be arrested, and it had over a thousand likes.

Maybe it was true. She'd stepped into a job she knew little about during the most crucial time in the university's history. What had she been thinking?

Her door flew open, and her father stepped into view without a warning from her assistant. He stopped in front of her desk and glared at her. "I've only delayed this until after your sister's funeral, but I can't wait any longer. This bankruptcy completely blindsided the board. We have serious concerns about letting you continue as president and are thinking about replacing you." He pointed his finger at her. "You've put the university in grave peril, Savannah. I'm very disappointed in you personally as well. My trust payments have plummeted, thanks to Hez and Jess's spurious claims, and now they've stopped altogether. That's completely unacceptable. I'm your *father*. I thought you'd look out for me." He glared at her when she didn't answer. "What do you have to say for yourself?"

She sank against the chair's back. He wanted her to blame all this on Jess, but she couldn't. Shouldn't she have known her sister had something planned? Shouldn't they all have seen this coming? This was all Savannah's fault because she'd allowed her love for Jess to blind her.

When she didn't answer, her father said, "The board is meeting on Monday to decide on a course of action." Then he wheeled on his black leather shoes and stomped out the door.

Savannah buried her face in her hands. She'd failed everyone—Jess most of all. If only Savannah had realized the depth of her sister's hatred. Not one of her decisions had been right since she first brought her desk into this grand room. Maybe she should resign without waiting to be fired. The social media haters had the same opinion as her father. Maybe an experienced crisis manager could save the university.

She lifted her head and turned to look out the window at the azaleas blooming in her garden. The problem was her father and the board wouldn't pick a good manager. They wanted their interests protected and would do whatever they could to ensure that happened. Her father wanted to keep his precious trust-fund dollars flowing into his pocket. None of them cared about TGU and its students and faculty.

What was she going to do? She closed her eyes and prayed for guidance, but the only response was a roar from Boo Radley.

CHAPTER 37

HEZ HOPED SAVANNAH'S DAY WAS GOING BETTER THAN HIS, but he doubted it. Missing that clause in the contract had added to the stress she faced on every side, and it seemed he couldn't fix it now. He'd spent the whole morning and part of the afternoon trying to come up with a coherent strategy for oral argument tomorrow. He'd failed. In the past few days he had collected nuggets of useful evidence, but forging them into a winning case wasn't easy. He spun slowly in his chair, surveying the documents spread out on the floor of his home office. All the puzzle pieces were here, but how did they fit together?

A pulsing ache radiated from his left temple, reminding him that his head hadn't fully healed. Could that be hurting his analytical abilities? Would he even know if it was? And what if he never fully recovered? Craniotomy patients often didn't get back to 100 percent of their preoperative functioning. What would it be like to be stuck at 90 percent forever? Could he still practice law? Would he even want to, knowing that he could miss something crucial at any time—just like he missed the trap in the Hornbrook loan documents?

The front door rattled. He jumped to his feet, holding on

to the back of his chair to steady himself against the head rush.

"I'm home," Simon called.

Oh, right. Hez looked at his watch: 3:40 p.m. Of course Simon was home. He walked out to greet his nephew. "Hey, bud. How was your day at TGU?"

"Fine." Simon dropped his backpack on the sofa without making eye contact with Hez. Then he bent over to pet Cody, who had materialized at Simon's feet and started pawing at his shins. Marley watched with half-closed eyes from a pool of sunlight. His tail thumped the floor, but the rest of him stayed motionless.

The dogs gave Hez an idea. "You know, Cody and Marley haven't been out in a while, and neither have I. Want to take them for a walk? We can pick up beignets downstairs if you like."

The mention of the sugary treats got Simon's attention. "Sure! I'm starved!"

"I'm always starved for beignets." Hez clipped leashes on collars. "Make sure to keep yours out of dog range."

Simon didn't need to be told which dog. He gave Cody a stern look. "I still haven't forgiven you for that slice of pizza. Or the cheeseburger."

Cody grinned and wagged his tail, clearly excited to hear his name in proximity to so many food words.

They headed down the iron stairs, the dogs' nails sounding like gravel poured on sheet metal. Mouth watering at the aroma of frying dough, Hez bought beignets from Petit Charms' takeout window and handed one to Simon, who held both leashes while his uncle paid for the food. He reached for his dog's leash. "Want me to take Cody?"

Simon handed over Marley's leash. "That's okay. I like taking Cody."

Hez slipped the leash over his wrist as they headed toward the beach. A balmy salt breeze greeted them. "They're both great dogs, but Cody is special."

Simon gave a rare smile. "Aunt Savannah says he's one of a kind."

"He definitely is, but that's not quite what I meant. He helped me get through some really tough times." Hez took a bite of his beignet, and a dusting of powdered sugar drifted onto his shirt. "We helped each other."

Simon looked up at him. "What happened?"

"You know that we had a daughter named Ella who died in September three and a half years ago, right?"

Simon nodded.

"It was my fault. I should have been watching her, but I got distracted. And there was nothing I could do to bring her back." Hez took a deep breath to steady himself as the memories came rushing at him. "I went into a dark place for a long time. I hid in my work and . . . other things. I hid from everyone who tried to help me. I even hid from Aunt Savannah, who I love with all my heart. I was all alone."

"Is that when you got Cody?"

Hez nodded. "I needed a friend, and he needed a home. It was hard for him—losing his old family and home and having to come live with me. None of it was Cody's choice and he didn't understand any of it. He was angry a lot, especially at first."

Simon squatted and gave Cody a hug. "Poor guy."

Hez patted Marley's side so he wouldn't feel left out. "Cody mostly hid under the sofa when I brought him home. After a few days, he decided my apartment was safe and he liked it there. Then he got very clingy and didn't want to be more than a few feet from me. He even got upset when I wouldn't let him follow me into the bathroom. I think he was afraid I'd abandon him like his first family did. It was a little rough on both of us."

Simon gave Cody a final rub and straightened. "I'm glad you didn't take him back."

"Me too. It took us a while to get used to living together, and it wasn't always smooth sailing—like the time he destroyed my most expensive shoes because I was ignoring him. But I love him and he loves me and we're happy now. I wouldn't give him up for anything."

Simon held him with those piercing, intelligent blue eyes. "Not for anything? No matter what happened?"

"Of course not. He's family—even when he steals food."

Simon looked down and snatched his beignet away just in time. "No, Cody!"

Cody, who had been stalking Simon's treat while the boy was distracted, huffed in disappointment.

They walked in silence while they finished eating. The breeze soughed in the seagrass. Simon dropped the last crumbs of his beignet for Cody, who grinned and gobbled them. "I'm glad you adopted him. I'll bet he is too." His gaze met Hez's for the first time since Jess died.

Hez had been quiet all evening, and as they sat on the condo balcony watching the pinpricks of boat lights out on Bon Secour Bay, Savannah sensed his worry in the line of his back and the set of his mouth. Tomorrow would determine TGU's future, but doubt of the outcome circled around them like a murder of crows.

She took a sip of sweet tea and put the glass on the table beside her phone. "Dad told me the board is thinking about replacing me, Hez. I think they're right to do it. I have no idea how to save TGU. I should have known better than to take on something so above my abilities."

He reached over and took her hand. "And who will they put in your place? One of your dad's cronies to milk the last of what life is left in the university? You care, Savannah. You're the only hope TGU has. It's why you took the job in the first place. I was so proud of you when you said you had to try. And you've done that with all your strength."

A boat horn blared out on the water, and the forlorn sound reverberated in her chest and intensified her sense of failure. "And I couldn't save it."

"The only mistake you made was putting too much faith in me and Jess. We're the ones who let you down." His voice went hoarse. "Jess's web of deceit and revenge was nearly perfect, and I-I'm damaged. Even after working all day, I'm not sure if I missed something that could save the university." He rubbed his head. "I don't know if I'll ever be the same man. I shouldn't have missed that clause."

She'd never seen him so uncertain of his abilities. He was right—he'd been operating at less than full capacity after the brain injury. This wasn't his fault or her fault. Evil won a battle now and then.

She rose and settled on his lap and cupped his face in her hands. "Putting my faith in you is never a mistake. If we lose TGU, I know God still has a purpose and a plan. The war isn't over as long as we're still breathing."

She kissed him, and the tension eased out of his shoulders as he pulled her closer. She wound her arms around his neck and felt the pulse in his neck quicken to match her own. Neither of them could wait until they were finally married. She sank deeper into his embrace until a sharp report from somewhere had them both on their feet. The glass in the sliding door behind them shattered, and she recoiled at the sound.

"Get down!" Hez bore her down on the balcony floor and covered her with his body.

His breath was raspy in her ear, and she struggled to get up when another gunshot rang out and someone down on the street screamed. Other voices shouted to take cover. An engine revved and tires squealed below them. She turned her head to peer between the iron railing, but it was dark and the angle was off.

She tried to get up. "I have to get to Simon!"

Hez held her on the floor as he reached up and grabbed her phone off the table to hand it to her. "Call 911. I'll check on Simon, but I'm sure he's fine. The office is on the back side of the condo."

The weight of Hez's body moved off her, and he helped her to her feet and propelled her down the hall to the bathroom. "Call the police and I'll be right back with Simon. We'll stay here until the police arrive. There are no windows, so we should be safe."

She perched on the edge of the tub and typed in 911 with a shaking hand. She reported the shooting incident and tried to calm her racing heart. The distant sound of sirens blared, and the sound of Simon's sleepy voice behind the closed door reassured her he was okay.

Who could have shot at them? Hornbrook was about to get everything he wanted, so why bother with something that could land him in jail?

CHAPTER 38

ADRENALINE, CAFFEINE, AND FATIGUE MINGLED IN HEZ'S
blood as he sat in the courtroom, waiting for the hearing on
Hornbrook's motion to start. The police and evidence techs
had been in his condo until 2:00 a.m., taking statements, digging bullets out of the living room ceiling, and so on. They
stationed a squad car on the street for the rest of the night, but
no one in the condo could sleep. One of the officers, a young
cop named Jackson Brown, had speculated that the shots had
been intended to knock Hez off his game before the hearing.
Hez hoped the shooter had failed.

As if sensing his thoughts, Savannah reached over and
squeezed his hand. She sat next to him at the counsel table,
and he appreciated her supportive presence. "You'll do great."
She kept her voice down so the opposing lawyers at the table
on the other side of the lectern couldn't hear her.

The Honorable Alice Sticklesby's courtroom reflected her
no-nonsense personality. The two counsel tables each had
fresh copies of the judge's standing order in the exact center
of the tabletop—and no water pitcher or cups, which were
customary in most courtrooms. A lawyer had once spilled in
her courtroom, and the pitchers vanished the next morning.

A piece of tape on the utilitarian gray carpet showed exactly how far lawyers could move from the lectern without asking permission. There was a place for everything, and everything was in its place. Including attorneys.

At precisely nine o'clock, Judge Sticklesby walked through the door behind the bench. She was a tall, very fit woman of about sixty who had been a scholarship volleyball player at Auburn. Her stark black robe was, of course, freshly pressed and spotless.

"All rise," the clerk intoned. Hez got to his feet, and so did the Hornbrook attorneys at the other counsel table. There were three of them, and they were all flying back to New York immediately after today's hearing, judging from the roller bags lined up behind them. "The Bankruptcy Court for the Southern District of Alabama is now in session, the Honorable Alice Sticklesby presiding. Calling the matter of In re Tupelo Grove University, motion for relief from automatic stay. Counsel, state your names for the record."

Hez cleared his throat. "Hezekiah Webster on behalf of the debtor, Tupelo Grove University. I have with me the university president, Savannah Webster."

"Allen Boswell on behalf of movant, Hornbrook Finance, LLC," said the oldest Hornbrook lawyer, a tall silver-haired man in a navy suit. "With me are my colleagues Robert Greenwood and Judith Smith."

Hez glanced back at the courtroom gallery. Empty. The other side had only sent lawyers—no one from Hornbrook Finance had bothered to come. They must view the hearing's outcome as a foregone conclusion.

Judge Sticklesby frowned at Boswell. "Have you read my standing order, Mr. Boswell?"

"No, Your Honor." Boswell gestured to the bags behind them. "We are only in town for this hearing, and we haven't had a chance to review your order. My apologies."

The judge tapped a nail on the polished wood of the bench, making rhythmic clicks. "The order is online and specifies that counsel may not bring any items past the bar except briefcases. Please move those bags into the gallery."

Hez repressed a smile. The other side's lawyers must have been glad they didn't have a client representative watching the hearing.

"Yes, Your Honor." Boswell gave a curt nod to the young woman he'd identified as Judith Smith. She was already on her feet and scrambling to move the offending luggage, a panicked look on her face.

Hez felt a little sorry for Smith as she struggled with the three bags. She was the junior attorney on Team Hornbrook, so it probably had been her job to be aware of things like Sticklesby's standing order. He opened the gate to the gallery for her and gave her a friendly smile. She nodded her thanks as she passed.

"All right, let's get down to business. I've read the papers, so no need to repeat anything that's in your briefs." Judge Sticklesby nodded to Boswell. "It's your motion, Counsel. Any argument?"

Boswell got to his feet and stepped to the lectern. "Not much beyond what's in the briefs, Your Honor. This is a very simple motion. My client is the sole secured creditor and has a right to immediate possession of all the debtor's assets."

The judge leaned forward. "But if I allow your client to exercise that right, Tupelo Grove University will effectively cease to function, right?"

"Yes, Your Honor, but that is precisely what the law provides in this case. As set out in our papers, recent events made our client understandably concerned about the university's financial future. The shocking murder of the CFO with whom my client negotiated, the exposure of a massive artifact-smuggling scheme that—"

"As I said, I've read the papers," Judge Sticklesby interjected. "You're telling me why your client may have the right to seize the university's assets at some point. But your motion asks me to let Hornbrook seize those assets right now—before the university has a chance to propose a reorganization plan. Why should I do that?"

Boswell's grip on the lectern tightened slightly as the judge pressed him, but he kept his voice smooth. "Because those assets are already insufficient to satisfy Hornbrook's secured claims, and they're decreasing in value every day, Your Honor. TGU's trademarks are worth less than they were a month ago, and they'll be worth still less a month from now. The university's bank accounts will be drained to pay staff salaries, utilities, and so on. That's money out of my client's pocket. Further, there's no realistic prospect that the university can reorganize. Its filings show that students, faculty, and donors are all fleeing. They'll lose their accreditation and government grants soon too. Keeping them on life support while they try to cobble together a plan will merely delay the inevitable."

"Thank you. I'll hear from the university now." The judge turned to Hez. "Mr. Webster?"

Savannah gave Hez a tight, nervous smile as Boswell vacated the lectern. Hez responded with what he hoped was a reassuring pat on her arm, gathered his papers, and took Boswell's place. "Thank you, Your Honor. We have critical new evidence. I apologize for not submitting this earlier, but we only just received it." Hez held up a thick document. "May I approach the bench to provide the court with a copy? I have one for counsel as well."

The judge's eyebrows went up, but she nodded. "You may."

Hez crossed the well and handed a copy to the judge's clerk, who gave it a cursory look and passed it up to the judge. Hez delivered another copy to a frowning Boswell and resumed his position behind the lectern. "I just handed the clerk a copy of Bruno Rubinelli's affidavit. Mr. Rubinelli is an expert in computer forensics. His résumé is attached to the affidavit as exhibit one. I asked Mr. Rubinelli to examine the laptop computer owned by Jessica Legare, the former CFO of Tupelo Grove University. As Mr. Boswell just conceded, her murder and the smuggling of artifacts through the university were the justifications for Hornbrook's demand for immediate payment. In fact—as Mr. Rubinelli discovered— Hornbrook was deeply involved in the artifact smuggling and had extensive undisclosed contacts with Ms. Legare, which we're still investigating."

Boswell scoffed and started to stand, but Judge Sticklesby

COLLEEN COBLE AND RICK ACKER

waved him away without taking her eyes off Hez. "Hold on. I have questions for Mr. Webster. How solid is your proof of these allegations?"

"Very solid," Hez replied without hesitation. "Mr. Rubinelli is a recognized expert in the field and we can make him available to testify in the near future. He found numerous documents on Ms. Legare's computer that incriminate Hornbrook. Hornbrook acted as a middleman for over a dozen sales, arranging for purchases of smuggled artifacts by its clients. Ms. Legare, who unfortunately was involved in the smuggling herself, kept records of the sales. Several dozen of those are attached to Mr. Rubinelli's affidavit as exhibits."

The sound of tense whispering and pages flipping from the table of Hornbrook lawyers rose behind him. He cut a quick glance at them and saw their heads together while the middle lawyer tapped furiously on his phone. "Hornbrook's founder and CEO, James Hornbrook, actually kept one of the artifacts for himself—a very nice Aztec jade mask. A picture is attached to Mr. Rubinelli's affidavit as exhibit forty-seven."

Judge Sticklesby slowly leafed through Bruno's affidavit. "I see. What about the contacts between Hornbrook and Ms. Legare that you mentioned?"

"Those are described in paragraphs sixty-one through eighty-two of Mr. Rubinelli's affidavit. It's a little technical, but the gist of it is that on at least a dozen occasions, Ms. Legare used an encrypted videoconferencing service to speak with someone from Hornbrook."

The judge continued to skim Bruno's affidavit and the exhibits. "It appears that Mr. Rubinelli is basing this conclusion on the fact that Ms. Legare's computer connected to this encrypted server at the same time a Hornbrook computer was also connected. Is that accurate?"

"Yes, Your Honor."

"There's no record of what they discussed?"

"Not that Mr. Rubinelli or I have been able to locate to date, Your Honor."

"And also no record of whether anyone else participated in those conversations?"

"No, Your Honor."

The judge nodded. "All right. Anything else you'd like to add?"

Hez took a quick look at his notes. "Just that Mr. Rubinelli's affidavit casts serious doubt on the validity of the Hornbrook loan and indicates that the university may have claims against Hornbrook, which should be adjudicated before Hornbrook is allowed to seize essentially all of the university's assets."

"Thank you." The judge turned to Boswell. "Any response, Counsel?"

Boswell stood. "Absolutely, Your Honor."

Hez gathered his things and resumed his seat next to Savannah. He'd just thrown Boswell a huge curveball, and there was no way he could give a substantive response immediately. He'd want to go through the affidavit with a fine-tooth comb and then question Bruno about it under oath. Boswell and his colleagues would also need to consult with their client and come up with a story that explained away the evidence Hez had just presented. They might be able to do it, but it would take at least a couple of weeks—probably a month or more. That would give Hez much-needed breathing space to prepare his legal counteroffensive. He, Bruno, and the Justice Chamber had been hard at work, but their plan wasn't ready for prime time yet.

"Mr. Webster says he just obtained this alleged evidence, and I will not question his integrity," Boswell said in a tone that made clear he was very much questioning Hez's integrity. "However, I first saw this affidavit a few minutes ago when Mr. Webster handed it to me in this courtroom. That is far too late. The court should disregard it."

The judge nodded. "Deadlines exist for a reason and the general rule is to ignore evidence or briefs that are submitted late. However, that rule has exceptions, and I suspect Mr. Webster is prepared to argue that one or more of those apply here."

Hez half rose. "Yes, Your Honor."

The judge jotted down a note. "I'm inclined to continue this hearing to allow both sides to brief whether I should consider the Rubinelli affidavit. If I do, I will allow adequate time for Hornbrook to do discovery sufficient to test the accuracy of the affidavit. Is that acceptable to the parties?"

Hez started to relax. It would take time to brief the admissibility of Bruno's affidavit and more time for the judge to rule. He might get the month he needed even if she ultimately excluded the affidavit. He popped to his feet. "That's acceptable to the university, Your Honor."

Judge Sticklesby turned to Boswell. "What about Hornbrook?"

"One moment, Your Honor." Boswell huddled with the other two attorneys. "We have some new evidence of our own, Your Honor." He shot a sidelong glance at Hez. "We have been in touch with James Hornbrook via text. He is the founder and CEO of Hornbrook Finance, and he says that he had no idea that these artifacts were smuggled. He trusted Ms. Legare, just like the university allegedly did." He held up a phone and read from the screen. "His exact words are, 'Please tell the judge that if I had any hint that these items were looted, I never would have told my clients about them, let alone purchased one myself. I am horrified.'"

The judge drummed her fingers for a moment. "What about the encrypted videoconferences with Ms. Legare?"

"He says those related to the negotiation of the loan the university was seeking—which makes perfect sense because Ms. Legare was the university's chief financial officer."

The judge frowned in thought for a few seconds. "Is he willing to repeat all of that under oath?"

"Yes, Your Honor. To quote him again, 'I'll swear everything on a stack of Bibles.'"

"All right, anything else?"

"Yes. The university's counsel did not deny—or even address—our main argument: that Hornbrook Finance is the sole secured creditor and that it is being harmed every day as the value of its collateral decreases."

"Thank you. I have a few questions for Mr. Webster."

Boswell sat and Hez stepped to the lectern. "Yes, Your Honor?"

Judge Sticklesby flipped through Bruno's affidavit. "Is there anything in here indicating that anyone at Hornbrook Finance knew these artifacts were looted? For example, an email saying, 'I'm smuggling another statue to you,' or 'Here are the forged provenance documents you requested'?"

If only. "No, Your Honor."

"And do you dispute that the amount of the university's debt to Hornbrook exceeds the liquidation value of the university's assets?"

"I don't think liquidation value is a fair benchmark, Your Honor. The university's—"

The judge speared Hez with a look. "That's a yes or no question, Mr. Webster."

Hez swallowed hard. "No, Your Honor."

"Thank you." The judge dismissed Hez with a nod and he resumed his seat. She turned to Boswell. "Your client's CEO says he's willing to swear on a stack of Bibles. I want him to actually do it. You have forty-eight hours to file an affidavit from him stating exactly what you just told me. Once I receive that, I'll grant your motion."

Savannah gasped and gripped Hez's arm. "What are we going to do?" she whispered, her voice tight with panic.

If only he knew.

In spite of the warm spring sunshine on her arms, Savannah was so cold she couldn't stop shaking. She'd seen the failure and despair on Hez's face when they left the courtroom, and it felt like the end of all their dreams. What would she say to all the faculty and students? How could she tell them she'd failed them all?

Maybe she was wrong and there was some hope. She tugged Hez far enough away from Hornbrook's smiling attorneys that they couldn't be overheard. "Is the situation as bad as it seems?"

His mouth tugged farther down in his pale face. "Unfortunately, it couldn't be much worse. They'll have that affidavit the judge demanded by day's end. Judge Sticklesby will sign the order, and they'll be able to seize everything TGU owns." He rubbed his forehead. "I let you down, babe. Again."

She slumped against him and struggled to keep her composure. TGU would cease to exist. That shyster Hornbrook would have their bank accounts, their buildings, their future. She'd probably be locked out of her office, but she couldn't think about anything but the way things had crumbled around them. She straightened and clasped her arms around herself, giving in to the despair. How would they survive this blow?

She started to turn back to Hez and realized he'd moved away. She spotted him talking to Boswell. His intent expression told her he was on a mission, and she felt a glimmer of hope. Was there something he could do after all?

His jaw set in a hard line, Hez walked back toward her. "I asked for a settlement meeting, and Boswell is calling Hornbrook to see if he'd be willing to talk."

The glimmer of hope went dark. "A settlement meeting? Are you ready for that?" It was over, really over.

Hez shrugged. "I'd need another month to be really ready, but we have no choice. TGU will be long gone in a month. Maybe we can salvage something."

An undercurrent in his tone made her wonder if he had something up his sleeve, but before she could ask what he planned, Boswell came their way with a purposeful stride. The set of his shoulders and the arrogant tilt to his chin set her teeth on edge.

He swiped at a strand of silver hair that had been caught by the wind. "My client is sick of your delaying tactics, Webster. If you have a serious offer to make, you can do it in person at

Mr. Hornbrook's New York office tomorrow morning. Don't show up with an army of attorneys either. You can bring one other person, and Mr. Hornbrook will give you fifteen minutes. Take it or leave it."

"I'll take it," Hez said in a mild tone. "What time?"

"At ten. Fifteen minutes," Boswell warned again. "That's it."

"That's all I'll need."

A black SUV pulled up, and Boswell gestured for the other two attorneys to join him. They didn't look back as they departed the courthouse with heads high in triumph.

Hez's arm came around Savannah as she watched them drive off. "I've got one final shot tomorrow."

She yanked her gaze from the black SUV's taillights. "I'm coming with you to New York."

His lips flattened and he shook his head. "No, babe, you need to stay here and take care of Simon. He's still so sad, and he'd worry if we were both gone." He hesitated and glanced away. "If things . . . go south, people will need you. We can't run the risk of leaving Simon alone."

She gasped as his comment soaked in. "You think Hornbrook might k-kill you?"

"He's unscrupulous. He wouldn't want to be indicted for murder, but he could arrange for an accident. I'll be on my guard."

She grasped the rough material of his coat sleeve. "I need you, Hez. What if he makes sure you never make it to his office? I can't lose you. I just can't!"

His fingers tipped her chin up, and he stared intently into her eyes. "You're stronger than you know, Savannah, but I have no intention of dying tomorrow. I've been dreaming of our future together for too long to let it slip away. I'll be on guard."

She swallowed down the thickening in her throat. "You can't go by yourself. I don't trust Hornbrook, so take someone intimidating. Maybe Jimmy?"

"There's only one person who might scare these guys. I'll take Bruno Rubinelli, if he's free." He pulled out his phone and launched his travel app. "There's a flight in three hours out of Pensacola. I'll be back tomorrow in time for dinner. I'll text Bruno and ask him to meet me." Hez tapped out a quick text and his phone pinged a few seconds later with a reply. "Awesome, he can make it."

Bruno had done great work in setting up the fake website they used in taking down the smuggling ring. But how could a computer whiz protect Hez? God could, though, and she would try her best to lean on her faith in the next twenty-four hours.

CHAPTER 39

A GUST OF WIND FUNNELED DOWN THE GLASS AND STEEL
ravines of Midtown Manhattan and knifed through Hez's suit
coat. He shivered and stepped behind one of the massive col-
umns outside Hornbrook's building. Late March meant spring
in southern Alabama, but winter still held sway in New York.

Where was Bruno? He was supposed to meet Hez ten
minutes ago, and the meeting with Hornbrook started in five.
Had Hornbrook's minions somehow learned that Bruno was
coming and intercepted him on his way from the airport? Hez
wished they'd had more time to plan this out.

A cadaverously thin man of about thirty-five rolled up on
a skateboard. He wore a black beanie and baggy jeans that
flapped around his bony legs. An ancient Metallica T-shirt
showed through his unzipped snowboarding jacket. Hez
smiled with relief and stuck out his hand. "Bruno! It's great to
finally meet you in person."

Bruno popped up his skateboard and grabbed it with his
left hand while he gave Hez a perfunctory shake with his right.
"Hey, Hez." He craned his neck and looked up at the tower
in front of them. "So this is it, huh? Think there's a chance
things'll get rough in there?"

Hez pressed his lips together and nodded. He and Bruno hadn't had a chance to discuss the danger in detail. "Things could get very rough."

Bruno considered that for a long moment, and Hez was afraid he might back out. But Bruno just shrugged. "Not my first rough situation. Besides, if they kill us, they may regret it."

That wasn't the most reassuring thing to hear, but at least Hez wasn't going in alone. He took a deep breath and pushed back at the fear rising in his chest. "Let's go. We don't want to be late."

They checked in at the security desk and then rode up in a gleaming brass-and-marble elevator they had to themselves. It had no buttons for different floors, just a slot for a key card. The building's tenants apparently didn't want any surprise visitors.

The doors opened, and they stepped into the lobby of Hornbrook Finance, LLC. Steel letters inlaid in expensive-looking walnut paneling announced the firm's name, and black leather furniture surrounded a glass table in a small waiting area. The receptionist, a muscular man with sharp brown eyes, waved them over. Two more very fit men emerged from a door behind the reception desk. They gave Hez and Bruno a quick but thorough search and confiscated Bruno's skateboard. Then one of the men led Hez and Bruno through the door, with the other Hornbrook minion bringing up the rear. Hez hadn't seen a gun, but he had no doubt all three men were armed.

They walked down a short, windowless hall to a conference room with a large table and south- and east-facing floor-to-ceiling windows. Allen Boswell sat on the table's far side next to a silver-haired sixtyish man. James Hornbrook. Neither of them rose when Hez and Bruno entered. "It's 10:02," Hornbrook said without preamble. "You have thirteen minutes left."

The door clicked shut behind Hez as he and Bruno sat opposite Hornbrook. Their chairs were squarely in the glare from the sunlight pouring in through the windows. It was an old power move designed to distract opponents and make them uncomfortable. Fortunately, Hez was prepared. He pulled out a pair of sunglasses and slid them on as he took his seat. "Are we being recorded?"

Boswell's mouth quirked in irritation. "Why does it matter? New York is a one-party state. My client can record any conversations that take place in here."

Hez furrowed his brows. "Hmm. He can legally record any conversation that he's a part of, which isn't quite the same thing."

Hornbrook gave a contemptuous little chuckle. "Thank you for the free legal advice. Now make your offer. You've got ten minutes left."

"I'm getting to that, but the recorded conversation thing has bugged me ever since Jess Legare warned me about it. In fact, that was one of the last things she said before she was murdered. And it really bugged me once I realized you were recording conversations you weren't part of."

Hornbrook's icy-blue eyes flashed. "What are you talking about?"

Hez fought to keep his tone calm and confident. "Your MO appears to be to invite people to your office for a negotiation, present an offer, and then leave while the other side discusses it. Then you eavesdrop on their conversation and use it against them. You sometimes even blackmail people with the recordings. Those are felonies under New York law."

"That's a lie." Hornbrook's voice was flat and cold. "Who told you that?"

Bruno raised his hand. "Your video surveillance system has garbage security, BTW."

Boswell gave a predatory smile. "Hacking is a federal felony, and I happen to be friends with the U.S. Attorney for the Southern District of New York. And yes, your confession was just recorded."

Bruno rolled his eyes. "Don't bother calling him. He'll just refer it to the FBI, and the Bureau will send it to their Cyber Division. My name will get flagged there, and your complaint will get routed to Special Agent Martin Lee. So just call Martin and say you want to make a complaint about Bruno Rubinelli. I've got his direct dial in my phone if you need it."

Boswell's grin faltered. His mouth opened and closed.

"Oh, one other thing," Bruno said. "Martin will probably have some questions about exactly what I was hacking 'n' why, so you know, you should be ready to talk about that."

Hornbrook brought his right palm down on the table. "Enough of these games!" His gaze flickered to a spot behind Hez. A soft swish of fabric indicated someone moving behind him. "You have one minute left to make your offer."

Hez took a deep breath and made his final move. "There's one more thing you should know. We ran facial-recognition software over the entire video database and managed to identify nearly everyone you illegally recorded. We have emails or cell numbers for most of them, and we have a mass notice set to go out. If we don't hit the kill switch by eleven

COLLEEN COBLE AND RICK ACKER

o'clock, they'll all get links to a database containing the illegal recordings."

That was a bluff. The mass notice wouldn't be ready to go out for at least another three weeks—which was why Hez had hoped to wait a month before putting his plan into action. If Hornbrook killed them now, he could stop it. But there was no way for him to know that—or so Hez hoped.

Bruno leaned forward. "Fun fact: a bunch of the guys you cheated are connected to organized crime."

Hornbrook sat perfectly still for a long moment. A single bead of sweat appeared at his perfect hairline. "What do you want?"

Hez realized he'd been holding his breath. He relaxed just a little and finally made his offer. "Your company will forgive TGU's entire debt and make a twenty-million-dollar donation. You will repay everyone you cheated, erase your video library, and stop surreptitiously recording people."

Boswell cleared his throat. "And in return you'll destroy the database of video you illegally hacked and stole from my client?"

Hez shook his head. "Nope. We'll hit the kill switch on the mass notice and promise not to tell anyone about your client's spying."

"But if anything ever happens to either of us, the notice automatically goes out," Bruno added. "Just thought you should know that."

"We'll need to discuss this." Hornbrook looked past Hez again. "Take these guys out to the lobby."

Hez permitted himself a small smile as he and Bruno stood. "I'm more generous with my time than you are. I'll give you twenty minutes."

The trapped, hopeless look in Hornbrook's eyes told Hez everything he needed to know about how the rest of the negotiations would go.

———

Savannah's pulse kicked at the sight of Hez standing on the curb at the Mobile airport. His jubilant grin told her more than his quick call on the way to LaGuardia. He opened the back door and threw his backpack onto the floor, then climbed into the front passenger seat beside her.

He leaned over for a lingering kiss, tasting of triumph and Skittles, and her head spun with joy as she clung to him. She kissed him back until a horn blared behind them and someone yelled out a rude comment. Her cheeks heated, and she pulled away. "I still can't believe you saved TGU *and* forced him to give such a huge donation. My head is still spinning."

"And here I thought the color in your cheeks was because you loved me so much."

Smiling, she pulled away from the curb as he was buckling his seat belt. "You guessed right." She ran her window down to let in the spring air. "It's a gorgeous day. Let's take 98 down along the water. I want you all to myself to savor the victory."

His long legs stretched out under the dash. "Sounds good to me. I'm beat. The last twenty-four hours have been a blur, and I don't think I slept at all. But even though I'm tired, I don't think I could sleep if I tried. It all went perfectly."

She listened to him recount the confrontation and Hornbrook's reaction. "I'll bet you were sweating bullets that it wouldn't work."

"Bruno's comment about the FBI really rattled them. Everything changed in an instant. They realized we had an ace or two up our sleeves, and they suddenly didn't want to gamble anymore. It was priceless." Hez yawned and leaned back against the headrest.

The road spooled out in front of them, and the tires hummed along the pavement. The afternoon sun slanted through the window and warmed Savannah's arm. She went quiet and hoped he might catch a few winks of sleep. There was so much to do now. News of this would hit social media immediately, and there would be reporters, professors, and students to deal with. She didn't dare think about what the school would do with that sudden influx of money. It was almost too much to hope for.

On the south side of Point Clear, she slowed to catch a glimpse of her favorite house along this stretch of road. About the same time she spotted the round rose window, she saw the Open House sign in the yard and gasped.

Hez's eyes flew open. "What's wrong?"

"Look! My favorite house is for sale!" They'd driven by it plenty of times in the past, but he'd never been inside. The owner, Edward Mossberg, was an architecture professor, and he'd been a friend of her grandfather's. Grandpa Andre had brought her to visit several times when she was a child. "Do we even want to look at it? It's probably way over our budget."

"I'd love to see it."

"I'm half afraid to. It was a magical place when I was a kid, and I'd hate to see all its foibles now. I might see it through a different lens." But she turned into the lane anyway and parked in a space at the end of the driveway. From here it was just as charming as she remembered. She pointed out the folly perched on the hillside overlooking Mobile Bay. The miniature medieval watchtower had always felt so real to her, and it was still in pristine condition.

She turned off the car and opened her door. The green carpet of grass was soft underfoot. Bees hummed in the flower beds along the walk to the door, and hummingbirds fluttered around the red feeders. "I think there are several acres here. The yard seemed to go on forever when I was a kid. The owner tinkered with this place for fifty years, and every time we came, he'd added something new. I wonder if Mossberg Cove is still here."

"What's that?"

"It's a sea cave, and Professor Mossberg pretended it was a pirate hideout. His grandkids loved it, and so did I."

"It sounds idyllic." Hez squinted in the sun as he stared toward the house. "It's really different, though."

Different wasn't a strong enough word. *Unique, mesmerizing,* and *magical* would be more apt descriptions but still not the right words to describe how the home made her feel. "Let's go inside."

A woman wearing a slim tan skirt and an eager smile greeted them inside the front door and handed them a listing paper. "Have a look around and let me know if you have any questions."

Savannah nodded and stood enchanted by the play of sunlight through the prism window onto the inlaid floor, made from wood from myriad different countries. She remembered watching the Mossberg kittens chase beams of light around the room. "I think there are prisms in most of the windows."

"There are prisms in every window," the Realtor said. "You seem familiar with the house."

"I came often when I was a child," Savannah said. She thanked the Realtor, then led Hez through the living room and up a spiral staircase to a tiny observatory perched on top of the house. "No window is the same. There's the one with the stained-glass rose and another with a hummingbird, and then there are all those prisms. They make rainbows where you least expect them, and they never look the same in the summer as they do in the winter."

Hez stared up at the roof in the observatory. "Is that thing retractable?"

She nodded. "I was here once during an eclipse, and Professor Mossberg opened it. I wanted Grandpa to buy the house when I was ten, and he tried, but Professor Mossberg refused to sell it. Can you imagine Simon exploring this house? He would love it so much." And it might help heal him. Hez would do about anything for her, but she didn't want to ask him to bankrupt them over a house.

She'd been afraid to look at the price, but she had to know. Her gaze dropped to the listing paper, and she blinked. "Hez, it's not nearly as expensive as I thought. Look."

He took the paper and read methodically through the listing. "We might be their only prospects. It probably costs the earth to keep up. If we broke a window, it's hard to say how much it would cost to repair. That retractable roof on the observatory probably leaks, and I have no idea how hard it would be to maintain."

She stepped closer to slip her arms around his waist. "I know it's not practical, but I'm not feeling particularly practical right now. Maybe it's crazy, but I want this house, Hez. What do you think?"

He pulled her closer. "I think you're much more beautiful than the house and even more irresistible." He tipped her chin up and kissed her.

The breath left her lungs and all thoughts of the house flew from her head. Hez centered her, and where they lived didn't matter. His fingers trailed through her hair, and a rainbow of light touched his face when he drew back.

"Can't you just picture it, Hez?" she whispered. "Us slow dancing through rainbows on that gorgeous inlaid floor, having a picnic in the little tower, swimming in the cove, growing old together here."

He smiled and wrapped a lock of her hair around his finger. "I can see us living here with Simon and our kids forever. Even all that upkeep might not be bad. I need something to keep me out of the office on weekends. I can't believe I'm saying this, but let's make an offer. I'll bet we can get a good deal." His hand trailed down to her cheek. "I'd give you the moon if I could."

A starburst of joy jolted through her chest. This home would be their fresh start, and she imagined their children running through the grass with Simon. Their laughter was a faint whisper on the wind, but it was coming.

CHAPTER 40

HEZ PEEKED INTO SAVANNAH'S OFFICE TO MAKE SURE SHE was alone. Then he walked in, shut the door, and did a little dance.

She looked up from her monitor and burst into laughter, the sunlight catching the gold flecks in her green eyes. She applauded. "Very impressive. I love that you have an actual happy dance. What's the good news?"

He bowed. "The deal is done. The Hornbrook wire transfer cleared and we got the signed release of the loan and withdrawal of their claim. I'll file a motion to dismiss the bankruptcy, but that's just a formality at this point."

"Whew!" She sagged back in her chair. "I was scared they'd pull out."

"Me too, but they followed through despite some grumbling." There had also been blunt and unsettling threats about what would happen if he or Bruno ever leaked the hacked videos, but no need to worry Savannah. "I think they also want to put this behind them as fast as possible."

Her eyebrows went up. "But it's not behind them or us, is it? What about Jess's murder?"

"That's the other thing I wanted to tell you about. We still haven't found video showing anyone at Hornbrook Finance planning the car bomb or even being aware of it before it went off."

She shrugged one shoulder. "That could just mean they were careful enough not to record evidence implicating themselves in a murder."

"It could—but they recorded lots of evidence implicating themselves in other crimes. And we did find video of James Hornbrook hearing about Jess's death. The first thing he did was order one of his goons to go check his car to make sure it didn't have a bomb. He still has someone check it every day before he drives home."

"Huh." Savannah looked into the middle distance for several seconds. "So you think the killer is still out there?" Her voice held an edge of fear.

He shook his head. "I think the killer is dead or in jail. If Hornbrook is innocent, then the most likely suspects are the smugglers. I'm sure Hope will get to the bottom of it."

"I'm sure she will." Savannah's face brightened. "And I'm thrilled that you got the settlement finalized so fast! I had to tell the trustees about the basics, of course, and they've been clamoring for details. I told them they'd get a full report as soon as everything was set in stone, but I couldn't say more until then. I also made clear that you needed to stay focused on the deal and that I wouldn't tolerate anyone bugging you."

He chuckled at the thought of her laying down the law to the trustees. "Thanks. You're really growing into the role of president."

"I'm not sure my dad would agree." She looked at her watch. "He's actually on his way over now to try to get some answers out of me. He'll be here any minute."

As if on cue, Pierre's muffled voice floated in from the reception area. "She's expecting me." A second later, a knock sounded on Savannah's door.

"Come in," she called.

The door opened and Pierre appeared, looking like he just walked out of a photo shoot for an executive magazine. He wore a well-tailored gray suit with a red silk tie, and his silver-streaked brown hair was freshly trimmed. "Ah, you're both here. Excellent. The board is delighted to hear that this whole bankruptcy mess is being taken care of, but we must know more about the particulars."

Savannah nodded. "Your timing is impeccable, Dad. Hez just finalized the paperwork. This was your brainchild, Hez—why don't you fill him in?"

Hez described the settlement. He was deliberately vague about what James Hornbrook and his company were getting out of the deal, saying only that TGU had "agreed to protect the confidentiality of certain information." Pierre cocked his head at that, but he didn't ask any questions.

When Hez finished, Pierre flashed his perfect teeth in a wide smile. "Excellent work! I couldn't have negotiated a better outcome myself. So the university is on sound financial footing now?"

Savannah leaned forward. "Better than in decades."

"Well done, my girl! The trustees will be thrilled." An eager light gleamed in his eyes. "Then it won't be a problem to return the funds that were borrowed from my trust, right?"

So that was the real reason he was here. Of course. Hez cleared his throat. "No funds were borrowed from your trust,

Pierre. Funds were removed because they were never legally put into the trust in the first place."

Pierre turned to Savannah. "There's obviously been a mis-understanding." He spoke with the demeanor of a senior executive gently reprimanding a subordinate. "The university can afford to clear it up now, and I can assure you the trustees won't object."

Savannah met her father's gaze. "There was no misunder-standing, Dad. That money belongs to the university, and that's where it will stay."

The muscles in Pierre's jaw flexed. "That's Jess talking! I'm your father, Savannah. I gave my life to this university. I can't believe you're going to invoke legal technicalities to rob me of my retirement."

Savannah's eyes flashed. "Jess wanted to sue you to get all of the money back. I refused because a messy lawsuit wouldn't have helped anyone, least of all TGU." Her expression softened. "I love you, Dad, but I can't let you steal from the university."

Pierre's confidence and polish cracked. "I need that money, Savannah. It's all I have."

"I'm sorry, but it's not your money. If you need help, let me know."

Pierre stood, drawing himself up to his full height and leaning over Savannah's desk. "I don't want your charity. I want what's rightfully mine, and I'll get it—one way or another!" He turned on his heel and stalked out without waiting for a response.

Hez got up and closed the door behind his former father-in-law. He turned to Savannah. "I know that wasn't easy. I'm proud of you."

She gave a weak smile. "I guess every silver cloud has a dark lining."

There were now three graves for Savannah to tend in the cemetery—her mother's, her daughter's, and her sister's. The scent of fresh dirt lingered in spite of the flowers heaped on Jess's grave. If Jess had ever thought about it, she probably would have asked to be buried in the Willard part of the cemetery with its unkempt, crumbling headstones. If Savannah had it to do over again, she would have talked to Helen about where to bury Jess.

Jess's headstone would take some time to be installed, but the name on the temporary marker was one Savannah had never thought to see. Fresh tears hovered closer than she'd like, and she swallowed down the boulder in her throat as she tried to imagine Jess in heaven with Mom and Ella.

Someone had sent roses and the funeral home had heaped them with the rest of the fresh flowers on the grave. It was a kind gesture, but Savannah couldn't bear the smell. She didn't think she'd ever get over her aversion to the scent of roses after that moment by the rosebushes in Jess's front yard when she had to tell Simon his mother was dead. She held her breath as she lifted them off the mounded dirt and tossed them into a nearby ravine so she didn't have to smell them.

She prayed as she planted new flowers in the pots swinging in the breeze near her mother's and Ella's graves. All she could do was take each day hour by hour and cling to her faith as she walked through this storm of grief. She would have to bring

Simon up soon. She could talk about losing her own mother and their shared grief over Jess. Maybe he would open up. His withdrawal worried her, so she prayed for him too.

She wiped her hands on the soft grass around Ella's grave and spotted a small figure walking up the hillside path toward Jess's grave. Helen Willard. The tiny woman carried bundles of fresh flowers almost as big as she was. Without thinking, Savannah dove for cover and huddled behind a sprawling rhododendron. She peered through the glossy leaves and watched Helen stop first at the grave marked Marie Legare. Helen arranged fresh flowers in the vase attached to the headstone before moving to the fresh mound where Jess lay buried.

Was that a sob from the older woman? Savannah strained to hear and put her hand to her mouth when the choked sound of grief came from Helen again. Had she loved Jess, truly loved her? If only Savannah had known all this. Her chest squeezed with regret and grief.

Helen drew back from Jess's grave and moved to Ella's grave, where she stood for a long moment, staring at the fresh flowers Savannah had planted. She was close enough that Savannah could hear her ragged breathing. Why was she standing there motionless so long? Savannah wished she could see her expression better, but the foliage was too thick.

Helen spit out a string of profanity, and Savannah bit back a gasp. The tiny old lady screamed curses to the sky with her fist raised. Savannah gulped and waited for whatever emotion had caused the outburst to ebb. The older woman dropped her hand back to her side and continued to stare down at Ella's headstone.

COLLEEN COBLE AND RICK ACKER

A cramp seized Savannah's left calf, and she flexed her foot to try to ease it, but it worsened. *Please leave.* She gritted her teeth and kept flexing her arch without relief. When she was about to admit defeat and reveal her hidden spot, Helen finally moved from Ella's grave and picked her way carefully down the slope toward the campus.

Once she was out of sight, Savannah emerged from behind the foliage and put all her weight on her foot until the pain eased, then went back to Jess's grave. Helen had been truly grief-stricken when she was standing here.

Jess had been part of the Willard family more than Savannah knew, and it hurt to realize she'd been so unaware of this side of her sister's life. When they were young, Jess would vanish for an afternoon or even a whole weekend and then reappear with a fresh tan or a new barrette in her hair. Everyone knew where she'd been, but no one talked about it because that might trigger another ugly scene between Mom and Dad.

Savannah should have probed, especially once they were on their own, but she hadn't. Had it been habit? Fear of the pain she knew would come from unraveling their tangled family past? Both? It was too late now. More of the damage caused by her avoidant personality. She fell beside Jess's grave and buried her face in her hands as regret washed over her in a flood.

"Savannah?"

She jerked erect at the sound of Hez's voice and turned to see him coming toward her in a run. The love and concern on his face brought her stumbling to her feet, and she rushed to meet him.

He folded her in his arms. "I'm so sorry, babe," he whispered against her hair.

She shook her head. "It's not just her death. I failed her, Hez. I only realized how much after seeing Helen here a few minutes ago."

He stiffened. "Helen Willard was here? She came to Jess's grave?"

"And to Mom's. She put flowers on both graves before stopping at Ella's. While standing next to Ella's headstone, she raised her fist in the air and screamed out curses." Savannah stepped back and rubbed the gooseflesh on her arms at the memory.

"She *cursed*? Sweet little Miz Willard? I mean, she's been angry with the Legares, but I've never heard her swear."

"You didn't grow up around here. She was the iron lady of the Willard family, and they're a rough bunch. Still, it was peculiar. Ella had nothing to do with the Willards and had never even met them, so why would Helen do that at her grave? Why would she even visit it? It's not next to Mom and Jess."

"Did she have to search for it?"

"No, she walked to it like she'd been there before."

"Odd." Hez frowned and stared toward the spot where their daughter's body rested. "I don't like it."

"I don't either." She shook off her unease. "I wasn't expecting to see you until later."

He smiled. "I had news that couldn't wait, but it will cost you." He pulled her back into his arms. "A few kisses might be enough payment. But maybe not, because this is really big news."

She chuckled. "I think I can manage that payment, but I think you'd better tell me first so I can judge how many kisses it deserves."

"Oh, it's worth a lot." He kissed her thoroughly until she was breathless. "You ready for a huge change to our lives?" he whispered against her lips.

She released him reluctantly. "More than ready."

"We got the house."

Her pulse had started to slow but jumped again at his words. "You're sure?"

"The signed offer acceptance is in our inboxes. All we have to do is send over the earnest money." He lifted her in his arms and swung her around. "We've got a new house, babe, and a new start with Simon."

She let out a squeal. "Hez! It's the best news ever." When he put her down, she hugged him. "Thank you for going along with my very impractical longing for that house."

Her hand in his, they headed back down the hillside, and she glanced back one last time at the graveyard. Maybe she'd never know why Helen had screamed out curses by Ella's grave.

CHAPTER 41

"I AM PLEASED TO ANNOUNCE THE INDICTMENT OF JAMES
Hornbrook," Elliot Drake said, baritone voice laced with prac-
ticed gravitas. He stood behind a portable lectern with the
DA's seal, which had been set up on the steps of the TGU administration building. "Mr. Hornbrook was the mastermind
behind a smuggling network that stretched from the jungles of
southern Mexico to the art galleries of Manhattan and victimized this fine university. He is a coward and has fled justice, but
we will work tirelessly with our law enforcement partners to find
him and bring him back to face the consequences of his actions."

Hez smiled and leaned against the bole of a tupelo tree. This
was much more fun than the last conference he'd attended here.
He was a spectator this time, so he could relax and enjoy the
show. And Drake knew how to put on a good show. His gelled
black hair gleamed in the late-morning sun, and he squinted
slightly in the bright light, looking strong and resolute.

The ostensible reason for holding the press conference
at TGU was that Drake's announcement involved artifact
smuggling, but Hez suspected Drake also wanted to associate
himself with Savannah, who was now very popular for having
saved TGU. She stood to Drake's right, looking gorgeous and

professional in a blue suit accented with a red-and-white TGU pin. Hope stood on Drake's left, beaming.

Hez chuckled at Hornbrook's predicament. He'd paid a huge price to keep Hez and Bruno from airing his financial dirty laundry—and he *still* had to run. Hope had been putting together an indictment for artifact smuggling at the same time Hez had been battling in bankruptcy court, and she'd gotten an arrest warrant just days after Hornbrook's deal with TGU closed. It couldn't have happened to a nicer guy.

A hand touched Hez's arm and he turned to see Martine beside him. "Why aren't you up there?"

"This is mostly Hope's accomplishment. If Drake is going to share the credit with anyone, it should be her. Besides, having the university's lawyer up there might imply that the DA's office didn't do all the work."

An amused smile curved her full lips. "You know what DA stands for, right?"

Hez grinned at the old legal/political joke. "Definitely Ambitious. Think he'll run for AG?"

Martine's smile broadened. "You mean Aspiring Governor? I heard he's already talking to donors, and someone registered drake4attorneygeneral.com." She jutted her chin toward the press conference. "When do you think he'll indict Hornbrook for murder?"

Hez kept his face blank. "Whose murder?"

Martine's eyes widened in surprise. "Jess's, of course. Hornbrook had her killed because he was afraid she was about to turn on him."

That would have sounded right to Hez—except for the video of Hornbrook sending underlings to check his car for bombs.

Could that have been an act for the cameras, or was Martine lying? "How do you know?"

"I don't know—but my client does."

"Your client. So you're here on business, then?"

She gave him a coy look. "It's always a pleasure when I get to see you, Hez. But yes, I'll be billing for our chat."

"So why doesn't your client save himself the money and talk to me directly? The smugglers are all dead or in jail, and Hornbrook isn't a threat anymore. He's on the run. Rumor has it he isn't even in the U.S. anymore. The danger is gone."

She shook her head. "The danger won't be gone until Hornbrook is in a federal prison. Besides, my client believes that when you do good deeds, you should do them in secret. Do not announce them with trumpets like the hypocrites."

He let a hint of sarcasm creep into his voice. "Your client must be a very humble man."

"I never said my client was a man. You did." She leaned close and winked. "Nice try."

Martine's gaze went back to the press conference. Hez turned in the same direction. Drake was saying something about getting an Interpol warrant for Hornbrook's arrest. Savannah was looking toward Martine and Hez. Was she frowning or just squinting in the sun?

Martine patted Hez's arm. "I should be going. Good seeing you, Hez."

It seemed fitting for the three of them to be in the cemetery before the postponed engagement party. Savannah paid close attention to how Simon was doing as they stood beside Jess's grave with the scent of wildflowers in the air. If only he could cry and get out his grief, but he stood dry-eyed staring down at the flowers still heaped on the mound of dirt. Cody seemed to sense his mood and settled at his feet with his head on his paws. Marley followed suit and lay down near Savannah.

Simon stooped and plucked a daisy from the grass. "Mom would have put on a really great party tonight."

Hez let go of Savannah's hand and moved close enough to Simon to put his hand on his shoulder. "She did everything with a great sense of style and flair. She'd had a really great one planned the night she died."

"Out at Jesse's Restaurant. I've still never gotten to go there." Simon gave a jerky nod. "Are you going to sell the house?"

Savannah shot a helpless glance at Hez, who nodded encouragement. There was no reason to keep Simon in the dark. "We already have an offer on it. Your mom made sure you were taken care of."

"I'd rather have her than money."

Simon had no idea how much was in Jess's estate, and Savannah hoped he'd never ask. She wanted to keep him innocent of how wealthy he would be someday. "No one will ever replace your mom in our hearts. I know things are a little cramped in my cottage at the moment, but we'll show you the new house as soon as we can. You can select your new room and decorate it however you like."

A hint of a smile lifted Simon's face. "I can't wait to see the observatory."

"You can be in charge of it and show it to your friends."

The smile grew larger, and for the first time, Savannah

thought they might get him through this storm of grief. "Let's go to Ella's grave. There's something I want to show you." Savannah knew how the dog might react to her surprise. "Simon, maybe you should pick up Cody and keep your dog under control."

"My dog? I thought he was Uncle Hez's dog. Is he really mine?"

"He's yours," Hez said. "He has made his wishes clear in case you haven't noticed. When I tried to take him home the day you and your aunt moved to her cottage, he refused to leave you. I tried not to feel hurt, but he's abandoned me."

Simon picked up the dog and fell into step beside Savannah. "I'm sure he still loves you, Uncle Hez—he just knows I need him."

Hez curled Marley's leash around his palm and walked beside Savannah too. "You're a love magnet, kiddo, and the dogs are not immune to your pull."

"Love magnet," Simon sputtered. "Don't ever say that to anyone else, okay?"

Hez made a zipping motion against his mouth. "Not a peep."

Even though Simon had protested, Savannah caught the delight in his eyes. If they kept surrounding their nephew with constant love, he'd get through this. She stopped and set her hand on Hez's arm. "Close your eyes. This is your engagement gift from me. You too, Simon."

"I'm only ten. I'm not getting engaged for a long time."

"No, but you're getting an official uncle, so it fits. Close your eyes." When both males complied, she took each of their arms and positioned them closer to a new statue she'd placed here this morning. "Okay, open your eyes!"

Simon's eyes popped open first, and he gaped. "That looks just like us."

Hez opened his eyes and studied the statue for a long moment. Savannah tried to see it fresh through their eyes. She'd commissioned it from a talented sculptor at the school, and the artist had perfectly captured all four of them. Ella sat on Hez's lap while Simon knelt beside her and smiled adoringly at her. Savannah sat on the sculpted grass on the other side with her face turned toward the children. The peace on the stone face was something Savannah hoped to feel soon.

Hez still hadn't said anything, and she saw him swallow hard. "Do you like it, Hez?"

"I—I have no words." His voice wobbled. "It's wonderful." He glanced her way. "You're wonderful."

Cody let out a low growl and launched out of Simon's arms. He ran on his short legs to the statue and gave two ferocious barks.

"You and your statues." Hez took a step toward the dog, but before he could snatch him up, Simon stroked Cody's head and the dog immediately calmed. "Well, I'm gobsmacked. I usually have to cart him away. See, Simon, I told you he was your dog."

Simon squatted beside the dog and continued patting Cody's head. "Good boy."

Hez put his arm around Savannah. "Don't tell our nephew I'm going to kiss his aunt. This is the best present I could ever have except for you." And he proceeded to kiss her breathless.

CHAPTER 42

SAVANNAH LINKED ARMS WITH HEZ AS THEY EXITED their car with Simon in tow and approached the white tent set up in the park by the pier in Pelican Harbor. This wasn't the engagement party Jess had planned, but Savannah couldn't face trying to mimic the party her sister was going to throw her at Jesse's Restaurant. They had left Marley and Cody napping back at Hez's condo. Jamaican reggae music floated from the DJ station on the beach side of the tent, and the scent of seafood wafted their way. Different was good, especially tonight.

Most of their guests had already arrived, and expectant, smiling faces turned their way. Nora stepped out first to greet them. "The caterer is here, and everything is ready."

Savannah hugged her. "Thank you so much for putting all this together. Is Graham with you?" The police had cleared Nora's boyfriend as soon as they confirmed that Jess was the artifact courier in New York, and he'd insisted there were no hard feelings. He even volunteered that he would have done exactly the same thing in Savannah's shoes.

Nora gestured toward the tent where Graham stood by the DJ. "He's making some song requests." She smiled at Simon.

"You look very handsome, Simon. Are you going to be in the wedding party?"

He shrugged. "I'll do most anything for Aunt Savannah and Uncle Hez."

Nora grinned and gave Savannah a surreptitious wink. Hez hadn't asked Simon to be his best man while the poor kid was reeling with grief for his mother, but hopefully that storm would start to subside soon. "I like to hear that." She pointed out an arbor laced with daisies, baby's breath, and miniature lights. "I told everyone once you got here, they could form a receiving line there, so let's get you in place. I'll have the DJ make the announcement."

"I don't have to go, do I?" Simon asked.

Savannah shook her head. "Nope. Will is at the table closest to the music, and he saved you a seat."

"Awesome." Simon took off toward the tent.

"Good call." Hez took Savannah's hand. "I was afraid it would be boring for him."

Nora walked just ahead of them and glanced back with a smile. "Not with what I have planned. I had cornhole, a giant Jenga game, and beach volleyball set up on the other side of the tent. I asked Will to invite some football friends too, and Will promised to take Simon under his wing. It will be a night he won't forget."

"You are amazing," Savannah said. "Are Hez's parents here yet?" She was eager to see them, and she knew Hez was too. They lived in Oregon, and they were supposed to arrive in Mobile at four.

"They're on their way here in a rental car," Nora said.

Savannah stepped into the center of the arch with Hez, and people began to line up before the DJ had a chance to make an announcement. Jimmy was first in line. His bear hug about broke her back, but she didn't mind a bit.

Jimmy had tears in his eyes as he hugged Hez. "Didn't think I'd ever see this day, my friend. If you have any trouble with him, you come straight to me, you hear?" he told Savannah in a choked voice.

Tears sprang to her eyes too. "I'm sure you'll keep him in line. Thank you for pouring into his life, Jimmy."

"It was my pleasure." He moved out of the way.

Person after person filed through with congratulations and hugs. Hez's cousin Blake and his aunt Jenna were there with Blake's girlfriend, Paradise, and his younger siblings. The Justice Chamber crew had come with their dates, and Jane Dixon and her family added their warm wishes. Savannah could barely keep her hands off Jane's sweet little girl, Dolly. Their pastor was there as well as Hope and even Savannah's counselor, Melissa Morris. A few reporters roamed the tent's perimeter, snapping pictures and talking to guests. Savannah had been a bit of a celebrity ever since Hornbrook's arrest. Hez should have been the real star.

She stiffened at the last person in line. Her father. She'd told Nora not to send him an invitation. "Hello, Dad."

"Savannah." He embraced her, and his overpowering cologne made her stomach clench. "I know I have no right to be here after the way I behaved, but I couldn't stay away. I hope you can forgive me for it all." He glanced out into the twilight where Simon and Will played Jenga. "I want to be part of

Simon's life. And yours if you'll have me. All that's happened has been a wake-up call for me. Jess is gone, but her son is still here. I want to be part of his life."

Her initial warm feelings at his manner took a sharp turn. Was it always about what he wanted? But did she have the right to refuse his olive branch when Simon longed for more family? No, she didn't. "Thanks, Dad. I'm sure you will love Simon when you get to know him."

"I already do." He smiled and squeezed her shoulder with his fingers before he shook Hez's hand, then wandered off toward Simon.

Savannah watched him amble up to her nephew and saw the moment when Simon's face lit up. Had she just made a terrible mistake? The man had been nothing but pain in Jess's life. She'd be watchful and see how things went.

She spotted Hez's parents and squeezed his arm. "Your parents are here!" They both left the line and went to greet his mom and dad. Hez's father was an older version of his son, and he was still handsome and distinguished at nearly seventy. His mother was beautiful with Hez's blue eyes and a blonde cut that accentuated her delicate bone structure. They chatted a moment before going off to grab food and meet Simon.

Savannah started to follow them, but Hez snagged her hand and drew her out of the tent and into the shadows. "I have you to myself at last." He pulled her into his arms and rested his chin on top of her head.

The scent of his sage soap enveloped her as well, and she relaxed into the feeling that she was right where she belonged. She could feel his heart beating, and the strength of his arms around her was the haven she'd been craving since they got out of the car. She didn't need congratulations from other people when she had Hez right here. Being with him was all that mattered.

He kissed her, and she sank into the overwhelming love he poured into that kiss. When he pulled away, she reached for him again but he smiled. "I have something for you too, but I didn't want anyone else to see it." He reached under the bench behind him and held out a wooden box. "All the best memories of my life are with you."

She took the box and settled on the bench before she removed the lid. He switched on his phone's flashlight and sat beside her as she lifted out the first picture. It was the two of them on their first date at a football game. They'd been impossibly young and foolish. But happy, so happy. She felt that same joy bubble in her chest as she stared at her former self. If she'd known then what she knew now, she'd still marry him. She laid it aside and continued to lift out pictures and mementos—various tickets and pictures, the invitation to their first engagement party, photos at their tiny first apartment, the ultrasound of Ella in the womb, a copy of Ella's birth announcement, Hez holding tiny Ella in the delivery room, so many pictures of the life they'd built together.

By the time she was finished, tears streamed down her face. "I love it," she whispered. "We have so many more memories to make. This is just the beginning."

"But I don't want to forget the others either. They build on each other. Thank you for giving us another chance."

She leaned into his kiss again and imprinted this moment into her heart forever.

EPILOGUE

THE LEGARE CEMETERY MADE MICHAEL WILLARD'S SKIN crawl. It was a macabre museum honoring fraud and deceit. The decaying marble crypt of Louis Legare and his wife crowned the little hill, shaded by a stately oak. Louis helped to force Joseph Willard out of the university he'd founded and erased his name from the school, changing Universitates Nova Cambridge Willardius to Tupelo Grove University. Louis's son, Luc—TGU's second Legare president—rested next to the crypt beneath a pretentious granite obelisk, chosen to honor his sole scholarly achievement: a minor paper on Egyptian hieroglyphics. The graves of Luc's son, Andre, and most of his immediate family clustered just downhill from their forebears. Andre, Pierre's father, had started the deep corruption that had cored out the guts of the university. Below them and to Michael's left was a plot that could not be filled soon enough.

The space reserved for Pierre Legare.

He was the worst of the family, which was saying a lot. His death was already long overdue. Too bad he would be buried next to Marie and Jess. That spot should belong to Michael, but Legares had been stealing the places of Willards for over a century.

Michael's gaze moved to the graves of his lover and daughter, both adorned with fresh flowers from Mama's visit two days ago. He picked up a lily from Marie's grave. "'The Lilly white shall in Love delight,'" he recited in a husky voice. "'Nor a thorn nor a threat stain her beauty bright.'" His vision blurred and he dropped the flower.

Marie had taught him to love poetry and so much else—to love life itself. It had been an unexpected and wonderful lesson for a hard-bitten businessman bent on revenge. She had lit his life like a meteor burning across a moonless night—and vanishing all too soon.

He focused on Jess's fresh grave, and tears surged again. Had he been wrong to pull her into his desire for revenge? Should he have shown his love and pride for her more often?

No, soft parents make soft children. Willards were as hard and strong as steel, and the finest steel gained its strength and keen edge from the heat of the blacksmith's fire and the pounding of his hammer. Michael's father had raised his children with fire and pounding to make them strong, and it had worked. Michael did the same thing for the same reason. Besides, he didn't know any other way. Jess had never thanked him—just like he never thanked his father—but she must have understood.

He shook his head as anger dried his eyes and hardened his heart. The two of them should be celebrating now, toasting each other on a yacht in the Gulf of Mexico. She deserved so much better than this—and she would have gotten it if not for that over-clever lawyer who married her half sister. Michael should have killed the guy as soon as he became a problem. If Hez had died, Jess would still be alive. So would Tommy and Little Joe.

Michael's blood pressure ticked higher at the memory of his nephews' deaths. They had been good men—strong, tough, and loyal. Little Joe had even gotten a Punisher tattoo in honor of the uncle he idolized. Michael's nickname grew out of his reputation as a crime boss with a ruthless sense of justice and honor. Little Joe had passed up opportunities in legitimate business to follow in his uncle's footsteps. Guilt needled Michael as he remembered that. Should he have used his influence to set Little Joe on a different path?

He shook off the question. Little Joe lived and died as a proud Willard. The Legares bore ultimate responsibility for his death. The Legares and Hezekiah Webster.

Had Hez known about the bomb in his car? Probably. He'd spotted almost everything else, so he must have spotted that too. And he gave Jess his keys. Cold fury rose in Michael. Hez used the bomb intended for him to kill Jess. With her out of the way, he was able to take TGU for himself and his Legare wife. Michael's hands balled into fists.

Still, Hez had his uses—for the moment. The information Michael fed to Hez through Martine had effectively turned the law enforcement focus onto Hornbrook. That took the heat off Michael and the remaining Willards, which was a relief. Having a single Willard spy in the Pelican Harbor Police Department was little protection against a multiagency, state-federal task force.

Martine had warned that giving Hez evidence against

Hornbrook Finance might hand him enough ammunition to win the battle for TGU. It seemed she was right. Michael had fired two shots into Hez's condo the night before the hearing to disrupt his final preparations and make sure he didn't get any sleep, but even that hadn't prevented him from somehow forcing James Hornbrook to completely surrender.

Still, that had been an acceptable loss. Michael didn't mind letting TGU survive if he could destroy the Legares. In fact, having the university intact might make that task easier. The Legares would keep fluttering around the school like moths around an open flame, ready to be incinerated one by one. Just last night, they'd all been gathered at that party on the beach. Michael had noticed it as he drove by and pulled to the side of the road for a look. Even Pierre had been there.

Michael frowned. Pierre had been standing near Jess's boy, Simon. Was that something to worry about? Michael had spotted at least one reporter at the event, so he pulled out his phone and hunted for coverage. One of the local news websites had a bunch of pictures—including one of Pierre with his arm around Simon with the caption "Three years after tragic death of his only grandchild, former TGU president Pierre Legare connects with newfound grandson, Simon Legare."

Michael's blood boiled. "That boy is a Willard!" he hissed through clenched teeth. He made the mistake of leaving Jess in Pierre's clutches, but he would *not* let her son suffer the same fate. There would be no replacement for Ella Webster. "He is *my* grandson!"

He looked toward Ella's grave and noticed a new statuary grouping. He walked over for a closer look. The sculpture was exquisite—and infuriating. What made them think they could just take Simon? The presumption in that little stone family made him shake with rage.

Jess was barely cold in her grave and they were already stealing her son!

Michael wished he had a sledgehammer and could pound that statue into gravel.

His anger gradually cooled into icy resolve. He was going to take Simon away and make him into a true Willard. No one would stop it from happening. No one.

His gaze went to the smallest figure in the sculpture. What would happen if Hez and the Legares knew the truth about Ella's fate? How would they react if they knew she had been murdered?

A NOTE FROM THE AUTHORS

DEAR READERS,

Thanks for coming with us on the second stage of Hez and Savannah's journey! We enjoyed every minute, and we hope you did too. We do our best to make every detail in our books as authentic as possible. That involves a lot of research, of course, but we love it. Most of the questions we investigate aren't very interesting outside the context of the novel we're writing—for example, "How soon can a patient drive after a craniotomy?" or "What local rules and standing orders govern bankruptcy cases in the Southern District of Alabama?"—but sometimes we come across items that are worth sharing. Here are a few from this book:

Jess's Crucifix: The crucifix that haunted Jess is real. Rick saw it during a trip to Italy in 1987, and he still remembers how the enormous brown eyes seemed to follow him. We couldn't find a picture of it, but we did locate a strikingly similar crucifix in the Uffizi Gallery in Florence. It was created in the twelfth century by an unknown artist in Pisa, and it's known simply as Cross no. 432. Here's a picture of it: https://www.uffizi.it/en/artworks/cross_432.

Bruno's Hacking of Hornbrook: Bruno's successful hack of Hornbrook Finance's video surveillance system is based on a real case Rick investigated at the California Attorney General's Office as part of a multiagency team. The investigation details remain confidential, but the case is now public. You can learn more about it by searching "Glenn v. Cisco."

Artifact Smuggling: This is sadly a very real problem. Many magnificent pre-Columbian sites in Central and South America have been badly damaged by looters, and all too often stolen artifacts wind up in North American collections. Museums generally do their best to check the provenance of items before acquiring them, but private collectors are not always so scrupulous. The silver appliqué that Jess tried to sell in New York is real, by the way, though we have no reason to believe it was looted. Colleen tracked it down and you can find pictures of it by searching "Pre-Columbian Inca Viracocha Great Creator Deity Appliqué."

Cody: Cody is a real dog, and he's exactly like the dog in the Tupelo Grove novels, except that the real Cody is a little smaller and more neurotic. You can follow him on Instagram at @codythegoblin.

We hope you're having as much fun reading the Tupelo Grove saga as we are writing it! Shoot us an email and let us know what you think.

Blessings,

COLLEEN COBLE
https://colleencoble.com
colleen@colleencoble.com

RICK ACKER
https://rickacker.com
contactrickacker@gmail.com

ACKNOWLEDGMENTS

Our huge thanks goes to our HarperCollins Christian Publishing family for cheering us on with this collaboration! The team has been behind us every step of the way and supported us in more ways than we can mention. We are so very grateful, especially to publisher Amanda Bostic, who has always been there to steer us through the murky waters of publishing. Thank you so much!

A special thanks to our freelance editor, Julee Schwarzburg, who has such great instinct for story. She caught our vision early on with the first book and has guided us with a deft hand. Thank you, Julee!

Thank you to agents Karen Solem and Julie Gwinn for your invaluable suggestions along the way. We both appreciate you so much.

A heartfelt thanks to Anette Acker, Rick's sweet wife! She read every word and offered great suggestions and was a much-needed sounding board for direction and brainstorming. She's a silent, but much appreciated, third party in our cowriting endeavor.

A big thanks to Dave, Colleen's hubby. He hauled us all over the South for an exciting book tour with Denise Hunter right after we finished this. Dave has been a constant support in quiet ways all through our efforts.

And where would that tour have been without Colleen's granddaughter Alexa, who acted as our photographer during the tour! We were too busy talking to the many readers who came out to get any pictures on our own, but Alexa was always there in the background snapping candid photos and jumping in to haul boxes, set out swag, and make sure things got done. Pretty amazing for a fifteen-year-old!

We have such great friends in the author community who have been wonderful supports through this new journey. Denise Hunter in particular has been a steady influence and encourager through it all. We had way too much fun on our book tour together as we ate our way through four states. ☺

A heartfelt thanks to our beta readers as well. Thank you, Deb Blower, Cat Brown, Nancy Cantrell, Chandler Carlson, Kay Chance, Jodi Edwards, Kathy Engel, Marcie Farano, Gay Lynn Hobbs, Per Kjeldaas, Beverly Moore, Bubba Pettit, Gail Pettit, Dawn Schupp, Barbara Slone, Joni Truex, and Leah Willis!

And we are thankful to *you*, dear reader! So many of you have reached out and told us how much you loved *What We Hide*, and your encouragement is priceless.

Honestly, it has felt like God himself dreamed up this partnership, and we're so thankful for his guidance and provision for this new venture!

DISCUSSION QUESTIONS

1. Was it reasonable for Savannah to doubt Hez over the bottle she found in his trash?
2. Was it reasonable for Hez to be upset that Savannah didn't believe him when he said he didn't put the bottle there?
3. How has Savannah changed over the course of the first two Tupelo Grove books? Would she have been able to stand up to her father if the confrontation over his trust fund came at the beginning of the first book?
4. Was the dove Jess talked to in chapter 29 just a dove? Or was it something more?
5. Have you ever felt that God was speaking to you through nature? How about through the words of another person?
6. The desire for revenge and the need for forgiveness are recurring themes in both Tupelo Grove books. How have they impacted Jess? Hez? Savannah?
7. Is there a painting, sculpture, or other piece of art that has stuck with you for a long time, even though you only saw it once?
8. Did the revelation on the last page surprise you, or did you see it coming?

From the Publisher

GREAT BOOKS

ARE EVEN BETTER WHEN THEY'RE SHARED!

Help other readers find this one:

- Post a review at your favorite online bookseller

- Post a picture on a social media account and share why you enjoyed it

- Send a note to a friend who would also love it—or better yet, give them a copy

Thanks for reading!

LOOKING FOR MORE GREAT READS? LOOK NO FURTHER!

THOMAS NELSON
Since 1798

Visit us online to learn more:
tnzfiction.com

Or scan the below code and sign up to receive email updates on new releases, giveaways, book deals, and more:

@tnzfiction

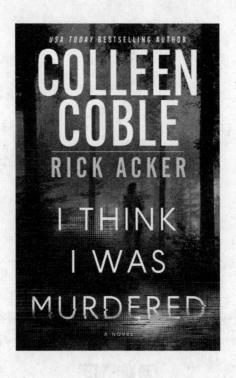

ABOUT THE AUTHORS

EAH Creative

COLLEEN COBLE IS THE *USA TODAY* BESTSELLING AUTHOR of more than seventy-five books and is best known for her coastal romantic suspense novels.

Connect with her online at colleencoble.com
Instagram: @colleencoble
Facebook: colleencoblebooks
X: @colleencoble

ABOUT THE AUTHORS

RICK ACKER WRITES DURING BREAKS FROM HIS "REAL JOB" as a supervising deputy attorney general in the California Department of Justice. He is the author of eight acclaimed suspense novels, including the #1 Kindle bestseller *When the Devil Whistles*. He is also a contributing author on two legal treatises published by the American Bar Association.

You can visit him on the web at rickacker.com.
Instagram: @rick_acker
X: @authorrickacker